To my old colleague with best wishes

YOU OWE ME

Kerry Costello

Kerry Costello Books

Copyright © 2018 Kerry Costello

All rights reserved

The characters and events portrayed in this book are fictitious. Any similarity to real persons, living or dead, is coincidental and not intended by the author.

No part of this book may be reproduced, or stored in a retrieval system, or transmitted in any form or by any means, electronic, mechanical, photocopying, recording, or otherwise, without express written permission of the publisher.

ISBN-13: 978-1999600006
ISBN-10: 1999600002

For my wife Lyn and our sons; Andrew, Timothy and Alexander

***

ACKNOWLEDGEMENTS

Lyn Costello

***

Others who helped Zsolt Monostory, Hanne Monostory and Jasia Painter

FLORIDA'S TREASURE

COAST

The term Treasure Coast was coined by writers at the Vero Beach Press Journal newspaper shortly after salvagers began recovering Spanish treasure off the coast in 1961. The discovery of treasure from the 1715 Treasure Fleet, lost in a hurricane near the Sebastian Inlet, was of major local importance and brought international attention to the area. Since the 60's, locals, professionals, and tourists have had gold fever!

Capitana gold The S/V Capitana crew of Dan Beckingham, Jonah Martinez, William Bartlett and Brent Brisben show the treasure (Photo: 1715 Fleet/Queens Jewels LLC) 2015

Yes, treasure is still, to this day, found all the time along the Treasure Coast. Most of it is literally a stone's throw from the shore in 10 ft of water. Don't believe me? Sometimes it washes up on the beach and handheld metal detectors can reveal gold, silver, and other artifacts.

PROLOGUE

Before - March 2003

"This is not the time to falter. This is the time for this house, not just this government or indeed this prime minister, but for this house to give a lead, to show that we will stand up for what we know to be right, to show that we will confront the tyrannies and dictatorships and terrorists who put our way of life at risk, to show at the moment of decision that we have the courage to do the right thing. I beg to move the motion."

◆ ◆ ◆

These are the closing lines of Prime Minister Tony Blair's' speech to the British Parliament on 18th March 2003. A majority of 179 votes approved his

motion. Subsequently, 45,000 British troops were sent to Iraq to fight alongside American and other forces in Operation Telic.

CHAPTER 1

*PRESENT DAY – MANCHESTER
UK 24 MARCH 2017*

Frankie Armstrong sat by the phone. *Surely she'll call back?* The phone rang, he resisted picking up. Forced himself to wait for it to ring four times. He lifted the receiver.

'Hello,' he kept his voice level, neutral.

'That you Frankie?' Frankie slumped back in the chair, half recognized the voice, but couldn't quite place it, then he could... no, not now? The American accent, the drawl, even after all this time. Shouldn't have picked up, but how the fuck was I to know it would be him? Shit! He forced himself to speak.

'Hello Joe. It is Joe isn't it?'

'Sure is friend, been a long time. But hey, aren't

you pleased to talk to your old buddy, you don't sound too thrilled?'

'Yeah, course I am Joe, sorry, you just caught me snoozing,' he lied. 'Great to hear from you. So, to what do I owe the pleasure, after all this time?'

'Owe, now there's a word, in fact, a very appropriate word. Remember that little favor I did you a few years ago Frankie?'

'How could I forget Joe?'

'You remember the very last thing you said to me when we last met? When was it now, 2003?'

'May 2003, and yes I remember. I said I owe you if that's what you mean?'

'It is. I owe you, right on Frankie.' Joe laughed. 'You owe me. In fact, you wrote me and said if I ever needed anything, I shouldn't hesitate. Promised you'd help. That promise still hold good Frankie?

'Yes sure, course it does Joe' You should've just let the guy kill me, thought Frankie, as he looked out of the window at the grey sky and the cold rain lashing down.

CHAPTER 2

BEFORE – IRAQ

15 APRIL 2003

'Move your fucking bony arses you lazy twats. In case you hadn't remembered, we're in the middle of a fucking great big war, and you pathetic excuses for soldiers are supposed to be fighting for Queen and country – God help us all. And..., we haven't yet managed to find a way of defeating the enemy from our fuckin' beds, 'ave we?!' The sergeant's voice had gradually increased by a million decibels as he spoke. He turned and pointed 'You, you and you,' Frankie was the second you. 'Prisoner escort duty'. Oh no, thought Frankie shit shit shit....

Fifteen minutes later they were lined up outside one of the portacabins that served as a barracks, waiting for the armored truck to ferry them to the front line. The transport arrived.

Shame there were no window seats. I could take in the scenery en-route thought Frankie, *dead camels, abandoned tanks, maybe some bodies piled up by the roadside, tracers screaming across the sky?* One good thing, rumour was rife, the war wasn't going to last much longer. They boarded the armored truck

'Prisoner escort Frankie. Fuck, you know what that means?' said his pal Barnsie, who was sitting next to him in the cramped seats,

'Yeah, I know all right. Too near the front line for comfort.' Frankie replied.

'Too fuckin right Frankie, like the front line doesn't move. It moves the wrong direction, and we'll be in the thick of it. Still, look on the bright side,' he continued

'What bright side would that be Mr. Barns?'

'We might be home by the end of May according to Alfie the know-all. Assuming we stay alive till then that is. Then you can take your bird to the seaside, you know all that lovely sand...' He dug Frankie in the ribs hard as he said it and laughed hysterically.

'Yeah very funny,' said Frankie, but Barnsie's words had conjured up an image of Penny, and the pain hit.

They arrived at their destination a couple of miles short of the front line. The prisoners, about fifteen in total, were corralled in a hastily constructed makeshift compound surrounded by barbed wire. They were docile, beaten, but occasionally one would sneer and make a remark in Arabic. Mostly they seemed grateful to be out of the war.

Frankie was looking over his section when one of the prisoners signaled that he needed to go to the toilet. He looked around and caught Barnsie smirking; He'd seen Frankie cop for the task. Then he pointed at some scrub about five yards away.

'Really?' said Frankie as Barnsie moved nearer.

'Well, you could wait till he shits his pants. Up to you? I'll cover the rest of your sorry lot. They're not going anywhere, well not until the transport turns up'.

Frankie pulled up a portion of the barbed wire and signaled with his submachine gun for the prisoner to duck under it.

'Over there, and make it quick,' he said, pointing at some sorry looking leafless bushes, not knowing if the man understood English. The prisoner went to squat behind the scrub. Frankie turned his head slightly, trying to ignore the stink. A jet fighter roared overhead, and Frankie looked up.

A vicious blow to the head felled Frankie. Too late he felt his gun being wrenched from his grip as he fell to the ground. Now on his back, he was looking up at the prisoner, his own submachine gun pointing at his head. The prisoner sneered as he saw the fear in Frankie's eyes. '*Kanith.*' he growled through grated teeth as he began to squeeze the trigger.

Frankie steeled himself for the impact of the bullets, knowing in that split second that he'd be shredded to a pulp. He'd seen it happen on the battlefield. Instinctively he started to raise his arm in a vain attempt to shield himself from the onslaught and closed his eyes.

He felt the blood splatter across his face a microsecond before he heard a single gunshot; he felt no pain.

'Fucker nearly had you there pal'. The incongruous relaxed American accent at odds with the moment. Frankie opened his eyes and looked up at the soldier, gun in hand. 'That's what you call a cheap lesson buddy. Never ever take your eyes off a prisoner when you're one to one. Not unless you've got the raghead cunt in handcuffs and leg irons. Give you a hand?' Frankie grabbed the proffered hand and was pulled back up to his feet. He felt dizzy. His head hurt, worse than his worst ever hangover. He registered some additional pain in his hand where the submachinegun had been wrenched from his grip. His legs felt like boiled spaghetti.

Frankie tried hard to regain his composure. The American soldier stuck his gun back in its holster, took a pack of cigarettes out of his top jacket pocket, and shook it to partially eject a cigarette. He offered it to Frankie, who held his hand up.

'No thanks I don't,' he said.

'Yeah, bad habit,' said the American as put the cigarette between his lips, flicked his lighter and lit up. Taking a long draw, he said.

'Name's Joseph H Nelson, Joe to you. Pleased to make your acquaintance,' he said without irony.'

'Frankie Armstrong, Frankie replied, 'and not as pleased as I am to make your acquaintance Joe. Thanks again. I..' he stopped talking and turned to look down at the almost headless body on the ground, the piece of wood the prisoner used as a weapon lay beside the body. Frankie bent down to retrieve his submachinegun, just managing to stop himself vomiting as he did so.

'You look a bit green pal, take five. Easy done, lose concentration for a few seconds and bam! they gotcha.'

Alerted by the gunshot, Barnsie and the sergeant arrived to investigate. Barnsie took in the scene

'Shit,' he said, looking down at the prisoner's body.

'This down to you?' the sergeant asked, looking at the American and pointing at the corpse. Joe nodded.

'Yeah, we're just passin' through, six of us checkin' for IEDs along the road. Stopped over there for a comfort break and coffee,' said Joe pointing at a small clump of palm trees that had mostly escaped the ravages of the conflict. The sergeant took out his notebook.

I'll have to make a formal report of the incident, name and rank please?'

'Say, is this really necessary?' said the American, gesturing towards the open notebook. We just don't have the time sergeant. Got to be movin' on. The cap'll go ape if I get tied up. Look I'll give you my details, but the situation was pretty clear. The guy there was about to shoot, er, Frankie here, so I had no choice, so. whaddya say?' The sergeant looked at the American.

'What division are you in?'

'Ordinance, bomb squad.'

The sergeant hesitated.

'I suppose I shouldn't hold you up then?'

'No sir, we're needed.' The sergeant handed his notebook to the American and asked him to write down his name rank and number. Joe scribbled his details down and handed the notebook back to the sergeant. He looked at the detail.

'Okay corporal Nelson, I'll be in touch if necessary.' They shook hands all round.

'Take it easy', said Joe to Frankie, and saluted them before walking away. They saluted back.

'Back on duty now,' said the sergeant pointing towards the prisoner compound. The sergeant marched off.

'Jesus, you were lucky there Frankie,' said

Barnsie as they walked back, how the fuck did that happen?'

'Took my mind off the job, no excuse.' The pain from the blow to his head was starting to get worse. He stopped and felt the back of his head. Barnsie asked to look.

'Whoa what a lump, you feel okay, you might have a concussion or something?'

'Nah, I'm okay, hurts like fuck though. Serves me right. Maybe it was all that talk about getting back home. Got a letter from Penny yesterday and, well like I say, a momentary lapse of concentration.'

'Well, lucky for you the American guy was there,' said Barnsie, 'you owe him big time Frankie.'

◆ ◆ ◆

It was nearly three months later that Frankie bumped into Joe again as he waited at Bagdad airport for his transport back to the UK.

'Hey, Frankie. That you buddy?' Frankie turned to see Joe, arm in a sling. Frankie suddenly felt strangely emotional. He realized he'd never thanked Joe properly. He'd intended to get his details from the sergeant and write, but somehow never got round to it.

'Hello Joe. What happened to you?'

'Fell out of a jeep a couple of nights ago, drunk

as a skunk, but I'll tell the folks back home I broke it in hand to hand combat, I'll work on the story on my way home.' Frankie laughed.

'Home, ain't that got a nice ring to it, Frankie?'

'Certainly has Joe. Look I never really thanked you properly for saving my life. I think I was in shock, so thanks.'

'Forget it, just in the right place right time.'

'No,' said Frankie 'I'll never forget it. I owe you.' Just then the PA system announced a flight departure.

'That's my flight Frankie, see ya buddy', said Joe holding out his hand. They shook. Frankie once again noting the strength in Joe's hand. He wasn't that tall but wide, built like a bull.

'And if you ever get over to Florida, look me up. Joe Nelson, like Horatio the one-armed limey guy. Nelson's Boatyard in Naples, don't forget.'

'Will do Joe,' replied Frankie, both of them knowing they'd probably never meet again. But when Frankie got home from the war, he'd written to thank Joe properly. He sent the letter, care of Nelson's Boat Yard Naples, Florida. He reckoned there'd be a good chance it would reach its intended recipient, but never had a reply.

The circumstances surrounding his brief acquaintance with the man who saved his life, eventually became just part of the kaleidoscope of events that occasionally swirled around in Frankie's head, whenever he thought about the war. A war which he mostly tried to forget. The destruction, the violence, the noise, the fear and the waste. And at times, the boredom and tediousness, punctuated by moments of controlled panic when you were called into action. You tried to look brave, gung-ho even. But in reality, you felt your bowels loosen and wondered if you'd ever get home alive.

CHAPTER 3

PRESENT DAY

MANCHESTER UK

Frankie took a deep breath
'What d'you need my help with Joe? Only I'm in the middle of...' *what the fuck am I in the middle of...?*

'Sorry Frankie, you said, in the middle of.., then I lost you. Bad line maybe, shall I call back?'

'Sorry Joe, no, carry on, please. *The least I can do is listen to the guy.*

'You sure Frankie? You still sound a bit; I don't know. You okay?'

'Yes, coming down with a cold I think, please carry on.'

'Okay well, I've got a situation, and I'm in deep. My nephew Billy Ray's a scuba nut, diving fanatic, a treasure hunter. Long story short, he and his pal Jerry found an old Spanish shipwreck, one with a valuable cargo, very valuable.

'Spanish shipwreck, really?'

'Yeah, seems the western shores of Florida are littered with old shipwrecks. Anyway, he needed funds, a better boat and some expensive equipment, so he comes to his Uncle Joe and convinces me to back him. I looked into it in some detail. I mean I've been around the block a few times, so I'm not easy to fool, and Billy Ray's a good guy, and so is his pal Jerry. Thing is, they've gone missing.'

'Very sorry to hear that Joe, but how does this involve me?'

'Like I said, and getting to the point. They've disappeared, boat and all and I'm out by over forty thousand dollars. Plus the boat is one I'm storing for a customer until he comes back for the next winter season, a motor cruiser worth a couple a hundred grand at least, so that's nearly a quarter of a million dollars Frankie. And this customer, he loves that boat, so apart from paying him for the missing boat, which I can't do, he'd likely kill me anyway.'

'Sounds like a big mess Joe. Look, I don't want to sound uncaring, and I know it's a lot of money, money and a valuable boat, but people let you down, I mean....'

'It's not the money or the boat,' Joe interrupted, 'they're important, but it's the boys, they've disappeared, gone, as in no trace. My sister's in bits, and I'm not exactly thrilled.'

'I'm really sorry Joe. Yes, of course, you must be very worried. I wasn't thinking straight. You'll have to forgive me, I've been a bit distracted... Obviously, you need to find your nephew and his friend; you must be worried sick. But I'm still not sure how I can help. I assume you've reported it to the police?'

'I have, but.' He could hear Joe take a deep breath.

'But what Joe?'

'Well, I only just reported them missing. I don't have a lot of faith in cops.'

'How long have they been missing?'

'It's well over a week since I spoke to Billy Ray, haven't been able to get him since. Thought I'd leave it for a few days to begin with, Billy Ray can be like that, you know just dropping off the radar, then bang, he's back in touch. But he's never been out of touch for this long before. Can't get a reply from his cell, nor from his buddy Jerry's cell. I'm worried Frankie.'

'What about a private detective Joe, you've got lots of private investigators over there, haven't you?'

'Sure and I did hire one for a few days, but it just got too expensive. Those guys don't come cheap. The simple truth is, I just can't afford it. There was a fire in the boatyard last year, and my insurance had lapsed. The money I gave my nephew was a sort of investment. I know it sounds a bit farfetched, but if they found treasure, which is not as unlikely as you might think, I could get my life back. I didn't know where to turn; then I remembered you and your promise.'

'But as I've said, what can I do?'

'I thought maybe you could come over and help me look for them?'

'Me, come over there? I mean...*he can't be serious* I don't know the territory Joe, wouldn't know where to start.... I don't know anything about diving, shipwrecks. I get seasick on a canal boat. Look, Joe, I'd love to help, and I know I owe you big time, but I have commitments....' Frankie ran out of words and realized in many ways he had very few commitments at the moment.

'I know I'm asking a lot Frankie,' Joe continued, 'but I can't do it on my own, I've got to keep the boatyard going. Otherwise, I'm on the street. Look I can fund your airfare, a couple of weeks stay in a motel or a condo or something, and some expenses. Won't be the Ritz but I'm sure I can find something acceptable, and you'll be near the beaches. Nowhere around here is that far from the beaches. Maybe you could think of it as a working holiday.... I..' Joe stopped talking.

'Joe, you still there?'

'Yeah, just realized what I'm asking. Sorry Frankie, not been thinking straight for a while now. Look forget I called, it was a crazy idea.' Now Frankie was silent.

'Frankie?'

'Yeah, still here', he said and looked over at the table where he'd placed the bottle of whisky, the pile of pills and the note he'd begun to write. *Get this call over; then I can get on with it. Leave me you bitch, how fucking dare you? I'll fucking show you what leaving means!*

'Frankie, I keep losing you Frankie.' Frankie swallowed hard and just about stopped himself from screaming down the phone. *Leave me alone; I'm trying to commit suicide you stupid cunt.*

'Frankie, I can't hear you?' Frankie held the phone to his chest and took a deep breath. *What the fuck?* Something switched in Frankie's brain. He shook his head.

'Fuck it!' Frankie said out loud. He brought the phone back to his ear

'Sorry Frankie, what was that?'

'Sorry Joe, just…. Okay, I'm on, let me get a pen, and I'll send you an email then you can reply and fill me in on some details.'

'You sure about this Frankie, I mean…?'

'I'm sure, absolutely.' He said and thought, *this is crazy, but what the hell…*

◆ ◆ ◆

There were practicalities to take care of, and

Frankie was grateful for the distraction. While he waited for Joe's email, he searched online for information on Naples Florida. Beaches bathed in sunshine, were in stark contrast to the current British weather, which was presently doing its best to reinforce Manchester's reputation as the UK's rain capital. Add to that the freezing temperatures, which even for March in the north of England were unseasonably low. The day before it had snowed, rained and snowed again before freezing overnight. A short while ago he couldn't have cared less about the weather, anywhere, about anything at all.

Frankie's laptop pinged as Joe's email came through. It gave the address of his boatyard and his telephone numbers. Joe said if possible, Frankie should fly to Fort Myers, which was the nearest commercial airport to Naples, about forty minutes' drive away. He said to let him know his arrival details, and he'd pick him up. And to pack for a beach holiday. Frankie still had a valid visa from their trip to New York, last December, a surprise present for Penny. It pained him to remember.

He'd called Derek the day before, told him that he was having some problems at home and would be taking a couple of days off. Derek told him to take all the time he wanted, said the business practically ran itself these days anyway. Now he called Derek again to tell him he might be away for more than a few days. This time it was his answering service.

'You're through to Derek Barns, Leave a message, and I'll get back to you.'

'Hi Barnsie, Frankie here, decided to take a bit of a longer break. Don't know how long, maybe a couple of weeks, maybe more. I'm planning to leave this Sunday. I'll call you again and let you know what's happening.'

He put the phone down and went to search for flights on Google. He found the Virgin Atlantic website and started to put in his dates. He stopped, took in a long breath, leaned back in his chair and breathed out trying to slow his speeding heartbeat. *Sweet Jesus, ten minutes ago I was thinking about ending it all. What the fuck, that's not me. Now I'm booking a fucking flight to America. Definitely more like me!* He shook his head in disbelief, then got back to the task in hand.

CHAPTER 4

BEFORE – FLORIDA

16 MARCH 2017

Billy Ray made his way along the outside of the wreck by handing himself along the side of the vessel. Then he floated up and on to the deck area to get a better look. Despite his headlamp, he found it difficult to see in the murky water. Much of the deck seemed intact, but no doubt rotten. Part of the bow had broken off and lay on the ocean floor, but he wasn't able to see inside and didn't want to go in in conditions like this.

He'd got enough information, for the time being, so he yanked three times on the rope and began his ascent to the surface. He gasped and spat out his mouthpiece and clambered up the ladder, over the side and on to the deck of Falling Star.

'Treasure, gold, silver, coins anything?' asked

Jerry.

'Don't know buddy,' Jerry helped him take off the oxygen cylinder, then Billy Ray began to strip off his wetsuit. His broad, tanned body glistened with perspiration in the late afternoon sun. Jerry, by contrast, was tall, wiry, gingery hair and pale Irish freckled skin. 'Couldn't see properly, that storm's messed the water up. Take a good few days to clear. Might be okay later this week or maybe next. But Jerry buddy, this could be it. International waters an all.'

'Will she stay where she is?'

'I think so. She's resting on a big mother of a shelf, a long, broad sandbank. 'Looks like she's been there for forever, sorta wedged in. But no telling bud, you know the sea. The only thing you can rely on is its unreliability.'

'Get her name Billy Ray?'

'Santa Maria de Santiago, I think. Can't be sure with all that crud covering the wreck Tried to rub it away, but I thought the wood might disintegrate. Maybe try to do some research, see if there's any info on when she sank and what she was carrying.'

'You think? Look Billy Ray; these ships were all carrying, we know that. I mean it ain't called the Treasure Coast for nothin'. So either there's good stuff in the hold, or someone's already had it. Or maybe the captain offloaded it before he set sail intending to get back to some chick he met, whatever?'

'Yeah right, but it don't really matter. Remember what we're looking for. Could be this wreck fits the bill, Jerry, my old buddy.'

'You going to call Uncle Joe and tell him?'

'No, not yet, let's go back, have a few beers and a bite. Look at the vid, not that you'll see much with all that murk. Anyways, we sleep on board tonight, rest up for a couple of days, then get some fresh cylinders ready to come back out in a few days' time, depending on the weather. We'll have another look, and if it seems like the one, we call Uncle Joe and give him the good news.'

'Okay Captain!,' Jerry gave Billy Ray a mock salute.'

'You sure you got the waypoints for this baby?'

'I sure have, yes siree cap'n.'

'Knock it off sailor, or you're over the side.' Jerry laughed, went to the wheelhouse and started the engine of the Consort 45 Cruiser and set course for their mooring at the Pelican Yacht Club in Fort Pierce on the east coast of Florida.

❖ ❖ ❖

Back in port they moored up and made their way to the lounge and ordered two beers and a bowl of nuts. Jerry watched the video on the cam for a couple of minutes, then switched it off and slurped his drink.

'Man that tastes good. You were right Billy Ray, hardly see a thing on the vid. Like you say, maybe clearer tomorrow?'

'Not a chance. Gonna take a good few days, and that's if there's not another storm. We really need that break Jerry, I'm running out of money and I don't want to go back to fixing engines, cleaning boats. Man, I've had it with all that shit, I'm ready for the high life.'

'Me too Billy Ray, me too. On another matter, you still messin' with that Valentina broad?'

'She ain't no broad, she's a nice lady, and yeah, we still see each other when we can.'

'I hope you know what you're doing there buddy. Playing with fire doesn't cover it.'

'He doesn't care about her Jerry; she's just a sorta trophy wife. He's got all these other women on the side, and Valentina was getting ready to leave him anyway.'

'Whoa Billy Ray, you really got it bad if you're thinking of doing what I think you're thinking of doing, didn't you say the guy is some sort of Miami gangster? How do you think a guy like that would react to someone taking his wife away?

'Listen, just leave it. I ain't taking anyone's wife away, leastwise not yet. I can't do anything anyhows until I get my hands on some serious money, but that's looking mighty more likely tonight.' They high fived 'Come on, let's eat.'

CHAPTER 5

BEFORE – FLORIDA

18 MARCH 2017

Billy Ray was worried. He hadn't heard from Valentina for a few days, and she wasn't answering her phone. He wanted to tell her about finding the shipwreck and how it might be the opportunity he'd been waiting for to make some serious money. He began to wonder if she'd cooled down, lost faith in him making it big, decided the relationship wasn't going anywhere. But none of that chimed with the passion of their last meeting. His cell rang, he looked at the screen but didn't recognize the number.

'Billy Ray?' her voice was punctuated by small sobbing sounds

'Valentina? Where have you been?'

'Billy Ray,' she replied, her voice still shaky, 'he found out and locked me up, but I escaped.'

'Locked you up, Jesus how did he find out?' Valentina whimpered. 'Forget that, not important now, you can tell me later. Where are you now?'

'A small motel outside Miami, please come and get me, Billy Ray, if he finds me, he'll kill me.'

'What motel, where is it and what's your room number? I'm getting off the boat and walking to my ride now. What are you calling me on, it's not your cell, the number would have come up?'

'I'm using the phone in the lobby, my cell's dead and I forgot to grab the charger when I left.'

'Good, keep it that way, people can be traced by their cell phones. Hold on Valentina I'll be there as soon as I can. Should be there in under two hours.'

'Hurry Billy Ray,' she said. He ran to his truck, got in and drove out of the parking lot, tires screeching.

◆ ◆ ◆

She was stunning, a slim, ebony skinned, raven-haired beauty. Their eyes locked across the dance floor. That magic look. A story told and retold over centuries. Songs composed and sung about a beautiful young woman married to an older man. A loveless trophy marriage, a deal, a financial arrangement and it works for lots of people, except when the beautiful young wife falls for a handsome young swain, what's new? And so it was that in Miami's Liv nightclub come disco, in 2017, that age-old scenario was played out once again.

Liv was considered Miami's premier nightclub disco. Movie stars, celebs, the Miami glitterati out in force. It was where fate brought together Billy Ray Ballantyne and Valentina Katerina Meszaros. Classic. It started with a look, then a dance, then a kiss, then... They were both well and truly hooked.

◆ ◆ ◆

He'd found the motel; a grubby looking two-story affair named The Rambling Rose. Ignoring the look from the guy on the reception desk, found the stairs and bounded up two at a time, found room 204 and knocked.

'It's me Valentina, Billy Ray, let me in. The door opened, and Valentina threw her arms around him. He hugged her back.

'Can we get away now please Billy Ray, I'm scared he might find me somehow?'

'You have any bags?' said Billy Ray.

'No, nothing, just my purse, I'm ready to go.'

'Okay, do you need to pay the bill?'

Valentina laughed.

'No, they made me pay in advance, a hundred dollars for this flea pit. They could see I was desperate.'

'Okay let's go.' Said Billy Ray taking her hand

and leading her out of the building to his truck.

During the journey back to the boat, she told him how her husband Zaros had found records of calls to Billy Ray on her cell and beaten the truth out of her, then locked her in her bedroom.

'Did he hurt you bad? He asked her.

'I thought he was going to kill me. Look at the marks on my neck.' Billy Ray turned briefly and could see red weals on her neck.

'Jesus Valentina, I'll pay the bastard back for what he did to you. How did you escape?'

'He forgot to take my cell away, and I managed to call my sister just before my cell died. She came over and used the service elevator and managed to get me out; then she drove me to the motel, then I called you. Gemma had to get back to the kids, she'd left them on their own to come and get me, and they're only babies really.'

'Okay, Valentina, you can relax now. I won't let anything happen to you.'

Billy Ray, I need to get my cell charged up. Got to tell Gemma I'm okay, that you've cone to get me.'

'No, here, use mine,' and he handed his cell phone to her. 'Like I say, better not to switch your phone on, might be traceable.'

'Thanks Billy Ray, you think of everything.' Billy Ray leaned across and kissed her gently on the cheek.

'I love you Billy Ray,' she said, then began to

call her sister.

◆ ◆ ◆

Two hours later they arrived back at the boat.

'Hey Billy Ray', said Jerry who was busy cleaning the handrails on the boat as Billy Ray approached the boat. 'Where d'you go?' One minute you were here, the next you'd disappeared.'

'Sorry Jerry, got an urgent call, 'I don't think you've met Valentina,' said Billy Ray as he and Valentina boarded the boat.

'No, I don't think I have,' said Jerry as he held out his hand to her. They shook. 'Nice to make your acquaintance, er Valentina.'

'Likewise, I'm sure. Heard a lot about you, Jerry.'

'That right,' said Jerry looking at Billy Ray.

'I'll show Valentina to my cabin; then I'll be right back up.'

'Sure thing Billy Ray,' replied Jerry going back to his polishing. After five minutes Billy Ray came back on deck.

'She's sleeping,' he said, 'had a tough time. Husband found out about us, roughed her up a bit but she escaped and holed up in a motel, so I went to get her.'

'Are you out of your fuckin' mind Billy Ray? Didn't you tell me her husband is some sort of murdering Miami mobster?

'Yeah, but what could I do, I mean..?'

'Well let's see, you could maybe choose somebody with a husband who's a pastor, maybe a Quaker, or a gardener, or maybe even a broad who isn't actually married to someone else.. I think they're called single women, and I'm given to understand there's lots of them out there.'

'Come on Jerry, don't be like that. And please stop calling Valentina a broad.'

'Okay, she's not a broad, but she's a big fuckin risk, that's for sure. So what do we do now Billy Ray? What about the shipwreck, the plan, the treasure? What the fuck do we do now, now we're likely to be targeted by a homicidal Miami gangster?'

'Sorry buddy, but we have to put those plans on hold till I figure things out. We need to go somewhere this maniac can't find us. For starters, too many people know we moor the boat here, so we have to get out of here, at least for the time being. He probably knows she's escaped by now and he ain't going to be too happy about that.'

'Billy Ray, you are the master of the understatement.' Replied Jerry, raising his eyes to heaven.' Billy Ray laughed, then frowned.

'We got to act quick; he won't have a big problem finding us.'

'Jesus Christ Billy Ray what were you thinking, getting involved with a Miami mobster's woman? What are you thinking?'

'I love Valentina Jerry. It's a simple as that.' Jerry shook his head. He knew his friend was beyond making sensible decisions where women were concerned.

'Okay, so what do we do now, where do we go Billy Ray?'

'Jerry, now I appreciate none of this is your fault, so I wouldn't blame you if you want to leave, for a while anyway, until I figure out what to do longer term.'

'Not a chance dude. Without me, you'll probably end up dead. I ain't leaving.' Billy Ray put his arms around Jerry's shoulders.

'Thanks buddy, said Billy Ray, 'I knew I could rely on you. We need to get out of here, find somewhere else to moor up for a few days, at least until we can decide our next move.'

'Okay Billy Ray, any idea where?'

'Yeah, I remember seeing a place north of here, a marina called Melbourne Harbor. Nice looking place, very busy with lots of boats, they'll never find us there.'

'Let's do it,' said Jerry. They went up to the deck, released the ropes, reversed the boat out of the mooring, navigated out of Pelican Yacht Club and headed north.

As they got underway, Valentina woke from her sleep and shouted up to the wheelhouse. Billy Ray left Jerry in charge of the boat, went down to talk to Valentina. He made her some coffee, then told her about their decision to move to another marina.

'Good idea Billy Ray, now you go back on deck and leave me now. I want a shower and a few minutes to get myself looking less like a street person.'

'Okay Valentina, give me a shout if you need anything.' After getting cleaned up, Valentina used Billy Ray's cell phone to look up Melbourne Harbor Marina on Google. The blurb said it catered for transient and permanent boats, had lots of facilities, including a complete laundry service and two restaurants. She smiled.

They arrived. Billy Ray checked in, paid, and they were allocated a berth. Jerry and Valentina went to explore the marina while Billy Ray went to fuel up the boat and buy some items from the ship's store. After a late dinner in the marina restaurant, they all felt exhausted.

'Okay, said Billy Ray, we've done enough for today. Got ourselves out of harm's way for a while anyway, so I suggest we leave any decision making until tomorrow, go back to the boat, turn in and get an early night.'

'Amen to that,' said Jerry. Billy Ray went to sleep thinking about what would happen to them if Valentina's husband caught up with them, and then had the beginnings of an idea as to where they might hole up for a while.

CHAPTER 6

BEFORE – FLORIDA

19 MARCH 2017

Chuck Mainous had turned in his badge early and had gone private, but still maintained good relations with some of his old buddies in the Miami Criminal Investigations unit, and still saw some of them socially. They understood his move was out of a desire to save his failing marriage and so far it looked as though it might.

'Hey, George buddy, how's it goin'?'

'Hey yourself Chuck To what do we owe the pleasure?'

'Just wonderin' how my old pals at the department were doin'.'

'You are the worst liar in the world Chuck. We talked last week at Jim's barbeque so don't give me all that bullshit. What do you want?'

'That transparent huh?' George laughed.

'You are Chuck, always were, so come on, I've got a shitpile of work to get through today.'

'Okay, George, well I'm on a mispers case, and I need to know if the guy I'm looking for, a Mr.. Billy Ray Ballantyne, has made any recent credit or debit card transactions, withdrawals etc. Need to get a fix on him.'

'Okay, full name address, bank details etc.' Chuck gave his friend all the information he'd been given by Joe Nelson.

'Okay, well I'll need some time to look into this. I'll call you back within the hour if I find anything.'

'Thanks George, I'll go for a coffee.' Chuck waited in a coffee bar in Fort Pierce, the last known location for Billy Ray. He'd checked out the marina Joe Nelson had said was the last place he knew of where Billy Ray had moored the boat and established he'd been there, but neither he nor the boat was still there. Twenty minutes later his cell chirruped.

'Hi George, that was quick.'

'We aim to please. Got a hit at a place called Melbourne Harbor. A marina north of Fort Pierce Florida.'

'That fits, when?'

'Yesterday, 15:43 hrs.'

'Thanks George I owe you.'

'Glad to help; have a good one.' Mainous looked up the precise location of Melbourne Harbor on his cell, then slurped the last of his coffee asked for the check, paid, left the coffee shop and got on his way.

CHAPTER 7

BEFORE – FLORIDA

19 MARCH 2017

Jerry didn't need much sleep and was always up at the crack of dawn. The next morning, he was padding around the cabin quietly so as not to wake the other two. That first cup of coffee was the best. He was about to switch on the coffee machine when he felt the boat move. He went over to Billy Ray's cabin, knocked gently and opened their cabin door.

'Billy Ray,' he said in a loud whisper.

'Wake up; there's someone up on deck.' Billy Ray shook his head to clear the sleep away and motioned to Valentina to be quiet as she started to open her eyes. Billy Ray got out of bed and dragged on some shorts then crept out into the main cabin, Valentina followed. Jerry had armed himself with a mace spray in one hand and a telescopic steel baton in the other, fully extended.

He motioned for Billy Ray and Valentina to go hide in the head then went to crouch under the stairway. The cabin doors to the deck opened quietly, and a man dressed in dark clothes slowly made his way down the wooden companionway into the main cabin. When he reached the bottom rung, Jerry came out from behind the stairway. The man swiveled around. Jerry pointed the mace at his eyes and sprayed. Then whacked him with the baton. The man screamed and folded. Billy Ray and Valentina came out of the head and helped Jerry pick the man up, drag him to a chair and tie him up. He came round, eyes streaming, gasping for breath. They searched him and found a cell phone and a gun in a shoulder holster, which they took and placed on a table.

'Water, please.' He managed to say in a croaky voice. Valentina got some water in a cup and brought it to his lips. He slurped noisily, then breathed out. 'Could you wipe my face with the rest?' he managed to ask. 'Jesus Christ my head,' he said as the initial shock wore off. Valentina got a flannel and wiped his face and eyes. Tears were still streaming from his now red eyes. Jerry took the lead.

'Okay pal, who the fuck are you?'

'The name's Mainous, Chuck Mainous I'm a PI working for your uncle. Assuming you're Billy Ray that is.'

'I'm not, he is,' said Jerry nodding in the direction of Billy Ray.

'Oh right, can't see too well at the moment.'
Billy Ray spoke.

'I told Uncle Joe not to come looking for me, Jesus what do we do now?' The question never got answered. One of the treads on the wooden ladder squeaked, and they all looked around.

'Lenny!' Valentina gasped as she recognized the man, now halfway down the stairs and pointing a handgun in their general direction, silencer attached. They froze. The man was no more than twenty feet away. Jerry was the first one to move. He turned grabbed his mace spray off the table with his left hand. Still holding the steel baton in his right, he raised the spray and the baton and lurched forward towards the intruder. Lenny didn't hesitate, took aim and shot Jerry just once through the forehead. The noise in the small cabin was deafening. Valentina screamed as Jerry collapsed in a heap on the floor. Billy Ray looked on in disbelief at the summary execution of his dearest friend. He recovered enough to pull Valentina to him, a protective arm around her shoulder. With her head buried in his chest, she sobbed uncontrollably. The man called Lenny kept his gun trained on them as he walked towards where they stood. He saw the gun on the table and put it in his pocket. He picked up the cell phone.

'This his?' he said nodding at the man tied up in the chair.

'Yes,' said Billy Ray. It was a flip phone. The gunman opened it, snapped it in half and threw the pieces on the cabin floor.

◆ ◆ ◆

By now Billy Ray had pushed Valentina behind him as if to shield her from harm. Chuck Mainous struggled with the ropes but had been well and truly immobilised. Lenny casually grabbed a chair and sat down facing them all gun at the ready. He seemed to be mulling things over.

'You two stay just where you are.' He said to Billy Ray and Valentina. 'And you are?' He asked Mainous, pointing the gun in his direction.

'Chuck Mainous, Private Investigator?'

'Working for?'

'This guy's uncle.' He nodded his head in the direction of Billy Ray.'

'And you are?' Mainous asked the gunman.

'Not sure you're in a position to ask questions,' he replied, 'but what harm? I work for this broad's husband. See, he's a bit ticked off at her running away with this bozo, so he sent me to find them. And now here we all are.' Lenny stood up stroking his chin, thinking. He spoke.

'Okay, well we have ourselves a little problem here Mr.. Mainous. I mean what am I going to do with you?'

'You're going to let me go. I'm an ex Miami Police detective, so if any harm comes to me, you can bet your sweet ass that my old police buddies won't let it go. They'll come after you, and you know what they'll do to you when they find you. Cops always look after their own, and cop killers live very short lives. Untie me and let me go.' Lenny stood there saying nothing, then seemed to come to a decision.

'You,' he pointed his gun at Billy Ray, 'untie him.' He turned back to Mainous. 'One wrong move...' Mainous nodded. Billy Ray undid the ropes. Mainous stood up rubbing his wrists. 'Now go while the going's good,' said Lenny. Chuck Mainous walked towards the stairway. As he got to the foot of the stairs, Lenny brought his gun up and shot Mainous in the back twice. Billy Ray gasped, Valentina screamed. Lenny walked over to Mainous's now inert body and kicked it. 'As if?' he said to nobody in particular and smiled. Then he walked back towards Billy Ray and Valentina who were clinging to each other.

'Right, here's the rules, he said, 'I'm gonna be very clear, so there's no misunderstanding, okay? If I see, or even think, either one of you is making a move against me, I'll shoot the other one in the leg, or maybe I'll shoot to kill, just like I did with these two? I'll shoot without hesitation, so don't give me any excuse okay?' He looked at each one of them in turn and waited for them to nod in agreement.

'Valentina, get your purse and cell phone and don't even think about trying to call anyone, or both of you are dead. And you,' he said still pointing the gun at Billy Ray, 'are going to reach into your pocket slowly and hand your cell phone over to me.'

'It's in the cabin,' said Billy Ray. Lenny nodded then shouted.

'Valentina, bring this guy's cell phone as well. Same rules apply. She came back with her purse and Billy Ray's phone which she handed to Lenny, then she dug into her purse and handed her cell phone over to him as well

'I'd better not see you've attempted to make a call.'

'It's not even switched on,' said Valentina.

He opened the flap on her phone and checked. Then put both cells in his trouser pocket.

'Okay, you,' he said pointing at Billy Ray with his gun 'drag your friend's body next to the other stiff. You,' he pointed at Valentina, 'sit over there, keep quiet and don't move.' Billy Ray did as he was told. 'Okay, now we're all going to go up to the wheelhouse or whatever it's called and go for a nice little sailing trip.'

'Where to?' asked Billy Ray.

'Just out to sea, far enough out that no one can see us dumping the bodies. Not too far, I don't like boats, get seasick.' Lenny signaled with his gun for Billy Ray to lead the way up to the deck and stood back, letting Valentina walk up behind Billy Ray. 'One wrong move and she gets it, then you. Understand?'

'Yeah yeah, tough guy with the gun,' replied Billy Ray defiantly.

'Hey, less of the lip or I just might shoot her anyway. Move it' Billy Ray led the way to the wheelhouse cabin. Checked the fuel, inserted the key, then started the engine. He reversed the boat out of its mooring conscious of the gun trained on Valentina. He changed to forwards and began to maneuver the boat out of the harbor and into the ocean. The sea was calm, though with a slight swell

'Head out there, and I'll tell you when to stop,' said Lenny pointing. Billy Ray steered the boat towards the horizon and gunned the engine. The boat's bow rose up as the craft picked up speed then settled into a steady cruise. After a few minutes, Billy Ray turned to the gunman and asked.

'Just out of curiosity, how did you find us?'

The gunman laughed.

'Same way our friend lying downstairs did I guess. Let me ask you a question. What was the first thing you did when you got to Melbourne Harbor?'

'I checked in with the port master and paid for two nights mooring. But I misspelt the boat's name, gave him a false name for me and paid in cash.'

'Smart move, and then what did you do?'

'Then I fueled up…. Shit?'

'Yeah shit… for brains. That's right; you used your credit card.'

'And you have access to that sort of information?

'Don't be dumb; you can buy anything.'

'And the PI?'

'Come on; he's an ex-cop, or should I say was an ex-cop?' Lenny chuckled at his own joke, 'so he probably just pulled a Favor. Lucky for me he got to you first, and bad luck for you. Could have been the other way round, me lying on the floor down there instead. Now enough with the questions, just shut the fuck up and drive.' After another five minutes, the gunman spoke.

'You got one of those depth finder things right? Switch it on.' Billy Ray did as he was told. 'Okay, that's the bottom, right?' asked the gunman, pointing his finger at the screen display.

'Yes,' said Billy Ray, 'that's the ocean floor.'

'Okay then. The next big dip *in the ocean floor*, bring this tub around and anchor up.' Billy Ray did as he was told. The anchor chain clanked nosily as it descended to the bottom of the sea.

'Find some spare chain. And don't give me all that shit about not having any. There's always chains on boats. Oh, and no heroics, don't forget what I said about shooting your pretty girlfriend here.' Billy Ray went to one of the lockers, found some chain and brought it back. 'More,' said the gunmen. Billy Ray went and got more. When Lenny was satisfied they had enough to weigh two bodies down, he shooed the couple downstairs and followed them, covering them all the time with his gun. He told them to haul the bodies up to the deck. Billy Ray took the heavier end of Jerry's body under the armpits, back walking up the ladder. Valentina struggled behind, holding the body by its ankles. They repeated the process with the body of the private eye.

Once both men's bodies had been hauled up on deck, Lenny told them to drag the bodies round to the side of the deck hidden from the shore. Lenny then instructed Bill Ray to wrap some chain around both bodies. Billy Ray did as he was told and wrapped some chain round the body of the PI, then tried to turn his face away from the gunman as he wrapped some more chain around his friend Jerry's torso, tears streaming down his face as he carried out the task.

'Okay, no more blubbing. You two, get these fuckers over the side.' Billy Ray caught Valentina's eyes and gave the slightest shake of his head. He and Valentina tried to lift the body of the PI, but Valentina kept dropping her end under the weight. They tried twice more, then Lenny lost his patience. Looking a bit green, he pushed Valentina out of the way, tucked his gun in his belt and got hold of the PI's ankles.

'Okay, lift bozo,' he said to Billy Ray. And they lifted, but instead of Billy Ray heaving his end over the side, he put all his weight into pushing forwards and threw Lenny off balance. Lenny fell backwards. His gun came free from his waistband, clattered on to the deck and slid away from him towards Valentina. She looked at it horrified. She'd never fired a gun in her life, or even handled one. She grabbed it, and to Billy Ray's dismay, threw it over the side where it plopped as it hit the water. Billy Ray launched himself at the gunman who was trying to get up, but he was wearing the wrong shoes entirely for boating and slipped on the shiny deck. Billy Ray took his chance and hit Lenny with all his might, full in the face with his balled fist. The man fell backwards, laid out cold. Billy Ray leaned over and hit him hard again for good measure. Billy Ray stopped and looked down at his right hand; his knuckles were skinned and bleeding. He stood back up and landed a vicious kick into Lenny's prone body.

'That's for Jerry, you murdering bastard.' He stopped to get his breath back then shouted at Valentina," Come on, help me get these chains off Jerry's body.' She recovered enough to help. As gently as they could in the circumstances, they unwrapped the chain. Then Billy Ray started to wrap the chain around Lenny's waist, through his legs and back around his waist. He made a crude knot, sufficient for his purpose.

'Help me drag him aft; the rails are a bit lower there.'

'I can't Billy Ray; I can't do this. I've never even seen a dead body before.'

'Look we got to get rid of this body and quick. Another boat could come along any minute. You want to go to jail?' She shook her head. 'then grab his other leg and heave.' They each took a leg and began to drag the gunman's body towards the rear of the boat.

'Stop!' said Billy Ray and kneeling down, he searched the man's pockets and recovered all three cell phones, including the gunman's. He got up and stuffed them in his short's pockets.

'Okay Valentina, pull.'

They managed to get him right to the rear of the boat then propped him up against the rail and turned him, so he half flopped over the side. Billy Ray squatted down, got hold of the gunman's ankles and lifted. As he did so, the gunman started to moan and wake up.

'Have a nice swim you fucking murdering bastard,' shouted Billy Ray as he gave the final heave. Lenny screamed as he was pitched over the side, the chains ensuring he made a speedy descent to the bottom of the ocean.

'What about the other two Billy Ray?'

'We have to throw them in as well, but I want Jerry's body to be found. I owe that to him at least.' They rested just long enough to get their strength back, then manhandled the other two bodies into the water. Billy Ray stood by the rails for a while looking at Jerry's body as it floated off. Valentina began to cry.

'Look I'm upset as well Valentina, but we ain't got time for grieving, we can do that later.

'Okay Billy Ray,' said Valentina.

'Good girl, said Billy Ray, kissing her on the forehead. 'Look, first we're going to have to get that carpet up and ditch it overboard, then I'll set a course for Fort Pierce. Once we get there, we leave the boat, and get my truck.'

They arrived back at Fort Pierce City Marina, moored the boat and disembarked as quickly and as quietly as they could, then made their way to Billy Ray's truck. He exited the parking lot and drove slowly through Fort Pierce.

'Why're you driving so slow Billy Ray?'

'Looking for a parking lot, a big one, preferably multi-story. I need to change my plate. Not taking any chances this time Valentina. Soon as I do, we can be on our way, and I think I know where we can go where no one will find us.'

CHAPTER 8

BEFORE - FRANKIE

His war experience dramatically changed Frank's outlook on life; more it seemed than the others he'd served with. At first, he'd kept in touch with quite a few of his army mates, then apart from Barnsie, gradually withdrew as he tried to forget and carve out a new life. He'd married Penny within three months of getting back.

A small wedding, by contemporary standards. Frankie's childhood friend Derek Barnes as best man. The ceremony was held in a quaint church out in the Cheshire countryside, followed by a meal in a 'gourmet' pub. There were only forty guests or so, but Frankie didn't care. As far as he was concerned the only thing that he cared about was Penny. Just the two of them would have been fine by him. After they'd returned from their honeymoon in Mallorca, Penny went back to her job, teaching in a local primary school and

Frankie set about getting a job.

'Any interviews in the pipeline Frankie?' asked Penny one evening just after she'd come home from work. Frankie was leafing through the local paper.

'Nope, nothing appeals, still looking though.'

'What about going back to the building trade? You did well there, starting as a bricklayer and ending up in management. Didn't your old employer say you could go back and work for them if you wanted?'

'Yeah, but I got bored with the building game, which is why I left and joined the army. Same with Barnsie, he was in a dead-end job, and the army was his way out as well. And we were both enjoying it, until they sent us to fight in an actual war. I mean how unfair was that, sending soldiers to fight a war?'

'Yeah, too right Frankie Armstrong. But seriously, you need to get something. It's not just the money, but it's bad for you to be doing nothing. You're fit, talented and intelligent, so come on get out there and get stuck in.'

'I will, but somehow I just can't get enthusiastic about anything. By the way, you missed out handsome.'

'Well at least your sense of humour's still just about intact, but seriously Frankie, I think you're suffering some sort of low level post-traumatic stress.' Frankie put the paper down.

'Are you kidding me?'

'No I'm not Frankie. The man I married wouldn't sit around all day while our savings get more and more depleted. The Frankie I married would be up and at 'em.'

'It's Friday, and I'm off to the pub, said I'd meet Derek for a pint. Don't wait up.'

As he walked to the pub, he regretted what he'd just said to Penny. He knew she'd been more than patient, appreciating the impact the war had had on him, *still, PTS, what a ridiculous thing to say* Frankie laughed a scoffing laugh as walked along, but inside knew she wasn't far off the mark.

Apart from Penny, the occasional interview, the odd phone call with his younger brother, his only other meaningful contact with anyone was with his old pal and fellow soldier Derek Barnes, or Barnsie as he was known to his pals. He met Barnsie for a drink in the pub most Friday evenings. This Friday evening would be a game changer.

'How long we been out of the army now Frankie?'

'Just over a year, I guess.'

'You still haven't found anything you want to do?'

'Nope, just can't find anything that appeals to me. How are you getting on with the warehouse job?'

'Great really, the boss gave me promotion almost soon as I started. Shift manager now. The problem being that little word shift. Earlies aren't bad but night shifts...man. So I've had an idea. We're both handy lads, both in good shape, capable, and in my case, extremely good looking.'

I'd agree with all that Barnsie, except your eyes are obviously failing, but the rest... So, what's the idea, Hollywood? You always did fancy being an actor even as a kid, soppy git.'

'Nah, Hollywood comes later, Security.'

'You want to elaborate on that?' Frankie asked.

'You know, we talked about it the other week, having our own firm. We even had the name, A&B Security Services.'

'I seem to remember that was after several pints of Groves Bitter.'

'Well I don't know about you, but I was serious. What we needed was a bit of luck to get started,' said Derek.

'Okay, and so...?'

'Well, remember Malcolm, posh lad who never really fitted in at school?' asked Derek.

'I do, yes, Malcolm White, glasses, clever bugger. Wasn't there long, moved to another school if I remember right. Just as well, he was always being picked on, poor sod.'

'You got him. Well, he isn't a poor sod anymore. Quite a rich sod in fact. I bumped into him in Manchester. Didn't recognize him but he remembered me. I was having a pizza with Rita, and he comes over. It's Derek isn't it, remember me he says? Anyway, once he said his name I did. And you know what, he remembered me sticking up for him a couple of times? Saved him from a beating from that well-known dickhead and shit for brains Bonzo, remember Brian Onslow?'

'I remember,' said Frankie, 'go on. I assume there's a happy outcome from this chance meeting?'

◆ ◆ ◆

'Listen, I'm sorry about earlier. I was an arsehole.' Frankie said when he got back that evening. Penny looked at him and stood up.

'I'm going to bed now. Apology accepted, but don't think that's going to get you into my knickers tonight. No sex for a month, make that six weeks.'

'Six weeks? Supposing I told you I'd got a job, could you shorten the punishment period to say, what, half an hour?'

'How could you have got a job while you were drinking with Barnsie in the pub? You going to be a barman, is that it? 'cos if it is, the ban has just been extended to three months minimum.

'I'm going into the security business' Frankie said. It was the first time she'd seen him excited about anything for a long time.

'Security' what kind of job's that?' she'd asked. 'Sounds worse than being a barman, what, doorman at some sleazy club?'

'Exactly that, in fact, a strip club, keeping the riff-raff out and protecting all those vulnerable, naked women.'

'In your dreams Frankie Armstrong, be serious. What are you going to do to keep me in the style I'm accustomed to? Scratch that, to keep me in the style I wish to get accustomed to?'

'I am serious; I'm going into business with Barnsie. A&B Security services.'

'What, you and Derek Barnes going into business, doing what kind of security exactly?'

'The kind that pays a lot. We've already got our first job. Barnsie bumped into an old school friend. Big knob in a merchant bank now and they've got a Saudi prince, some rich Arab guy coming to Manchester, well somewhere near Preston ultimately, visiting some racing stables to buy a horse he said.'

'Barnsie's got friends like that, since when?'

'It's a long story, but we're doing it. What's to lose?'

'Well, I suppose when you look at it like that. But this Saudi whatever person, surely he'll have his own security people?'

'Yeah, but they want some local support, and that's us.' Three grand for two days work.'

'Isn't that sort of work a bit...dangerous Frankie? What if people take the opportunity to attack him while he's away from his own country? Those sort of filthy rich people always have lots of enemies.'

'Don't you worry, we're more than a match for anyone. Do I look like a pushover?' Penny looked at him, just under six foot tall, dark brown hair, crooked nose from a scrap he'd had with an army mate when they were both a bit drunk.

'No Frankie you don't look like a pushover. So tell me more about this crazy idea.'

'It's not crazy. I'm as fit as I was in the army, fitter probably, and Barnsie, you wouldn't want to tangle with him. He could probably give the karate kid lessons. And this contract is only the start. Barnsie's mate says there's plenty more work if we do okay with this one.'

'You'd better get a new suit then,' said Penny, and smiled.

'What about the ban?'

'Hmm, I'll consider a temporary suspension,' she said and laughed. Frankie chased her upstairs.

◆ ◆ ◆

Four years later A&B Security Services had expanded its range of services to include; professional investigations, alarm monitoring and response, key holding, safe deposit boxes, credit checking, security guarding for business, twenty four hour CCTV Monitoring and personal security guards. The next business move happened almost by accident.

Derek Barnes's nephew Gareth was a computer nerd. No formal training, nineteen years old and a bit of a layabout. No job, and seemingly no interest in getting one. He'd been building computers since he was a kid and there was nothing he didn't seem to know about technology, PCs, the internet, programming, the lot. As a Favor to his sister, who wanted to get her son out of the house, if only for a short time, Derek got Gareth to set up A&B's network and computer system.

'You're pretty good at this stuff aren't you?' Frankie said to Gareth when he'd installed his PC and was finishing off installing some office applications.

'Yeah, okay I guess,' said the boy, his sullen manner and slow speech at odds with the speed at which his hands skipped over the keyboard. They were almost a blur at times.

'We had to get this new system,' explained Frankie, 'partly to upgrade the old kit, but partly 'cos we were afraid we might have been hacked into. The last techie guy we used said we'd be better starting afresh. Some bugs in the old system according to him.'

'Yeah, well you're clean now, and I've installed some good antivirus so you should be okay.'

'Anything else we can do to protect ourselves?'

'Yeah, just don't click on any email links unless you absolutely know where they've come from. Most people are so careless they leave themselves wide open, even the big guys who should know better. And get a password program, one that generates proper passwords and manages them. And keep your system properly updated.'

'Okay, you're the expert.'

'Too right I am,' Gareth said and laughed.

'Maybe you could come and check the system on a regular basis? Maybe every couple of weeks, make sure we're nice and secure. Could you do that?'

'Suppose so, but better ask Uncle Derek.'

'I'll talk to your Uncle Derek.' Later that day, Frankie told Barnsie about his suggestion.

'Good idea. Help keep him out of mischief, maybe an opportunity to talk to him, see what's going on in that clever, nerdy mind of his. He's a bit wary of me, being his mother's brother.'

'You might have that wrong Derek, seems to me he has quite a high opinion of his uncle, God knows why?'

'Boy's just got good judgement. But he still needs someone to talk to outside his immediate family

'But, why me?'

'Let's say it would be a favor to me if you'd try. Gareth's not a bad kid. I watched him growing up, and he was okay, then he had a bit of a problem at school. Never really found out what, but after that he changed, became a bit of a recluse. Stays in his bedroom most of the time these days, playing on that effing computer. I say playing, but my sister Sheila worries. She's convinced he hacks into computer systems for fun. She's heard him talking to his nerdy mates on the phone, boasting about systems he'd hacked into.'

'What about his dad, doesn't he talk much to him?'

'His dad's a useless tosser. Half-cut most of the time, not much of a role model. And Sheila told me last week that the kid's started mixing with some new and really odd types. Two older guys came to see him. She'd never seen them before, and she accidentally overheard them talking in Gareth's bedroom. I say accidentally, but she actually had her ear to the door.

Anyways, she swears she distinctly heard the words cyber blackmail, then they all started laughing. She couldn't hear the rest of the conversation. Sheila tackled him later, but he accused her of spying on him and went into a two-day sulk.'

'Okay I'll have a go,' said Frankie.'

Twice a month visits to check on their computer security gave Frankie the opportunity to talk to Gareth, and after a shaky start, they got on okay. Frankie was impressed at the depth and breadth of knowledge the boy had about computer systems, and it gave him an idea. Cyber security wasn't a million miles away from their existing business model of general security protection.

The yawning gap in their portfolio was cyber security, a whole new area of business they were missing out on, and one that was growing fast. The truth was they hadn't known where to begin, until now.

'You must be off your rocker,' said Derek when Frankie floated the idea, 'I mean I know the kid's good at that sort of stuff, but starting a new division with him in charge? I love my sister's kid, he's family, but he's a nerd, a layabout. A good day's work would kill him.'

'Look Derek; I've been watching him and talking to him. He's a bit of a genius on the quiet. Maybe he needs a break, a chance to show what he's really capable of? My idea is that using him; we can start small, dip our toe in the water so to speak. Short of advertising for some top professional and paying them a fortune, I don't know how else we could start in this cyber security game. And even then, we wouldn't know if the person was any good, I mean what do we know about computer systems?'

Barnsie muttered a reply.

'Fuck all,' in my case.' He said distractedly, obviously turning the idea over in his mind. 'Well, I suppose there's not much risk, well financial risk that is. But what if the kid fucks someone's system over. And then there are those dodgy types Sheila said he was mixing with?'

'Fair point Barnsie. You'd need to have a word with him, make sure he's not involved with anyone dodgy. And if he has got any friends who might pose a risk, then we don't do it, but my guess is he's okay. I'm a fair judge of character, and I think he's more lonely than anything else. As for making a mess of someone's system I've thought about that. We can minimize the risk, see if he's competent. Take it one step at a time. If he isn't as good as I think he is, our exposure will be minimum.

'I've done some thinking, Frankie continued, 'and I suggest we do it this way. We'll tell an existing client we're starting this new service and ask them if we can do a free check on their computer system, provide a report for them and see where we go from there. That will tell us a lot.'

'Hmm,' said Barnsie 'okay. But one of us needs to have a serious conversation with him, make sure we're not going to expose any of our clients to cybercriminals.'

'Agreed, leave it with me,' said Frankie. The next time Gareth came in to check on their system Frankie took the opportunity to talk to him. Gareth was doing some sort of scan, completely absorbed in the task.

'Gareth, when you've finished, I want to talk to you about the possibility of a bigger opportunity for you in the business.' Gareth looked confused.

'What sort of opportunity?'

'When you've finished. '

'I've finished,' said Gareth, 'it'll just run itself now for the rest of the scan.'

'Okay, well Derek and I have been discussing branching out into IT security, but as you're only too well aware, both Derek and I know very little about it. So, before we look for someone else to employ, we thought we might offer you a position.'

. 'Me,' said Gareth, 'a job?

'Yes, you a job, if you can do it. We want to take it slowly, and maybe you could be the one to get us started?' You interested?' Gareth hesitated.

'You mean full time?'

'Yes, one of those, where you get up early in the morning and come to work five days a week. And work hard.'

'Yeah, I think I'd like that.'

'Okay, Gareth, but before I make you the offer, I want to say something. I know you've probably hacked into systems you shouldn't have.'

'How would you know that?'

'Okay, let me put it another way. I'm going to ask you a question, and if you lie, that will be the end of any trust between us and the end of any opportunity there might be to get properly involved in this business, right? Gareth nodded

'Have you ever hacked into a computer system, or computer systems you shouldn't have?' Gareth looked at the floor, then raised his head and looked Frankie straight in the eye.

"Yes I have,' he said 'but I never actually did anything other than look. I think about it as a sort of challenge, a game, to sort of see how good I am at it, how far I can get into these systems.'

'Okay, well thanks for being honest, but you can see why that might be a concern for us can't you?'

'No I can't. I'm not dishonest. I might boast a bit to my friends that's all. Anyway, I would never do anything to hurt Uncle Derek or his business, your business. He's always been good to me, always, and I wouldn't ever let him down.' Gareth held Frankie's gaze, and Frankie thought Gareth was either a very good actor or entirely sincere.

Later that day, Frankie told Derek he thought they should give Gareth a chance

'If this little experiment goes wrong, Frankie, remember it was your idea.'

'Okay, and if it succeeds?'

'We'll put that down to my good judgement in agreeing to it.' Barnsie replied, then laughed like a drain.

And so it was that in a classic poacher turned gamekeeper scenario, Gareth proved to be quite a find. His first foray into ethical hacking was a huge success. The client, a private adoption service for whom they already provided tracing services, was found to have gaping security holes in their computer system.

Gareth provided a potentially devastating report along with recommendations for fixing the problems. All the more upsetting for the client, as they revealed, with some embarrassment, that they'd had someone else look at their systems only a couple of months previously and been given a clean sheet. A&B's cyber security business took off.

CHAPTER 9

BEFORE – FLORIDA

20 MARCH 2017

They'd been driving for over four hours, stopping only for essential bathroom breaks, fuel and food. They were now heading down the US 41 south of Naples and entering the Everglades.

'Tell me again, where exactly are we going Billy Ray? I don't have any spare clothes, nothing except the stuff I had on the boat.'

'Believe me, you'll still be overdressed for the place we're going to stay Valentina.'

'Not sure I like the sound of that. Can't we just take a flight somewhere, Puerto Rico, Bahamas, anywhere with a decent hotel we can hide out in?'

'No, too many opportunities for your husband to find us. He's got people everywhere on his payroll, and he'll have alerted them to look out for us. We got to stay off the radar, at least for a while. I mean look how easy those two guys found us. Just because I used a fucking credit card to buy gas for the boat for Christ's sake.

Having said that, we are going to have to use an ATM at least one more time to get some cash. But then we'll be so far away from it by the time they're alerted, they'll never find us. Talking of which, we need to stop and disable our cell phones, take the batteries out.'

'I thought you'd already switched them off?'

'Yeah, I did, but can't take any chances. I heard somewhere that phones can be tracked even when they're switched off. Look there's a gas station sign, two miles. Let's stop, gas up, use the bathrooms and sort these phones out.' A few minutes later they drove into the gas station, and while Billy Ray fueled up the truck, Valentina went to use the restrooms. When she came back, Billy Ray had moved his truck to the far side of the station forecourt and was sitting in the truck, door open, and in the process of snapping Lenny's phone in half.

He took the bits of the phone and the battery and dumped them in a nearby trash can. He put his own cell back into his right-hand jeans pocket and the battery in the left one.

'Okay, here's your cell back,' he said to Valentina, 'put it in your purse but keep the battery separate then there's no danger of it being tracked, okay?'

'Is this all really necessary Billy Ray?' He looked her in the eye.

'Yes, it is, if you want us both to get out of this alive.' She sighed, then put her cell and battery in her handbag, separately as instructed.

'Does this place we're going to have proper bathrooms and stuff Billy Ray? You lived there for a while right, is it.., I mean is it civilized?'

'It's not exactly what you'd describe as luxurious, but I can't think of anywhere safer for the time being. Your husband will kill us both if he finds us.'

'You don't know that.'

'Are you kidding me? If his man Lenny is anything to go by, he'll kill me without even thinking about it.'

'Is that regret I hear in your voice Billy Ray?'

'No Valentina, no regrets, but I think if your husband finds us he's not going to be satisfied with just killing us.' Valentina looked shocked.

'We've got to go to the cops Billy Ray.'

'Oh yeah, that'll work. How do we explain about the dead PI and Jerry and us killing your friend Lenny?'

'He isn't my friend. And that it was self-defense.'

'And they're going to believe us, just like that? First off, they'll arrest us, and while we're trying to get out of all that shit, trying to prove our innocence, we'll be in prison and how long would it take your husband to arrange for someone to have us knifed or worse? And if we ever did get them to believe us, proved we were innocent and got free, you think your husband would leave it at that?

No way. He's gonna come for us eventually, whatever happens, so no thanks. No one knows what happened and best to keep it that way. I need time to think. Come on, let's go, we've got another couple of hours at least and then I've got to remember the final part of the way. Look I need to use the restrooms, then get some cash from the ATM and hightail it out of here. Put as many miles as we can between here and where we're going. He started to get out of the truck. Shit, I forgot, we'll need some bug spray, lots of it, can you go back into the gas station see if they sell it.'

'Jesus Billy Ray, what kind of place are you taking me to?'

'A safe one I hope.' Valentina got out of the truck and headed for the gas station shop. When she was far enough away, Billy Ray muttered to himself.

'What the fuck have I got myself into?' He made his way to the restroom.

◆ ◆ ◆

The Florida Everglades comprise of over 1.5 million acres or, 800 square miles, of mainly subtropical wetlands. In the early 1900s logging camps were established, manned mostly by migrant workers. These camps were often violent places to work. The inhospitable climate didn't help – being home to hordes of mosquitoes, alligators, bears, snakes, spiders and all other manner of critters and creatures.

For additional discomfort add in some unbearable heat and raging humidity. The camps were long since abandoned, but now some people had found a new use for them, despite the continuing presence of hordes of mosquitoes, alligators, bears, snakes, spiders and other critters and creatures, plus of course, the still unbearable heat and raging humidity.

And so it was that Billy Ray and Valentina were driving along a dirt track in the forest, the light limited by the thickness of the surrounding vegetation, trying to find their new, if hopefully, temporary home.

'Are you sure you know where this place is?'

'It's been a while, but I think this is the right track.'

'And if it isn't?'

'Then we go back and try another track. Look a bear.'

'Jesus Billy Ray, I thought we were going to run

off to somewhere romantic, not the fucking jungle.'

'Relax, it'll be okay when we get there. A bit basic, but we'll be safe.' Valentina seemed unconvinced.

It was late afternoon by the time they arrived. A large wooden gate with barbed wire barred their way into the compound. Billy Ray sounded his horn and got out of the truck. Valentina got out to stretch her legs and was immediately surrounded by insects. She wafted them away. A man dressed in camouflage clothes arrived, a rifle tucked under his arm.

'Hi friend, name's Billy Ray, is Joshua still here?'

'He is. Billy Ray you say, and this is?'

'Yeah, my... er wife, well wife to be. Her name's er Lola.'

'Nice name. I'll go get Joshua.' Valentina waited till the man was out of earshot.

'What's with this Lola shit, what's going on here Billy Ray?'

'I just thought, you know, you have such a distinctive name, maybe someone would connect the dots. Maybe your husband's reported you missing, told the newspapers, has a reward out for information, I don't know. I just thought it would be better if we didn't say who you were. It's only for a few days, so what's the big deal?'

'The big deal is I don't like being called Lola.

Makes me sound like a stripper. Anyway, how are they going to know about news reports, rewards whatever? You telling me they have the internet out here in jungleland?'

'It isn't a jungle."

'You could've fooled me. Anyway, do they?'

'No, at least they didn't used to. The idea is they don't live like the rest of us. They want to live in peace and don't like all that modern stuff, say it's disruptive and so on. But they do have cell phones, at least some of them do, and that gives them access to the internet, I guess. I don't think they're supposed to look up things on the web, but people are people, and they might be curious enough, about you in particular. So just be Lola for a few days, it won't kill you, okay?'

'Yeah, okay I suppose. And this wife stuff?'

'Well they can be a bit, I don't know, traditional, old-fashioned. This lot are devout Christians, which is a good thing. Very moral, so try to look wifey.'

'Look what?! Exclaimed Valentina, 'did you say wifey?' Just then the gate man came back with a person she assumed was Josh. He was tall, wore a Stetson, and dressed in jeans and a suede leather jacket with tassels on. Valentina stared *I got it wrong, it's not jungleland, it's the wild fucking west.*

◆ ◆ ◆

'Well well, Billy Ray Ballantyne,' said the man, 'what on earth you doing back here?' Then without waiting for an answer, he turned to the man with the rifle.

'Jeb, open the gate and let our friends in.'
Valentina stayed in the truck while Billy Ray stood a few yards away talking to the man called Joshua. She noticed both of them occasionally swatting bugs away from around their faces. *Jesus, what have I got myself into?*

'So Billy Ray, to what do we owe the pleasure? I didn't expect to see you back here I must admit. I mean apart from the dengue fever problem, I got the impression you weren't really cut out for this sort of life?' Billy Ray thought he'd be better telling the truth, or as near to it as he could.

'Well, it's a bit delicate Josh. See Val, I mean Lola and me, we're sorta on the run. She's married, and she wanted to leave her husband, He beat her, and she told him she wanted a divorce, but that just made things worse. When we met we fell for each other, and she ran away from this guy, and he's chasing her....'

'I get it, so you want to hole up here awhile till he cools down and gives up the chase?'

'Yup, that about sums it up. You okay with that?'
'Well, strictly speaking, I don't believe in divorce. Marriage in my world is for life, for better or worse, but I don't stand in judgment of others.

And I always did like you Billy Ray, so yeah, it's okay with me. How long you think you want to stay?'

'Oh, a week or so I guess, just till I get things figured out.'

'No problem Billy Ray, now you gonna introduce me to this lady of yours, er Lola was it?' Josh winked as he said her name.

'Sure thing,' said Billy Ray who turned around and waved for Valentina to come and join them. She got out of the truck.

'Hey, come and meet Josh here. He says we can stay as long as we want. I told him it was only till we could figure out our next move.' She approached them, and Josh held out his hand.

'Nice to meet you,' Josh said, surprising her with his formal greeting and cultured voice.

'Likewise, I'm sure,' she replied.

'I'm afraid you'll find things a bit basic around here ma'am, but it isn't too bad once you get used to it. I'll get my wife Tess to show you the ropes. We have a spare trailer you can use. Billy Ray and I will need to give it the once over, make sure it's clean, get some fresh bed linen and so on. You can wait in my trailer with Tess until we're done. Follow me, and I'll introduce you. Josh asked them to wait outside while he went inside the trailer

'Just give me a minute to explain the situation.' He came back out followed by a smart looking lady dressed in jeans and a lilac shirt.

Introductions were made, and the men left to attend to the task of preparing their trailer.

'You'll want to use the restroom after your long journey, down there on the left. I'll get some coffee on.' The trailer was huge, and if not exactly luxurious, was much better appointed than Valentina had imagined. More like a small house. She came back, and Tess invited her to sit. The coffee was good.

'Josh told me briefly what the situation is. Sounds quite exciting if you don't mind me saying so.' Valentina very much doubted Billy Ray had told Josh the truth, nor did she know what interpretation of the story Josh had told his wife. Being on the run from a murderous husband and three dead bodies weren't exactly her idea of exciting. Nevertheless, she decided to play along and say nothing until Billy Ray could tell her what he'd said. If they knew the truth, she had little doubt that these sort of people would feel obliged to get the cops involved.

'Yes, it is exciting, well sort of. We only intend to stay for a short while, just till we decide what to do.'

'I quite understand dear. Is it okay if I call you Lola?'

'Of course.'

'You just call me Tess and please don't hesitate to ask me anything. Oh by the way, did you bring any mosquito repellent, only I have some spare?'

Valentina shuddered involuntarily.

'Yes, we got some on the way here thanks.' Tess smiled approvingly

◆ ◆ ◆

The camp was much smaller than Valentina had imagined but also a little more civilized than she'd expected, at least during the day. However, it was a very far cry from the luxurious life she'd been used to. The first night they spent in the trailer had been an entirely new and frightening experience for Valentina. She woke up, just after midnight, in a state of near panic. Billy Ray patiently explained to the terrified Valentina that the strange piercing screeches, hoots, screams and other weird noises, were just birds and animals going about their nocturnal activities and presented no danger to them.

Unconvinced, she went back to bed, pulled the blankets over her head and tried her best to sleep.

Valentina found life at the camp variously scary, tedious and boring. Apart from cleaning their own trailer, she was obliged to muck in on general chores, prepare food along with the other women and do her share of cleaning the kitchen, while Billy Ray helped with the manual work and went hunting for food out in the Everglades. A weekly delivery ensured the camp was stocked up with supplies of more general food items and household supplies and fuel for the generators.

By the third day, Valentina had had enough. That evening after they'd finished their meal she decided it was time.

'Look Billy Ray; we just got to get out of here and back to civilization. I mean these people are very nice an all, but no air con at night, just a fan. I can't do this. Have you figured anything out yet?'

'Yeah, I have, well sort of. See, I figured coming here would let the trail go cold. So in just a few more days' time, I reckon it'll be safe to move on. We could leave and find a payphone to call my uncle Joe. I'm sure he can suggest somewhere we can go to. I could get some money from him, and maybe he could lend me another boat, and we can find a marina with lots of facilities, just like the Pelican Yacht Club. Swimming pool, bar restaurant but much further away. Or maybe we could go island hopping in the Caribbean, keep on the move for a while. What do you say?'

'You sure your uncle Joe would do that for you?'

'Yeah, I'm sure. We have, what you might call, an on-going business arrangement. Joe needs me, so believe it.'

'Well, why didn't you ask him before now?'

'Cos, he'd have cussed me and told me not to get involved. I didn't think things were going to get as bad as they have, but now, well we need his help. Anyway, I have an obligation to Uncle Joe, and I need to get things back on track somehow. Uncle Joe has a plan to make a shitload of money, and he needs me to help him.'

'Making a lot of money sounds good to me Billy Ray and a nice marina or island-hopping sounds like a big improvement on this place. What about afterwards?'

'Well like I say, I have this thing going with Joe, and we're gonna make lots and lots of money, so just have some patience, and I'll soon have you back in the lap of luxury.' Valentina smiled for the first time in four days.

CHAPTER 10

PRESENT DAY – FLORIDA

24 MARCH 2017

The sun was just rising as Larry and Clint arrived at their boat dock in Fort Pierce City Marina. The sea a coppery yellow, slick and calm in the morning light. The sky blue above the orange tinted horizon.
'Beeeyoootifull day brother Clint. A wonderful day to be alive and another great day to go fishin'.'

'Amen to that Larry. Got the bait?'
'I have. Four dozen shrimp, one dozen pin fish and some frozen ballyhoo.'

'Well dump the live stuff in the baitwell, and let's get to it buddy, no good reason to keep those fish waitin' any longer than necessary.'

Larry unhooked the ropes from the cleats and threw them on the dock, while Clint started the engine, switched on the Garmin and chose the pre-entered waypoints that would guide them to their Favorite fishing spot. Two hours and a whole lot of fish later, Larry whooped.

'You into somthin' special?' shouted Clint

'You could say that brother Clint. Jesus Clint, a huge mother this time... Hope this pole can take it. Man, it's heavy. Hey, pass the fighting belt please. Second thoughts, I can't let go. You'll have to put it on me.' Clint reeled in his own fishing line, put his rod in a rod holder and got the belt.
'Up with the arms buddy, can't get it on with your big fat hams in the way. There we go, what d'you think it is?'
'Not sure, not much fight, maybe one those goliath groupers, might be a sand shark, shit... Friend of mine had a goliath grouper on one time and reckoned the fish was so big it hadn't even registered the hook. Didn't know it was caught even! Jesus this is heavy, but it's coming, too slow though man.'

'Look Larry, maybe if you can get the pole in the boat rod holder at the stern, and I put the engine on nice and slow, we could haul the motherfucker up that way? Carry on like this, and your arms'll pop out of their sockets....'

'Good thinking brother Clint, let's do it.'

◆ ◆ ◆

'911 emergency service, how can I assist you today?'

'Hi, yeah, well, I think we just caught us a human body.'

CHAPTER 11

MANCHESTER

26 MARCH 2017

Frankie found Manchester airport security a pain. It took him over an hour to be processed. Once through security, he went to the pharmacy bought some last-minute items, then he got to the gate just as they were beginning to board the plane and joined the queue. He boarded and found his seat, a window seat next to an empty seat. Good no small talk.

He fastened his seat belt, the nervous tension he'd felt for the last few days drained away, and he felt pleasantly exhausted. The pilot and stewards made the usual announcements, then the plane taxied to the take-off position, the engines roared, and they were airborne. His eyelids felt heavy. He leaned back in the seat and closed his eyes.

Penny was running away from him, up a grassy

incline towards the edge.

'Stop Penny; stop!' but she couldn't hear him, too far away. He knew the cliff edge wasn't safe, been eroding for years. He'd seen a warning sign. He tried again to shout a warning...

'Sir, sir..' he woke disoriented and looked up at the stewardess. 'I think you had a bad dream, sir.'

'Sorry', he said feeling foolish.

'Can I get you anything to drink? He asked for some tea. He read for a while, then looked out of the window and began to think back. He'd gone home early from work that day to get his gym things. Thought he'd been looking a bit flabby of late and had decided he needed to start doing more exercise.

The folded note was on the mat when he'd opened the front door. He'd picked it up, put it on the hall table and went upstairs to get his things. He was back on his way out when he remembered and picked it up again.

Penny often left him notes about shopping they needed or if she was going to be late back from work. He'd opened it and read. He didn't believe it was genuine. *Some sad bastard's idea of a sick joke?* It ended with *Love Penny, please call and I'll try to explain. It looked like her handwriting.* He'd gone into the living room and sat down. He called her, confident she'd confirm it was a fake. She'd answered almost immediately. He remembered every word.

'Penny?'

'Hello Frankie, just a minute need to get somewhere I can talk.' He'd heard a door close. 'Okay, I can talk now.'

'Right, well listen, this is a bit, I don't know... weird. But I found this letter just now on the doormat, looks like your handwriting, says you've left me. Not sure what's going on, I mean who would send something like that, why would anyone..?' Penny interrupted his flow.

'Frankie, look I'm really sorry, it is from me.' He'd hardly heard the next few words she'd spoken. 'I should have had the courage to tell you in person, but I just...couldn't, so Jill suggested I leave a note. I'm a coward I know but... '

'You've left me.... for a woman?' Frankie had stopped talking remembering how he felt his chest tighten. He found it difficult to speak, to breathe. 'Frankie, Frankie you still there?' she'd said. 'Look I'm really sorry....' He'd found his voice and raged.

'Never a word, never a hint. Married all this time and you suddenly decide you're a fucking lesbian. Then you just leave me this stupid fucking note!' His voice had grown louder and angrier, and he'd felt as if his heart would burst out of his chest. He'd stopped and taken some deep breaths. 'Just, just when we should be looking forward to having..., having a good time. I mean, what was all that work for, building up the business? We've got all the money we need to have a great life. I thought we were free.. and now?'

'Look, Frankie, it's not your fault; she'd said, 'it just happened. I don't know....'

'Not my fault...not my fault!? Too fucking right it's not my fucking fault.' He'd replied.

'Frankie, calm down, you're going to have a seizure or something. Look I had no idea this would happen, but it did. It did, and there's nothing I can do about it.'

'There is something you can do. You can come to your fucking senses and come back home, that's what you can do. Is this because we didn't have kids? Cos remember, that was your choice, not mine. Mind you the way things are turning out maybe it's for the best.'

'Frankie I still love you....'

'Love, love! You don't know the fucking meaning...' Frankie remembered being suddenly so overwhelmed; he just couldn't speak anymore. He'd put the phone down and almost immediately decided what he was going to do. Looking back now, he realized his decision to kill himself was mostly to teach Penny a lesson, punish her for the hurt she'd inflicted. He closed his eyes and tried to forget. Sleep took over.

◆ ◆ ◆

He woke with a start as the plane landed heavily on the runway. Disorientated, he wondered where he was, then remembered. Looking out of the window, he marveled at the size and scale of Atlanta airport. So many simultaneous flights taking off and landing, everywhere he looked, it seemed. He checked his watch, asked a passing steward for the local time and reset his watch accordingly.

He then checked his onward flight ticket for the next leg of his journey to Fort Myers and estimated he had one and a half hours to make the connection. They deplaned efficiently, and after waiting for what seemed an eternity in the long queue to pass through immigration, he was interviewed briefly by a very pleasant immigration officer who asked him some questions.

He then had his fingerprints electronically scanned, and the officer stamped his passport and welcomed him to America. *Nice change for an official to be so well mannered and friendly* he thought. It was a short walk to the carousel to collect his luggage, which was then put on another carousel and was told it would automatically be sent on to his final destination. Deciding he needed to stretch his legs after sitting down for so many hours, he set off to navigate his way to the departure gate for his next flight on foot, rather than take the underground railway.

The underground passages of Atlanta airport were teeming with people, and as he walked along, he took in the huge pictures of Atlanta's civil rights heroes which adorned the walls. False jungle foliage hung from the ceilings in some of the transit tunnels, with works of modern art scattered here and there.

On one walkway wall were old posters of fifties movie stars. He eventually arrived in terminal 'F' where there was all manner of services and shops. Shoeshine stands, sandwich bars, restaurants, cafes and shops selling just about everything. Frankie found the whole Atlanta airport experience fascinating. It was like a small city in itself. He eventually arrived at the departure gate for his onward flight and was soon on his way to Fort Myers where Joe said he'd be waiting to meet him.

◆ ◆ ◆

The flight arrived at South West Florida International Airport, which everyone referred to as Fort Myers Airport, fifteen minutes early. They quickly deplaned, and Frankie followed the signs for the exit and baggage collection. He walked up the slight incline and into the main terminal then made his way to the luggage collection area, and he saw Joe waiting for him by the carousel. He recognized him immediately, a little older and maybe a little heavier, but the same big grin. To his surprise, Joe hugged him, then stepped back and held him by the shoulders giving him a good looking over.

'Well look at you old buddy... you've worn well Frankie. Look at me, fat as a barrel. Jeez, got to get me on a diet.' The carousel alert pinged and luggage started to spill onto the belt.

'Let's wait till we get your luggage then talk some more in the car. There's been a small development,' said Joe, and despite Frankie's protests, Joe insisted on carrying the luggage. 'That's my truck over there, the big silver one,' he said. They walked over to it. Joe put the luggage in the back and Frankie went to open the passenger door and saw the seat was already taken. Joe opened the driver's door. 'Charlie, get down on the floor. Sorry buddy, Billy Ray's mutt, we were looking after him when Billy Ray went missing. He's no trouble. Just ignore him.'

The little dog jumped down from the seat and lay in the passenger footwell. Frankie slid into his seat, placing his feet each side of the animal, being careful not to tread on him. The dog looked up at Frankie with doleful eyes, then laid its head against his leg and closed its eyes.

Frankie shifted his leg a little to make the dog more comfortable, then leaned down and briefly stroked its soft blond curly hair. The dog opened its eyes briefly, then sighed and went back to sleep.

'You a dog lover?' said Joe as he maneuvered

the truck out of the parking lot.

'Don't really know, never had one,' said Frankie.

'Better off not being, break your heart when they pass.' They drove out of the airport, stopped to pay at the pay booth to hand over some dollars, then they drove along the slip road on to the I-75 and headed south towards Naples.

'So, what is it you do now?' asked Joe.

'Oh, I work for a security outfit. Couldn't think of anything else to do after I left the army.' Frankie had decided on the flight over it would probably be better to downplay his security experience.

'Security, well that's great, means you got experience. I know a lot of ex-army guys over here went to work in security. What kind of security, do you specialize?'

'Nah,' said Frankie, 'just general stuff, meet and greet mostly, driving people around, that kind of thing, nothing exciting'.

'Uh huh, you ever get married?' asked Joe.

'Yes, got married almost as soon as I got back from the war,' said Frankie

'Kids?'

'No, you? asked Frankie

'Just the one daughter,' said Joe, 'nice girl but a bad picker. She married a loser, but between them, they managed to produce two beautiful kids, one of each, five and seven now.' Frankie

wanted to g
'So, a devo
'Yeah, a fr.
called Max. H
day before the
cent info we hav
where Billy Ray a
Max guy was able t
bit more accurate.
were looking for w.   , near
Fort Pierce.'

'Why did the Max   so long before telling you about the call?'

'He's another diving nut. Been on a trip to Cuba looking for shipwrecks apparently, only got back a couple of days ago. Saw a newspaper report about a couple of divers missing. He read it and realized it was probably Billy Ray and Jerry, so he called the cops to let them know what he knew. The cops called me to let me know he'd contacted them and gave me his number. So, I called him. Billy Ray had mentioned Max a couple of times in conversations, but I'd never met the guy. Anyway, he couldn't really tell me any more than he'd already told the cops, but maybe if you go visit him, you might get more out of him, you know, face to face?'

'Okay, somewhere to start I suppose,' Frankie replied. 'So why this Fort Pierce area in particular?'

ome spectacular finds
ast few years, Spanish gal-
o the reefs. Some guys find stuff
s of dollars off the coast of Florida.
e finds was big news a couple of years
uess that's what the attraction was.

Look let's leave it for now, you must be bushed after that journey, just relax. Let's get you moved into your condo, and if you're up to it, we can discuss some more detail tomorrow. You're going to need a computer to do some research and stuff I guess?'

'No worries Joe, brought my laptop from home, so all I need's access to the internet and I'm fine.'

'Well you'll need a car, so I thought you might as well use Billy Ray's spare ride. It's a Mustang convertible, so take it easy till you get used to it, it's a bit of a beast.

'What's Billy Ray driving then?' asked Frankie.

'Oh, he uses an old Chevy truck for the day job. He needs the truck to carry all his diving gear. The Mustang is his toy, only uses it when he ain't working on boats or diving for wrecks, all that stuff. Change of subject. So you say you married your girl when you got back?'

'I did, Penny yes.'

'And she doesn't mind you dropping everything to come out here to help me?'

'I wouldn't put it quite like that but let's just

say it's not a problem.'

'Oh, okay', said Joe realizing he'd stepped into somewhere off limits. 'You fish?'

'When I was a kid, keen as mustard, but haven't fished for years.'

'Well everyone's a fisherman, in Florida, even the women. Some great places to fish. You heard of Naples Pier?'

'I did see something about it when I did a bit of research on Naples before I left the UK.'

'Well when you get a few hours, go and have a fish, no license needed and great fun. Some big fish caught there. Billy Ray's fishing poles are in the trunk. Plenty of equipment too, so borrow the stuff anytime and have yourself a fish whenever you feel like it.'

'I will Joe, thanks.' They carried on chatting about this and that and eventually Frankie fell asleep. He woke as they pulled into the parking lot. The little dog was on his lap.

'Sorry about Charlie. He managed to climb on to your lap at some point, and I didn't want to wake you up by shooing him off. He's taken a real shine to you Frankie.'

'It's okay Joe,' said Frankie stroking the dog's ear, then lifting him gently off his lap as he got out of the car, putting him back on the seat. They went to the trunk to take out Frank's luggage.

'Oh, before I forget', said Joe and went back to his car, returning with a small box. 'I know you've probably brought your own UK cell phone, but I wasn't sure how those things work over here, so I took the precaution of buying you a local cell. Put a hundred bucks credit on it, so it should last you a while.' He handed the box over to Frankie. If you're not sure how to use it, look on YouTube. I never read instruction manuals these days, too easy to look at an online vid. Do that with everything I buy these days.'

◆ ◆ ◆

The Cove Inn was an old-fashioned three-story clapboard affair, with an exterior walkway all around the sides giving access to the upper story rooms. Frankie stood and took it in.

'Nice place this,' said Joe, 'all the condo rooms are owned by individuals but managed by the Cove Inn, so you get the best of both worlds, your own place and an income when you're not using it. A friend of mine from Connecticut owns the one you're staying in. Round the back, it has a great little balcony and a nice view of the Naples Dock.'

They walked to reception and went through the formalities of booking in. When they'd finished signing Frankie in, the man behind the reception counter came round to the front, gave Frankie the room key and pointed at the lift. He told them about the famous Cove Inn breakfast room called the Coffee Shop, and the outside area at the back, overlooking the docks, where guests could sit and sunbathe, plus he said there was a pool bar to the left of the recreation area.

'I'll get the maid to get some dog bowls put in the room for your little friend here.' He added. 'You'll have to keep him on a leash when you walk him though, and no walks on the beaches. Naples has quite strict rules about dogs.' Frankie and Joe looked down at Charlie, who had somehow managed to get out of the car and followed them.

The dog had firmly planted himself at Frankie's feet, looking up at him with something akin to adoration. Frankie started to protest, then looked at Joe who just smiled.

'Up to you buddy. Like I say, Charlie's taken a shine, and he's no trouble. Maybe you could use the company? He's a real easy dog, eats once a day, cleanest dog I ever knew. A walk in the morning. Like I say, up to you?'

'Well, I've never had...' He looked down at the dog.

CHAPTER 12

PRESENT DAY – FLORIDA

27 MARCH 2017

Frankie woke at three a.m., then again at five. He woke again at six and needed to pee and got out of bed. It was still dark. He maneuvered his way around the unfamiliar furniture to the bathroom. On his way, he saw a strange shape stir on the bed, then remembered. He came back from the bathroom, got back under the covers and snoozed until shafts of bright sunlight leached through the gaps in the window blinds making thoughts of sleeping in somewhat unrealistic.

He made a mental note to close the blinds fully in future. The light intensified as the sun rose in the sky and the clinking of the rigging on the yachts moored outside mingled with the morning birdsong chorus. Frankie gave up, got up and opened the sliding doors to the small balcony overlooking the dock.

He stood for a while stretching; eyes closed, enjoying the warmth of the early morning sun. He opened his eyes. A flock of small noisy parakeets flew by the balcony and settled in a tree on the right hand side of the dock. Seagulls wheeled in the sky over the water screeching noisily at each other. He went back inside, made some coffee, sat on the edge of the bed and drank. It tasted good. Charlie had padded over and sat at his feet.

'What the hell am I doing here and what have I got myself into Charlie?' he asked, looking down at the dog. Charlie didn't reply. He shook his head then went back to the bathroom to brush his teeth. *Shorts are the order of the day* he thought, and went through his still unpacked suitcase, dragged on a pair of Marks & Spencer's finest and pulled his Favorite old yellow Ralph Lauren tee shirt over his head. He looked in the mirror and ran his hands through his hair *perfect*.

'I suppose you want to go to the bathroom as well?' he said to Charlie. The dog was now sitting on his hindquarters at Frankie's feet, paws stretching up resting on Frankie's legs. Frankie bent down and ruffled Charlie's head, and tried to remember where Joe had put his lead. He found it and clipped it on to Charlie's collar. 'C'mon let's go for that walk'. Frankie found his sandals, picked up both phones from the bedside cabinet, turned them on and put them in his pocket.

The little dog wagged its tail in anticipation. Joe had shown him the basics before he left the previous day. They'd taken Charlie on a short walk, during which Joe demonstrated the necessary clearing up with a plastic bag. Frankie had never been squeamish, and although it wasn't something he'd taken into account when taking on fostering the dog, he guessed it was something he could cope with well enough.

They walked through the parking lot and round the corner to the Naples Dock entrance, which consisted of a wooden structure with a large sign over the top, reminiscent of the ranches he'd seen in old western films. It opened up on to a long wooden pier with fancy boats and yachts moored on each side, with more wooden piers at right angles to the main pier. At regular intervals, more boats were moored. To the left of the entrance was The Dock Pub and restaurant. Frankie made a mental note to give it the once over that evening.

A pretty young girl walked out of the restaurant entrance and immediately caught sight of Charlie. She smiled, came over, hunched down and held her hand out. Charlie licked it.

'So cute,' she said, 'what's his name?' Frankie was getting used to this. He'd already been stopped several times on his short walk from the Cove. *Naples' natives were obviously dog lovers.* He told her Charlie's name. She tickled Charlie under the chin then stood up, smiled and said goodbye. He watched her walk away.

'I think you and I are going to have a mutually beneficial friendship Charlie.'

The receptionist had given Frankie directions about where to find the beach, the Old Naples shops and the famous Naples Pier. He walked down 12th Avenue opposite the dock entrance and towards Old Naples. He felt the light and the warmth of the early morning energize and relax him.

The city workers were out in force, tending the verges, mowing lawns, blowing the leaves off the sidewalks, their noisy machines in sharp contrast to the otherwise peaceful morning. Old Naples was a mixture of low-rise shops and restaurants, cafes, art galleries and realtors. Pretty, opulent and quaint was his immediate impression. He turned left and walked along Third Street until he came to the junction of Third and Thirteenth, then another left on to Gulf Shore Boulevard and then left again and down to the entrance to Naples Pier.

Dogs weren't allowed on the pier or the beach, so he had to be content with viewing both from the road. He could see the beach on each side of the pier. White sand bathed in sunlight with early morning joggers and walkers doing their thing along the shore. He took a long slow deep breath.

'Does it get much better than this Charlie?' At the mention of his name, the dog looked up at him. 'C'mon, let's go back and try to find some breakfast.'

As they walked back, his new cell phone rang.

'Hello.'

'Mornin' Frankie, hope I didn't wake ya. How are you and Charlie workin' out?'

'Morning Joe, Charlie and I are fine, bosom buddies now. Just coming back from our morning walk as it happens. What's the agenda?'

'Well I'd really like you to get going ASAP, so I called Max to say you'd call him to fix up a time to meet today, but he's out all day picking a car up to take back to his garage, but he says he'll be okay for tomorrow. Anyway, be a good idea to take the day to get over the journey and recharge those batteries, then we start at it with a vengeance tomorrow.'

'Okay Joe, I was looking forward to getting stuck in, but I don't suppose a day will make any difference.'

'How about I text you Max's cell number, and you can call him tomorrow, first thing, to make arrangements, then I'll come to the Cove at ten with Billy Ray's car. You can drive me back to the boatyard, and we can talk some more.'

'Okay, I'll be ready to start tomorrow.' Frankie

arrived back at the Cove Inn and went to reception to get the low down on dogs and Naples. It was a different receptionist to the one the night before, so he repeated the initial information given to him.

'No dogs on Naples beaches or the pier,' said the man, 'but you can take dogs on the beach at Bonita, leash off I believe. There's some leaflets on the area in the holder over there; he said pointing to a shelf on the opposite wall containing a whole host of information guides. 'And then there's Delnor-Wiggins Pass State Park, just north of here, not too far. I believe you can take dogs on there but on a leash.' Frankie thanked him and asked how much it would cost for a taxi to Bonita Beach.

'Around forty bucks each way I guess,' said the man. Frankie decided a day on the beach with his new friend was well worth it. He asked the receptionist to book a cab for an hour's time. Breakfast called. He took Charlie back to the room, promising to bring him some breakfast back. *Why am I telling a dog that?*

The Cove Inn Coffee Shoppe made no concessions to cholesterol lowering food. It was a monument to hearty breakfasts, a celebration of bacon, eggs, sausages, pancakes, fried potatoes, fried bread, grits, toast, coffee and jam. *Heart attack on a plate* thought Frankie as he tucked into his bacon and eggs, *the best fried eggs he'd ever tasted in his life.* He asked for some extra sausages to take back to the room. That would have to suffice for dog food until he could get to a supermarket, he thought.

The cab arrived an hour later and took them to Bonita Beach. Charlie enjoyed his newfound freedom, running after other dogs along the beach and barking at the waves. Frankie was a bit nervous about letting him off the leash but needn't have worried. Charlie periodically came back to check that Frankie was still there. Frankie had taken one of the Cove's beach towels with him and lay on the white sand for a while watching the ocean and thinking about Penny, then decided life was just too short to go on wondering. *Here I am in a place as near to paradise as it gets, why worry about things I can do nothing about?* He got up, looked around and spotted a shady spot from where he could keep an eye on Charlie, then sat down with his back resting on an old tree washed up by the tide. He'd brought a book he'd found in his room and began to read, but knowing he'd probably fall asleep, as he almost always did when reading, he called Charlie, put his leash back on and hooked the other end around his ankle. Charlie seemed content to have a rest in the shade after all his manic running around and flopped down beside him. Some time later, Frankie woke and looked at his watch. He'd been asleep for over an hour. Charlie was asleep snoring gently. Frankie stood.

'Come on Charlie, better start walking back and try to get a cab.' It was late afternoon before they got back to the Cove Inn. Frankie felt tired and elated at the same time. *A couple of beers in the Dock pub and a takeaway pizza, then an early night, I think.*

'Busy day tomorrow Charlie,' he said. As he put the key in the door to his condo, he heard the distinctive Great Escape theme ringing tone of his UK mobile on the other side of the door. Opening the door, he moved to the table and grabbed the phone. The screen read Penny. He hesitated, then laughed and thought *why not?*

'Hello, Penny.'

'Hello Frankie, I wasn't sure you would answer. How are you?'

'I'm okay thanks..., you?' He leaned down, took Charlie off the leash and sat on the bed.

'Fine, I..., I wanted to make sure you were okay, I mean I was worried, you know, after our last conversation, you seemed to be a bit, well a lot upset really. I thought you might do something stupid.'

'As in?'

'I don't know, but you sounded so distraught, I thought maybe you might....'

'Might what, kill myself?'

'I know it sounds silly now I know you're okay, but at the time.... I nearly came round to check on you, but then I thought maybe not. Maybe it was me, feeling... guilty I suppose.' He was about to reply to say she should feel guilty, but she didn't let him speak and carried on talking 'Look, I know it was a shock when I first told you, and well, there wasn't a good way to say it.'

'You're right Penny, it was a bit of a shock, but then I thought about it and, well after a while, I realized these things happen, so no big deal. I assume you'll want to talk about divorce? I'll sell the house, and we'll split the proceeds fifty-fifty. This is one of those times when we should be grateful we didn't have kids.'

'Yes, I guess it is. But look, I would obviously have wanted to bring up the subject of divorce, and the house at some time, but there's no rush. And that wasn't the reason for the call. I just wanted to make sure you were okay.' She stopped talking, obviously thinking of what to say next. Frankie kept quiet. 'Listen,' she continued, 'if I'm honest, I'm a bit surprised. I mean you seem to be taking it all very... I don't know, you're being very, well, mature about everything. If that doesn't sound too patronizing?'

'No, it doesn't. Maybe you just don't know me quite as well as you thought?'

'Fair point, maybe I didn't, don't.... Anyway, where are you? The ringtone sounded as if you're abroad somewhere?'

'I am, taking a long vacation. Sun, sand and

you know…relax a bit, chill out as they say these days.'

'Wow, is this really the Frankie I was married to for what, thirteen years?'

'Fourteen actually, and yes, it is. How's Jill? Have you moved into her place or found somewhere new?'

'I've moved into her flat while we look for somewhere a bit bigger, but we'll stay in the area. I'll let you know when we move to somewhere more permanent. Oh, and by the way, I bumped into Barnsie a couple of days ago, and you'd obviously told him something. He was suitably discreet and didn't ask me anything.'

'That's Barnsie, discreet.'

'Yes, he is, well sometimes anyway. You're lucky to have such a good friend.' Then realizing what she'd just said, she continued. 'Look, Frankie, despite everything, I still love you, but just not like that anymore. And I'm still your friend if you want me to be. I mean in some ways I was probably just as surprised as you were, finding out I had those sort of feelings for another woman.'

'Maybe not quite as surprised as I was, but hey, water under the bridge.'

'Well, I didn't expect to have this sort of conversation I must admit' said Penny. Frankie could almost hear the disappointment in her voice, time to go for the kill.

'No worries, listen I have to go, someone's waiting for me.'

'Oh…, you're with someone then?'

'Yeah, a friend introduced us, and it was, well I know it sounds corny, but sort of love at first sight.'

'No…' said Penny.

'Yep, not been together long but things seem to be working out okay.'

'So, you're on holiday together?'

'Yes, self-catering place, really nice, great views.'

'Where?'

'Naples Florida.'

'Florida! I always wanted to go to Florida.' There was another silence, and Frankie waited 'So tell me about her, blond, brunette, old, young?' said Penny trying to sound casual but failing badly.

'Look I know this is going to sound really crazy, but he's not a her. And yes, he's blond, well blondish.' Now there was a stunned silence. He looked at Charlie and nearly lost it. It was all he could do to stop himself from laughing out loud. Eventually, Penny recovered enough to speak.

'You're fucking with me?'

'No, I'm not, and before you say it, or think it even, it's not a reaction or some sort of twisted revenge. I had absolutely no intention of getting involved…, with anyone, of any gender. It just happened.

'But I always thought you were a bit, well, old fashioned about that sort of thing?'

'I was, but you know...people change.'

'And are you..., are you staying together, I mean.... Sorry, ignore that question. None of my business.'

'No, it's okay. Yes, we're staying together in a one room condo. All mod cons, but just the one bed. Last night was the first night we slept together. It worked out well.' There was another silence. 'Penny, you still there?'

'Yes, sorry, still here.' Penny's voice sounded a bit shaky.

'Listen Penny, got to go. Don't want to keep Charlie waiting,'

'Charlie?' said Penny.

Yes, Charlie, and we haven't eaten yet. Listen, let me know your new address when you move and give my love to Jill, bye.'

'Bye,' said Penny. Frankie made sure the call was finished then erupted in laughter. He fell back on the bed, then got up and walked around the room and laughed until tears ran down his face. Charlie jumped up at his legs and looked up at Frankie, concerned. He bent down and patted Charlie's head to reassure him, but he couldn't stop laughing and carried on till he couldn't laugh any more. He collapsed full length on the bed and closed his eyes. He felt like a man who'd just woken from a nightmare. He vowed he would never let anyone or anything get him so low again.

CHAPTER 13

PRESENT DAY – FLORIDA

28 MARCH 2017

Frankie and Charlie were waiting outside the Cove the next morning when Joe drove a shiny lime green convertible Mustang into the parking lot.

'Some statement', said Frankie as he approached Joe. They shook hands.

'Yup, Billy Ray, never shy, always the showman.' Frankie walked around the Mustang, Charlie wagging his tail furiously, obviously recognizing his master's car. Joe handed the keys over to Frankie. 'Jump in, take her round the block, make sure you're okay with it. Easy on the gas pedal though.' Frankie got into the driver's seat, adjusted it while Joe got in beside him and Charlie jumped on to the back seat. The exhaust growled as they exited the parking lot and Frankie had to brake and re-assess his pressure on the accelerator. 'See what I mean,' said Joe.

They took her up 9th to the traffic lights left on to 5th and back around in a loop to the Cove Inn. Frankie wasn't used to giving way at four way junctions and would have cruised through all of them had it not been for Joe shouting in horror after going straight through the first one without stopping.

'Well, we all survived' said Joe as he got out of the car.

'Yes, sorry about that Joe, we don't have those in the UK.'

'Yeah I think I got that,' said Joe and grimaced. They went into the reception area, sat down and ordered some coffee. Joe took a black notebook out of his pocket and handed it to Frankie.

'I've made some notes, anything I thought might be useful. Billy Ray's cell number, his diving buddy Jerry's cell, Max's number, my number, the Detective in Fort Pierce I spoke to about Billy Ray going missing and a few other things I thought might be useful. I gave Max a call and told him to expect a call from you. I said you'd be going to see him today, so you need to call him and agree a time. He lives in Lauderdale, has his own business, so he's flexible. I've tried Billy Ray's cell and Jerry's, any number of times but no answer.'

'Okay,' said Frankie, eager for Joe to go now so he could make a start. 'I suppose I should leave Charlie with you?' he said to Joe.

'Can do if you want, or you can take him along, he's no trouble as you know, and there are not many folks who object to him being around. Take him with you why don't you?'

'Well if you're sure.'

'Can't see any reason why not. Oh, and by the way, like I said, Billy Ray's fishing poles are in the trunk so be as well to make sure the trunk's locked when you leave the car anywhere.' Frankie said he'd be sure to. 'So good luck and keep me posted. Not sure where this thing's going to go, but just do your best. Try to find the guys; find out what's happened to them.'

'Will do Joe.' They shook again, and Joe left. Frankie went back up to his room, checked with Google who told him the drive to Fort Lauderdale would take the best part of two hours. He called Max and said he'd see him at around one. Max told him he ran a small specialist car repair garage, gave him the address and they agreed to meet there. Frankie changed into some smart shorts and a plain light blue tee shirt, then walked Charlie round the block, before getting into the car. He tapped in Max's zip code into the satnav and set off. Charlie sat down on the passenger seat and fell asleep.

It didn't take long to get on to the interstate 75

otherwise known as Alligator Alley. As he drove along towards the east coast, he began to wonder what Penny would be doing now, *does she miss me or is she relieved we split up, and happy with Jill and her new life?* A huge articulated lorry's horn blared loudly as it passed, so loud he could feel the vibration. The sudden noise brought him rudely back to the present. He'd lost concentration and was straddling the line between the lanes.

'Shit, come on Frankie, let's not get killed by accident now,' he said out loud and laughed. He looked down at Charlie who was still fast asleep. He put his hand on his head and ruffled his fur.

'Fuck 'em all Charlie,' he said. The little dog woke briefly at the mention of his name, looked at Frankie then went back to sleep. Frankie switched the radio on, found a country music channel and sang On The Road Again along with Willie Nelson. The Interstate 75 took them towards Miami then a turn off to Fort Lauderdale and soon they were in the suburbs then as they got closer to the center, drove across numerous small bridges built over the many canals that crisscrossed the city. Fort Lauderdale was less busy than Frankie expected, and he took his time noting the contrast between the low rise buildings, malls, shops, offices and the contrasting high rise apartment and office blocks dominating the skyline.

The satnav took him to the beach road where he stopped briefly to put the roof down. Then he drove along by the miles of glorious sandy beaches. A few white clouds drifted slowly across the deep blue sky. A sea breeze kept them cool. Life in Fort Lauderdale looked pretty good. They arrived at their destination, which was situated a couple of blocks back from the beach.

Max turned out to be a tall black man, with a big smile and engaging manner. He was working on an old red Chevrolet, in a small garage with the roller door open to the street. He wiped his hands on a rag, and shook hands with Frankie, looked down at Charlie and smiled.

'That Billy Ray's pooch, Charlie right?'

'Yes, he sort of adopted me, surrogate owner you might say.'

'Cute dog, Billy Ray hardly went anywhere without him.' Max leaned down and tickled Charlie under his chin, the dog's tail wagged. Frankie waited while Max went to clean himself up and change out of his overalls. Then they walked a block down the road to an IHOP with outside tables. They ordered. Charlie parked himself in the shade under the table. Max asked.

'You two guys met in the army right, Gulf war, you and Joe?'

'That's right, different army, but on the same side.'

'Yeah, hard to miss the fact you're a limey bud,

that accent...' Frankie smiled. 'Anyways, Joe filled me on what he's asked you to do. I didn't know Billy Ray was missing till I got back from Cuba, then I tried to call him, hook up with him and Jerry for a beer, tell him about my trip, catch up, but I couldn't get an answer. Then I saw this report in the newspaper. The cops were asking for anyone who had info to call, so I did. Then I had a call from his uncle Joe. I told him Jerry, and Billy Ray had called just before I left for Cuba, but didn't say anything that might help. They were just shootin' the breeze was all, nothing specific. Joe asked about my call to the cops, and all I could tell him was that they didn't seem that interested, maybe I got the wrong impression.'

'Has Billy Ray gone missing before?'

'Yeah, well missing's maybe an exaggeration, he'd disappear sometimes, but only for a few days, maybe a week. And usually, that was 'cos he'd met some broad and fell in love - again. This time's different though ain't it? Been a while now according to Joe.'

'How close were you to Billy Ray and Jerry?'

'Not that close, but we diving guys in this neck of the woods, most of us know each other.'

'Describe Billy Ray to me. Anything, good or bad. What was he like as a friend, you know, reliable, honest, a liar, ambitious, loud, you know what I mean?'

'Yeah, I get ya. Well, Billy Ray was a happy

dude. Dependable? hmm, I'd say generally yeah, but would he steal my girl if he could? Yes, he would. Honest, I guess he was, at least as honest as the average guy, though he could spin a good yarn. You know, good at embroidery as my granny used to say. And yes he was, sorry, he is, ambitious, wants the lot. He's pretty confident and a likeable guy. Not sure if I can tell you any more than that.'

'Joe said Frankie lived with his parents in Naples some of the time, but that he stayed in a place in Fort Lauderdale, but he didn't know the address.'

'Sounds about right for Billy Ray. He moved around, depended on where the work was. He lived on his boat mostly, but I know he had an arrangement with some old girlfriend in Fort Lauderdale, where he stayed sometimes. And his buddy Jerry, he had a place on a trailer park. Billy Ray would crash there as well from time to time.'

'So, what did Billy Ray do for a living, to make money?' Max laughed.

'Anything to do with boats. He'd clean 'em, you know dive underneath, clean off the barnacles all that sort of stuff. Big demand for that beginning of the season. He'd do some repairs, engines, hull repairs if they weren't too damaged. Like I said, most anything to do with boats. And he knew his stuff.'

'What does he look like? Joe gave me a description, showed me some old photos but...'

'Hang on,' said Max and flicked on his cell phone. 'Give me your cell number.' Frankie couldn't remember it, so he handed his cell over to Max who scrolled through a menu then tapped the number into his own phone, clicked and gave Frankie's cell back to him. 'Just look on your images man, and you'll see a couple of recent pictures of Billy Ray. Here,' said Max and showed Frankie where to look.

Billy Ray had a similar build to his uncle, not tall but broad and muscular. He had dark hair, suntanned completion, deep set eyes and looked fit. He was smiling, had a beer in his right hand, Charlie under his left arm and was leaning against the Mustang. Max pointed at the picture and continued.

'We're all crazy. Divers - fairy tale seekers of sunken treasure. Maybe our moms and dads read us too many stories about shipwrecks and pirates. I did some diving for wrecks with Billy Ray off the Cuban coast a few years ago. That's where I got to know him and Jerry. We kept in touch, and they'd come around for a beer and a catch-up now and then. Billy Ray was always dreaming of the big one. We all were I guess, but Billy Ray, well he was more intense somehow, determined. Said he was going to make his fortune before he was too old to enjoy it. And he meant it.'

'How realistic is this searching for treasure,

sunken Spanish galleons and all that stuff?' asked Frankie, 'I mean it sounds like a lot of fun, but is there any serious prospect of finding treasure?'

'Yeah man. I read somewhere there are about six million shipwrecks on the ocean floor around the world. And around here there are hundreds of shipwrecks, maybe thousands, mostly Spanish, and still lots of them undiscovered. Most of them were carrying valuable cargo, including gold and silver back to Spain. I know some guys in Florida who've made fortunes, some officially declared, and lots of finds undeclared, but I never said that.' He winked and laughed then continued. 'Look up the shipwreck stats on Google man; you'll be surprised.'

'I had no idea it was such a serious thing. Don't you have to give stuff you find back?' Max laughed again. 'What, why is that funny?' said Frankie.

'Not so much funny, just so many answers.'

'I'm in no rush. I think I'd like to understand what it's all about if I'm going to have a chance to find Billy Ray. So, if you have the time?'

'Okay well depends on the age and what kind of ship. Might be something more recent than an old Spanish ship, so some outfit, or country might still own the rights to whatever's on it, especially if it's considered salvage, then you might have to give it back. If you declare the find that is?' Frankie smiled and nodded. 'Then if you do find a really old shipwreck with valuable stuff on it, you can report it, make a claim, but then the authorities know and depending on where it is, you might have to pay something. If you find a wreck in international waters, you're probably in the clear, but that depends again if it's considered salvage or not. It's complex.'

'I had no idea it was such a serious business, or potentially so rewarding.'

'You going to go get yourself some scuba diving lessons now?' Max asked, smiling.

'Not me Max, a landlubber if ever there was one. But thanks for the information, really fascinating.' The pancakes and coffee came. They ate, and Charlie had some scraps. The waitress brought out a bowl of water for Charlie, and he noisily lapped away at it.

'When was the last time you saw Billy Ray?' asked Frankie

'Not sure of the exact date, don't really live that kinda life, but I'd say about a couple of weeks before he went missing, somewhere around then anyway. I got a call from his mom asking if I'd seen him recently and that she hadn't been able to contact him for a while. Billy Ray was a bit of a mommy's guy in some ways and usually called her every few days or so if he could, so it was unusual, not unheard of, but... '

'And what was his demeanor the last time you spoke to him?'

'Demeanor?'

'Mood, was he normal, happy, depressed, what?'

Oh, right. No, excited I'd say. Said he was on his way, might be on his way, something like that.'

'On his way? What does that mean?' asked Frankie.

'To making it big, big find maybe, something good anyway.'

'Did you believe him?'

'No reason not to. I mean like I say, he was like the rest of us, a dreamer, but he wouldn't make things up just to impress, least I don't think so. But I guess you never knew with Billy Ray. Sounded genuine. Said he had a backer too, or maybe a few?'

'Backer, how d'you mean?'

'Well it's all very well locating a wreck, maybe even one that looks as if it might have valuable cargo, gold, silver, artefacts, whatever, but then you have to get the stuff out, Get it to shore. Get it to somewhere safe, preferably without anyone else finding out. And that takes money. Sometimes you can be lucky, and you can bring the stuff out yourself. It happens, but usually, you need specialist equipment.'

'And how much money would you need, to get stuff out I mean?'

'Oh brother, how long's a piece of string? Depends on the wreck, the location, the potential, the kit you need. And not just that, it might take a while to organize, and you got to live in the meantime. So some people sell shares, get investors on board rather than just backers.'

'So it wasn't just Joe who'd backed Billy Ray?'

'I don't know anything about that. I know his uncle Joe loaned Billy Ray a boat from time to time, but I didn't know about anything else.' For the first time, something in Max's body language didn't seem quite right. Frankie decided to leave it. He needed to keep Max talking. He could come back to that question another time.

'And have you seen anything of his friend Jerry?'

'Nope, the last time I saw him was with Billy Ray, the time I told you about.'

'You wouldn't have Billy Ray's old girlfriend's address or anything would you, the girl he sometimes stays with?'

'Fraid not. Her name's Deanne I think. I met her, but I don't know where she lives.'

'And the trailer park where Jerry lives?'

'Yep, been there, Windy something. Nope, Breezy Hill, yeah, Breezy Hill RV park, nice place.'

CHAPTER 14

PRESENT – FLORIDA

28 MARCH 2017

Frankie insisted on paying the bill, and they walked back to Max's workshop chatting about sports cars. They shook hands and Frankie, and Charlie got back into the Mustang. Frankie got the notebook out and looked for the number of the Fort Pierce Police Department Joe had provided. He tapped in the number and waited.

'Fort Pierce Police Department how may I direct your call?'

'Could I speak to Detective Sharkey please, Detective Pete Sharkey?'

'And your name is?'

'Frank Armstrong, it's about a missing person, a Mr. Ballantyne.'

'Okay, please hold.' Frankie waited, and the receptionist came back on the line.

Detective Sharkey is very busy right now, could you be a bit more specific about why you want to speak with him?'

'Yes, the uncle of the missing man has asked me to help him find him, and I really need to talk to Detective Sharkey. I promise I won't take up much of his time.'

'Please hold,' said the receptionist.

'Sharkey here, how can I help you Mr. Armstrong?' He sounded exasperated. Frankie asked if he could come to meet the detective to talk about Billy Ray.

'And you are? I mean are you a relative, a PI, what?

'No, I'm neither, just a family friend. Joe, Billy Ray's uncle that is, he asked me if I could help out. He's got his boatyard to run, and he asked me if I could help to find out where Billy Ray might be, so that's the reason I'm calling. If there's a problem I can give you Joe's number and you can check with him.'

'You a Brit?'

'Yes, I am. Joe and I met in the war, the Gulf war.' Frankie thought he noticed a slight change in attitude. Americans had great respect for their military. It seemed that might also apply to him.

'I'm a very busy man Mr. Armstrong, and you're probably wasting your time and mine coming to see me.'

'Well, I'd still like to come to see you.'

'Okay okay, but don't think I'll be able to tell you much more than you know already. You know where to find us?'

'I do thanks.' Back at the Cove Inn, Frankie had Googled the zip code for the Fort Pierce police headquarters which he now entered into the satnav. The journey took him just over an hour and a half along the I-75 then turning on to Okeechobee Road. At exit 129 the satnav lady instructed him to turn on to Sunrise Boulevard and eventually he arrived at his destination. The Fort Pierce Police Department was a large functional looking two story building set in spacious grounds of neat lawns interspersed with large parking areas.

The receptionist didn't seem the least bit fazed by Frankie asking if Charlie could accompany him into his meeting with Detective Sharkey.

'Sign in please, take a seat, and I'll tell him you're here.' Frankie obliged 'Detective Sharkey, your visitor Mr. Armstrong is in reception. Yes, I'll show him to your office. He does have a canine companion and wanted to know if it's okay to bring him along? No, a cute little thing. Yes right away.' She got up, smiled and beckoned Frankie to follow her. They walked down a corridor. She knocked on the door.

'Come in.' said Detective Pete Sharkey who remained sitting at his desk writing. Behind him on the wall was a large cartoon picture of him as a shark. Frankie entered the office, and the detective stopped writing. He remained behind his desk and extended his hand to point at the chair opposite. 'Please sit down Mr. Armstrong.' He noticed Frankie staring at the back wall. 'Police humor' said Detective Sharkey, 'and this is?'

'Charlie, he's actually Billy Ray's dog, the missing Billy Ray. We... er became friends and well....'

'Got a pooch myself. Dogs are much more trustworthy than humans in my experience' Frankie sat down. Sharkey leaned back in his chair. He looked Italian, thought Frankie, swarthy with slicked back dark hair. Shorter than Frankie but wider, looked as if he enjoyed his food. His office was a compact affair but had room enough for a decent sized desk and two chairs either side, plus some filing cabinets and a small bookcase. Charlie made himself comfortable under the chair. Sunlight streamed through the slats of the window blinds casting shadows across the pale cream walls. A ceiling fan whirred above. 'You want some coffee, water?' Sharkey asked.

'No. I'm fine thanks' replied Frankie, looking at the small mountain of files on Sharkey's desk, the detective noticed.

'See what I mean Mr. Armstrong? So, what would you like to know?' Sharkey didn't try to hide his impatience.

'Well, first of all, thanks for seeing me. Has

there been any progress at all?' Frankie got the feeling the detective was about to say he had, but stopped and instead of answering the question, came back with one of his own.

'So how did it come about, you helping the family find the missing guy?' Frankie gave him a potted version of meeting Joe during the Gulf war and the phone call out of the blue. 'So if you two hadn't been in touch all that time, how did he know you'd have any experience in finding a missing person?'

'He didn't, I mean I don't.'

'What do you do Mr. Armstrong, for a living I mean?'

'I'm a partner in a security company.'

'And does this security company get involved in tracing people?

'It does, but not my personal specialty. I mean I don't really have any personal speciality as such. I'm really more of a businessman. We have operatives who do the actual security stuff.'

'But still, a happy coincidence then, Mr. Nelson must be pleased you turned out to be a security expert, even if missing persons isn't exactly your specialty?'

'Well I didn't tell Joe I owned a security company. I thought it might build up his expectations, so I just told him I worked for a security company, meet and greet, drive people around, that sort of thing.'

'So why did you tell me?'

'Well I assumed from your initial questions, you'd check up on me, and lying to you wouldn't be the best thing to do.'

'You got that right.' So you asked if there'd been any progress tracing Mr. Ballantyne.

'I did, and have you? Asked Frankie, sensing maybe something had happened.

Well, yes, there have been a couple of developments. But coincidentally, I've only been appraised of them since speaking to you on the phone an hour or so ago. So that means, I haven't had time to fully assess the implications, nor have I had a chance to think about informing your friend Joe Nelson.' Sharkey stroked his chin before continuing, 'and as you're aware, there are two missing men, but we've established that Jerry Keenan has no living relatives as far as we can tell, so I guess Joe Nelson becomes the default contact and recipient of information relating to that individual also.'

'So are you saying you can't tell me about these developments?'

'Well it kinda puts me on the spot shall we say. It would be wrong for me to provide this information, at least without informing Joe Nelson first.'

'Okay, well how about we call Joe now and he can vouch for me, and you can tell us both about these developments.'

'The problem is, normally I'd take a little more time to assess the implications before informing the relatives. So, I really don't want to do that yet. On the other hand, I don't want to impede your search for the missing men.' Sharkey stopped talking, Frankie waited.

'Okay, Mr. Armstrong, I just hope this doesn't blow back in my face, but the main priority has to be getting these men back safely, if that's at all possible. So, despite our very short acquaintance, I'm going to go with my instinct and tell you what we have, off the record as it were. But, and it's a big but, you have to keep this to yourself until I decide to make it known to any third party, including Joe Nelson. Can you do that?'

'Yes, I can.'

Sharkey gave him a hard look, then sighed.

'Okay, well as a matter of routine, we did the usual description of the two men, an APB on their vehicles and plates and we've been monitoring any activity relating to Billy Ray's debit or credit card transactions. We couldn't monitor those of Jerry Keenan as we couldn't get any bank details for him, but Joe Nelson was able to provide details of Billy Ray's bank account. Using that, a transaction came on our radar. There was a purchase made at a marina some miles north of here, on the 19th March. A place called Melbourne Harbor.' Frankie had taken his notebook out and made a note of the name of the marina. 'Maybe if Mr. Nelson had informed us sooner.., anyway as soon as we got the information, we sent an officer to investigate, but there was no Billy Ray Ballantyne, or Jerry Keenan nor any boat called Falling Star.'

'No trace of them being there at all?'

'There was a boat called Morning Star moored there for one night.' No great description of the people on board. The office manager seemed to think it was just one guy.'

'And the other development?'

'Could be something, could be nothing to do with the missing guys. Bodies turn up drowned in the ocean all the time around here, but a couple of fishermen pulled a body out of the ocean a few days ago. Quite a distance away from the area of Melbourne Harbor but with the sea currents and tides, that really doesn't mean too much. The location of the find meant a bit of a delay in us being informed.

We've only just been sent an initial report. Apparently, The body's in a mess, not much of his face left, one arm completely gone, legs chewed off, you get the picture. Sharks, who knows?

There were some papers in the pocket, a bit waterlogged, but forensics say it was part of a receipt in the name could be Keenan or similar name, all a bit washed out, so the odds are... But we might know for something more definite by tomorrow when we'll hopefully get a match for DNA. Until then it's just a John Doe body.'

'Okay..., but no trace of Billy Ray?'

'No. Now there's something else, and this again is also sort of off the record. It seems you're not the only one looking for Billy Ray Ballantyne and his friend.'

'Oh...?'

'We've had word that at least one other guy is sniffing around. And my man says this guy usually works for people that are not..., how can I put it? Not the sort of people you'd want to have looking for you.' Frankie took his time digesting the implications of this information and wondered once again what he was getting himself into.

'And what significance do you attach to this information?'

'Well, it could alter our thinking. Is this really a missing persons case or is someone running, hiding from someone?'

'Yes, I can see that. So where do we go from here?'

'I'm not sure if I'm honest Mr. Armstrong. I think we'll reserve judgement until we get the results of the tests on the body recovered from the ocean and take it from there. Like I say, we should know something in the next couple of days on that. If you want to call me, I might be able to let you know if it is Billy Ray's partner, okay? In the meantime, if you find anything of significance, you let me know right?'

'Yes, of course. May I ask another question?

'Shoot.'

'Off the record, why might these people be looking for Billy Ray Ballantyne? I mean what sort of people are they?'

'If I were to guess, I'd say gambling debts, but I don't have any evidence to support that, just would be a typical reason these sort of people would be on your tail.'

'Okay, thanks Detective Sharkey, and thanks for placing your trust in me. I won't let you down.'

'You'd better not,' said the detective, giving Frankie a look that he interpreted as a serious warning. They shook hands and Frankie left with Charlie.

Once outside, Frankie sat in the car and absorbed all this new information. It was a lot to take in. He tried to decide if it was worth a trip north to the Melbourne Harbor Marina *not much point if the police have already established the boat and Billy Ray and the boat have gone. Anyway, the trail will have gone stone cold by now.* He looked at his watch,

'Too late to go anywhere now Charlie' he said. Charlie looked up and yawned.

'Yeah, me too. Let's go find somewhere pet-friendly to stay.'

The Sleep Inn hotel was basic but adequate,

had Wi-Fi and even sold pet food. They checked in and were given a room. Frankie decided to do some research online. Hooking his laptop up to the hotel's Wi-Fi he began to Google the subject of Spanish galleons, shipwrecks and sunken treasure. He leaned back and whistled in astonishment at the sums involved *Max wasn't exaggerating*. Alerted by the whistle, Charlie came over and sat at his feet looking up.

'Okay Charlie, got the message. Let's go down get you some food and see what's on the menu for humans, then after we've eaten, a walk around the block and an early night. Tomorrow, we'll go see Max again. I need more information. Okay with you?' The dog wagged its tail. 'I'll take that as a yes.' He said, then closed his laptop lid and took Charlie down to the lobby to see what was on offer.

CHAPTER 15

PRESENT – MIAMI FLORIDA

28 MARCH 2017

'Hi Zaros?'
'Speak Bernie, and you'd better have something good to report.'

'Maybe? The last place we knew the runaways were, was on a boat in a marina in Fort Pierce.'

'Yeah I know all that Bernie, but by the time Lenny got there, they and the boat had gone.'

'Right, but the cop in the Fort Pierce police department, the one on the pad, you know the one who told us about Billy Ray being reported missing?'

'Yeah I know, what about him?'

'He called me today, gave me a heads up.'

'And? Come on Bernie, I got to drag this out of you one sentence at a time?'

'Sorry boss, well he told me a limey turned up.

Guy with a little dog came to see a cop called Sharkey about Billy Ray, the detective who's in charge of missing persons.'

'And he knows this how?'

'He's got a thing going with the receptionist, and she told him about this guy with a funny accent and a little pooch coming to see this detective and the subject was Billy Ray.'

'You get a name?'

'Yeah, Armstrong, Francis.'

'Okay, anything else?'

'Yeah, my guy calls me back a bit later and tells me there's a body been pulled out of the ocean. The cops aren't saying anything official yet, could be a John Doe but they're not ruling out the possibility of it being Billy Ray's buddy Jerry Keenan.'

'I thought you said you burnt his trailer down, with him in it?'

'Yeah, I did boss. But maybe the guy wasn't in the trailer?'

'You didn't check?'

'Yeah, well no, well sort of. It was three in the morning see; I waited outside, check if there was any sign of someone in there, waited nearly an hour, then I heard movement then it went quiet again, so I thought the guy's got up to do a whizz…'

'So you set the thing on fire and burnt someone to death, but you have no idea who it was?'

'I guess that sums it up, yeah?'
'You are one dumb fuck Bernie.'
'Yes boss.'
'You heard from Lenny?'
'Nope, not a peep.'
'Fuck! If he'd found them, he'd have told us, or if not, he'd still have told us. So what's happened to Lenny? For fuck's sake, it's been over a week now and nothing, zip, nada. Am I employing professionals or idiot amateurs? Don't answer that; it's called a rhetorical question.'

'A what boss?'
'Never mind, anything else?'
'Nothing else, but my cop friend is going to try find out some more information on the limey. Who he's working for, that sorta stuff so should have an update soon, maybe tomorrow.'

'Yeah okay, but that body worries me. We send Lenny to find Valentina and this Billy Ray guy then nothing. Lenny should have been on the horn by now, so something's not right, then this body turns up. What the fuck is going on?'

'Beats me boss, but maybe the body isn't this Jerry guy, maybe it has nothing to do with Billy Ray or Valentina, or Lenny either? Maybe he did die in the trailer fire, someone did. I'll know soon enough. My guy says they'll try to match the DNA and as soon as they do, he should be able to let me know.'

'Right Bernie, well let me know. And find my

fucking wife and her boyfriend, pronto!'
'Yes boss.'

CHAPTER 16

PRESENT – FLORIDA

29 MARCH 2017

Frankie woke early the next morning and was out at sunrise to walk Charlie round the block. He decided a trip to Melbourne Harbor would be unlikely to turn up anything useful and thought a further conversation with Max might prove more fruitful. Frankie checked out of the hotel and drove to Fort Lauderdale. He found Max still working on the same red Corvette

'Hi Mr. Armstrong, back already?'

'Call me Frankie, please. And I'm sorry to take up more of your time. Just a few more questions if you don't mind? This place was on my way back anyway.'

'Mind if I keep on working while you're asking, only I got a deadline on this? Should have been ready yesterday.'

'Yes sure. You mentioned Billy Ray had investors. Any idea who they are?'

'Not really,' said Max studiously examining something deep in the engine compartment. We never discussed them in any detail. It was just, you know, talk like.'

'Surely he must have given you a clue? Look Max, I appreciate you don't want to compromise your friends, but if you know anything that might help me find him, you'd be doing him a Favor. I'm not the only one looking for him, and the police say the other party may not have good intentions towards Billy Ray and Jerry, so if you know anything....' Max looked up.

'All I know is that Jerry was into building websites and stuff, so I think they were inviting people to invest online, you know like crowd-funding, that sort of thing. But I don't know much more than that, okay?'

'Okay, any idea what the website was called?'

Treasure for something..., treasure for profit? Something like that. Now I've told you everything I know Mr. Armstrong; I really need to get on with my work now.'

'Just one more thing, Billy Ray's girlfriend, the one he used to stay with sometimes. Deanne you said her name was?'

'Yeah?'

'You wouldn't have her last name would you, and where she lived? This is important Max. I need to find her, see if she knows anything. Anything you can remember might help me find Billy Ray and Jerry.' Max stopped what he was doing.

'Well after you'd gone yesterday, 'I remembered her last name. You know how it is, you stop trying and suddenly it comes to you. Anyway, her last name is Dvorak, like the composer.' He laughed, 'I wouldn't have known who the fuck Dvorak was or how to spell it, but Billy Ray said people always said something like that that when she told anyone her name, and she always had to spell it out.' Frankie made a note in his pad.

'And can you remember where she lives?'

'Nope, not sure Billy Ray ever said, but I can remember where he met her, and she might still work there. A diner called The Floridian, Los Alos Boulevard. Nothing fancy but great food 'specially the steaks. Man, it's making me hungry just talking about the place.'

'Great, thanks Max. And the trailer park where Jerry lived,' Frankie looked at his notebook, 'Breezy Hill you said it was called. Is it far from here?'

'No not too far. Near Pompano Beach if I remember correctly. You'll find it easy enough. Here, I'll google directions for you on my cell.' Max fiddled around with his cell phone then showed the results to Frankie, who wrote down the zip code in his notebook. 'Thanks Max, you've been a great help.'

'No problem, and be sure to let me know when you find those two rascals.' They shook hands and Frankie left

♦ ♦ ♦

Frankie pulled up and parked outside the trailer park entrance, from where he could see the permanent and visiting RVs. He had a sudden thought. *After this is all over I could just buy me a big RV and take off around America with Charlie. Stay at places like this, swap stories over a few beers. Maybe meet someone?*

'What d'you think Charlie, the open road, no one to answer to, no nothing?' Charlie looked up at him as if trying to understand. 'Yeah I know, got to find these two missing men first and I will Charlie, I will. Come on boy, out you get, you must be bursting.' He took Charlie for a walk around the grassy area at the entrance to the trailer park then made his way to the reception building.

'Hello friend, help ya?' The man behind the counter got out of his chair slowly. He wore a white Stetson and sported a large moustache plus a well-worn leather waistcoat over a plaid shirt. Frankie felt he'd walked on to a cowboy film set from the fifties.

'I was looking for a friend of a friend. I'm told he lives here. Mr. Jerry Keenan.'

'And you would be?'

'Well, I'm really looking for Jerry's friend Billy Ray. They've both been missing for a while. I'm a friend of Billy Ray's Uncle. He's worried, and asked me to help out, try to find Billy Ray.'

'Jerry does live here, well most of the time anyways. I ain't seen him in a while, but not that unusual for Jerry, goes treasure huntin' and the like I believe.'

'Yes, he does. Would it be possible to see where he lives, maybe speak to his neighbors?' The man looked at Frankie, a steady stare eye to eye, then looked down at Charlie, whose tail began to wag. The man looked at Frankie

'You look okay I guess.' Frankie was tempted to respond but held his tongue. 'Thing is, the man continued, 'Jerry's place burnt down the other day, well night to be more accurate. We're lucky we managed to confine it to just the one unit.' Frankie took a while to process this information.

'What day was that exactly, sorry night?'

'Early morning fire chief said about three a.m. not last night but the night before.

'Have the police got involved?' asked Frankie

'Yep. They came early the next morning, but a sorta coincidence. They didn't know anything about the fire just came to examine Jerry's trailer for some reason.'

'There goes their DNA sample...' Frankie said out loud without realizing.

'What was that?'

'Sorry, nothing, just thinking out loud. Could I maybe have a look where Jerry's trailer was, talk to the neighbors?'

'Sure thing, just turn right when you go out the door, find the swimming pool and two blocks behind that, but all you'll see is the burnt-out shell. Can't miss it, but take it easy with any questions to the neighbors, they're still pretty upset?'

'Was someone hurt in the fire?'

'Little Banjo, burnt to death.'

'Banjo?'

'Yeah, Jerry's dog. I say Jerry's dog, but he was away so much, it was the neighbors looked after him mostly. Sorta community dog, great little feller, they all loved him. But he always went to sleep in Jerry's trailer. He'd howl the whole place down if he couldn't get into the trailer at night.'

'Oh, I'm really sorry to hear that. I'll take care with my questions.'

'Be sure you do.' Said the man, sitting back down in his chair and picking up a newspaper.

He followed the man's direction and found the trailer. All that was left was a large burnt out shell where Jerry's home had once been. As he looked around, an elderly man came out of the trailer next door.

'You from the insurance people?'

'No sir, I'm actually looking for Jerry's friend Billy Ray. They were partners, sort of.'

'Yup, I met Billy Ray, nice enough feller.' He pointed at the burnt out trailer. 'Deliberate in my opinion,' he said 'must have been trying to kill Jerry, but who would want to kill a nice guy like Jerry, let alone a sweet little dog like Banjo?' He bent down to stroke the hair on Charlie's head. 'Banjo had the same sort of fur, curly but black, a something crossed with a poodle. Everyone loved that little pooch.'

'Any idea where Jerry was when this happened?' Frankie asked the man.

'No, probably off on one of his treasure hunts likely. Cops were asking the same question.

'Told them everything we knew, which was zip really,' said the old boy. 'Jerry's a nice guy, good neighbor. I hope you find him soon, but he's going to be gutted when he finds out about Banjo.' Frankie couldn't think what to say, so he thanked him and walked back to his car.

Breakfast at The Sleep Inn hotel had been a self service all you can eat affair, but he hadn't had an appetite to do it justice and settled for some cereal and a glass of orange juice. He'd wrapped some sausage in a napkin and smuggled it out of the small breakfast room as a breakfast for Charlie. Now he was starving hungry

'Don't know about you Charlie, but a late lunch involving a nice big juicy steak sounds good. What do you think?' Charlie wagged his tail. 'I'll take that as a yes; let's go.' Frankie went

back to the trailer park reception to say goodbye,
but the office was closed, and the cowboy gone.

CHAPTER 17

PRESENT – FLORIDA

29 MARCH 2017

The Floridian was easy to find. The outside walls painted deep yellow with a turquoise canopy over the outside dining area, made it hard to miss. Frankie parked down the street and walked the short distance to the café where he took an outside table and hooked Charlie's leash around his chair leg. Two minutes later an attractive waitress came out of the main restaurant, menu in hand.

'Hello my name's Wendy,' she said with practiced ease, 'and I'll be looking after you today. May I get you a beverage while you look at the menu? My what a cute little dog.' Frankie was desperate to order a beer, but she kept on talking. 'the special today is lobster and steak, sorta surf 'n turf but with our chef's delicious homemade sauce…' Frankie held up his hand to stop the flow.

'What I'd like, er, Wendy, is a cold beer, then a nice T bone steak, medium rare, with fries, and mustard on the side.'

'Yes, sir. I like a man who knows what he wants. You're a Brit, aren't you? I mean that accent, just so cute' Cute seemed to be Wendy's Favorite word thought Frankie and felt a bit overwhelmed, not only by the attention, but by Wendy herself as she bent over to pick up the menus and deployed her ample cleavage in very close proximity to his face. As she walked away, he remembered why he was here.

'One more thing Wendy. Do you have a waitress called Deanne working here?'

'We do, but she's on a day off today.'

'Oh,' Frankie said, 'any chance you could call her? Maybe I could speak to her on the phone; it's really urgent I talk to her?'

'I guess I could. I don't think she was doing anything special today, wait here I'll go call her and see. Who should I say wants to speak with her?'

My name's Frankie, Frankie Armstrong. A friend of Deanne's, a guy called Billy Ray, he's gone missing, and I'm helping his uncle to try and find him. Deanne might know something, so...?'

'Yeah, I know Billy Ray. Let me get your beer, put your order in then I'll call Deanne.' The beer came then the steak. He took a swig of beer then proceeded to tuck into his steak, sharing some with Charlie under the table. Wendy came back.

'I got hold of Deanne, and she says she'll come and meet you in about thirty minutes. She only lives a couple of blocks back. Says she's been a bit worried about Billy Ray herself. Enjoy the rest of your steak Frankie.' She winked. Frankie carried on eating. It was delicious. He fed Charlie some more scraps. When he'd finished he ordered coffee. A new waitress brought it to his table

'Hi, I'm Deanne. You're Frankie, right? You want to talk to me about Billy Ray?'

'Yes and thanks for coming to meet me on your day off. Can I get you a drink or some food?'

'That's very kind, I'll just have a soda, but no food thanks.'

'Please take a seat.' She sat, and Frankie ordered her a soda.

'Hey, is that Billy Ray's dog?'

'Yes, we kind of adopted each other.' Frankie could predict her next three words.'.

'He's so cute.'

Frankie smiled.

'He certainly is,' he replied

'So, ask away,' said Deanne. Frankie explained the situation, how he was a friend of Billy Ray's Uncle Joe who he met in the Gulf war and was helping him out, trying to find out what had happened to Billy Ray. Then he told her about going to see Max, which was how he found her name. He also told her about his visit to Jerry's home at the trailer park and finding Jerry's trailer burnt out.

At this point, she put her hand to her mouth in shock.

'Jerry's trailer burnt down, why would anyone do that?' she asked.

'That I can't tell you yet,' Frankie replied, maybe an accident, who knows?'

'This is looking bad for Billy Ray isn't it?' said Deanne shaking her head slowly.

'Not looking great, which is why we have to find him, and soon. So your relationship with Billy Ray?'

'Yes, sorry. Billy Ray and I, well we were an item once, but somehow that changed. But we were still good friends, still are. More like brother and sister now. Sounds like you've already got a good idea of what Billy Ray was like. Nice guy. Bit of a gipsy, a bit of a womanizer, and a bit of a dreamer, but good fun. He stays at my place quite a lot, sometimes goes back home to stay with his Mom. And sometimes he stays on his boat. Comes and goes as he pleases, and that's okay with me. But he hasn't been around for a couple of weeks, maybe more.'

'So he doesn't normally stay away for that long?'

'No, but he has been a bit, well, preoccupied lately. He told me about this woman he'd met. Sounded like the real thing, or as real as it gets with Billy Ray. I got the impression it was complicated. Maybe gone and got involved with some married woman?'

'Why do you say that?'

'He didn't tell me directly. Let's just call it women's intuition. And you're now telling me Jerry's trailer burnt down, so I really don't know what to say. What happened to his little dog, Banjo?' Frankie grimaced. 'Oh no, not Banjo, what the fuck's going on, forgive the French. But it sounds like they're in a heap of trouble.'

'It does, which is why I'm here Deanne.' He took a sip of his coffee, then said. 'Course, it could it be that Billy Ray has simply run off with this woman and is hiding from her husband and the trailer fire has nothing to do with Billy Ray?'

'Is that what you think? She asked

No, not really, not a great believer in coincidence,' he said

'Neither am I. Did the other guy find out anything?'

'What other guy?' asked Frankie.

'The PI, came to see me a week ago, no maybe a bit more than a week ago. Said he was trying to find Billy Ray, same as you.' Frankie's expression clearly signaled this was news to him. 'You didn't know about him?'

Frankie felt wrong-footed and foolish. 'No, I didn't. Does he have a name this PI?'

'Yeah, gave me a card. Still got it I think. Why would Billy Ray's uncle not tell you about the PI?' She said as she rummaged in her handbag.

Frankie was thinking the same thing. She found her wallet and took out a small light blue colored business card and handed it to Frankie. Complete Investigations it said, Chuck Mainous licensed PI, address phone numbers.

'Can I keep this?'

'Sure thing, she replied.

'And he definitely said he was working for Joe, Billy Ray's uncle?'

'Said he was working for Billy Ray's family, not sure he said uncle specifically.'

CHAPTER 18

BEFORE

ZSOLT MESZAROS

In the years since 9/11 and the increase in terrorism in general, the focus of the US authorities had largely shifted away from tackling organized crime. But it was still there, flourishing under the surface in towns and cities throughout the country as it's always done. Florida was no exception, and nowhere more so than Miami.

◆ ◆ ◆

"Organized crime families have always had their tentacles in South Florida. It's kind of a playground for them. It's still lucrative territory. The great weather, the tourism, every kind of scam goes on here — there's a lot of money to be made," said Cicini, the former supervisor in charge of South Florida's organized crime task force. Sun Sentinel August 2016

❖ ❖ ❖

Zaros, or Zsolt Meszaros to give him his full name, was a vicious, ruthless psychopathic mobster. He'd grown up in Rosario, Argentina's most violent city. It was a good place to learn the business, a hard school as they say. But he'd been a bright child of relatively wealthy parents.

Ambitious for their clever son and eager to get him away from Rosario and his dubious friends, they packed him off to medical school to the Herbert Waldheim School of Medicine in Miami where he excelled in surgical studies, but soon became bored. He failed to complete his course, returning to Rosario without any qualifications. He soon picked up on lost time and re-joined his old friends, who by now were even more skilled in ways to make quick black money.

❖ ❖ ❖

'So, you're back Zaros?' asked the leader of the Sangre Roja gang when they met in the back room of the Bueno, Bonito y Barato bar, which the gang used as its unofficial HQ.

'I look like a hologram Sebastion? Yes I'm back,' he said, turning to include the other four members of the leadership in his reply, 'and I'm taking over.'

'Taking over what amigo?' said Sebastion, laughing and turning to his compatriots, his eyebrows raised, hand inside his jacket.

'The gang Sebastion, the Sangre Roja,' said Zaros to his back. Sebastion swiveled back to face Zaros, gun in hand, pointing at Zaros's heart.

'I thought you might try something like this Zaros, so as you can see, I prepared a response,' replied Sebastion, nodding down at the gun pointing at Zaros.

'As did I Sebastion, I suggest you turn round.' Sebastion looked round quickly to see four revolvers pointed at him. He turned back to Zaros, who in one fluid movement knocked the gun out of Sebastion's hand with his left hand, while simultaneously stabbing him through the heart with a stiletto knife, which had miraculously appeared in his right hand. With the merest cough, Sebastion dropped to the floor where he twitched once then lay still.

'Get him out of here,' said Zaros to the remaining gang members.

His uncompromising ruthless streak served him well, and under his leadership, the gang prospered and expanded their territory. But eventually and inevitably, Zaros's Sangre Roja gang clashed over territorial rights with the Demonios Negros gang, whose leader, Santiago Garcia, swore to eliminate Zaros's entire gang. Garcia's men planned and executed a devastating raid on the Sangre Roja gang headquarters, slaying most of Zaros's top gang members.

Zaros knew he was finished in Rosario. That it would take too long for him to build up his gang infrastructure to mount any serious challenge to the Demonios Negros, so decided in the circumstances, a tactical withdrawal the only option. For a while now he'd considered there were ultimately richer pickings to be had elsewhere, combined with a more luxurious lifestyle to boot.

He disappeared, and after a while, Garcia assumed his enemy had fled the country. A serious miscalculation. One month later, when Zaros guessed Garcia would have relaxed and dropped his guard, he put his revenge plan into place. Capturing Garcia's much loved younger brother, and using his expertise with a scalpel, Zaros made sure there would never be any trace of his victim found. Garcia would be left to grieve, wondering, and never knowing the fate of his brother. That was until Zaros decided to enlighten him by sending him a verifiable body part, but that cold dish could wait a while.

◆ ◆ ◆

Hooking up with one of his old medical college friends, Zaros began his task of establishing himself in Miami. He clawed his way up, first by taking menial jobs in restaurants and clubs to earn a modest living and to get his own apartment. He worked hard eventually becoming manager of The Seagulls nightclub in downtown Miami, which provided him with the ideal opportunity to become involved in drugs, prostitution and blackmail. As he moved into the gangland underworld, he knew he needed to make his mark and looked for the opportunity for a shortcut to the top.

That opportunity happened one night in a conversation with one of the nightclub's more nefarious clients. Rodrigues Lopez.

'You run a nice little operation here,' said Rodrigues, leaning on the bar next to Zaros, surveying the dancers as they cavorted to the salsa band.

'Yes, it's a great club Mr. Lopez, we are very fortunate to remain so popular. Nightclub people can be so fickle.'

'I was referring to your own private operation as you well know.'

Zaros smiled.

'That too goes well.'

'You know I work for Mr. Alfonso Lombardi, yes?'

'I am aware of that, and?'

'You must also be aware that club forms part of our territory, and you Zaros are effectively stealing our clients, so Mr. Lombardi wishes to pass on a message.'

'I'm listening,' said Zaros.

'Okay, well you have two choices. Stop what you're doing or work for us.' Zaros was silent for a minute as if weighing up his choices. But in fact, it had presented him with the opportunity he'd been waiting for.

'Naturally, I'd like to know the terms of my deal, but in principle, the answer is yes, I'd love to work for Mr. Lombardi.' Within months, Zaros had worked his way to the top of the Lombardi operation. He earned respect and the trust of Garcia Lombardi. So much so, that he invited Zaros into his inner circle, even inviting him to his family home on occasion.

It was one such invitation that presented Zaros with the opportunity he'd been waiting for. Garcia asked him to dine with the Lombardi family to celebrate his wedding anniversary. Zaros planned his anniversary gift with some relish. The event shocked even the Miami Crime Scene unit, who thought they'd seen just about every kind of perverted atrocity.

Lombardi woke up one morning to find his personal bodyguard and four members of his close family, his wife, his daughter and two sons, slaughtered, with their tongues cut out and their throats slit. The scene had been arranged in the bedroom, facing the bottom of Alfonso's bed. The three children were on a sofa with their arms around each other's shoulders. And his wife and bodyguard sitting on individual chairs, all in pools of their own blood to demonstrate the slaughter had happened in the bedroom, while Alfonso had snored the night away.

It wasn't just the violence, but the careful planning that impressed the criminal fraternity. Zaros had slipped some sleeping pills into Alfonso's dinner the previous night to ensure he didn't wake during the execution and setting of the macabre scene. Obtaining Alfonso's trust to get past the gang leader's elaborate defenses was also considered an amazing feat in itself. Alfonso and the people slaughtered were previously thought to be untouchable.

It was generally accepted that retribution by his extended family to anyone harming any member of the Lombardi family would be brutal in the extreme, but this didn't stop Zaros. And as if this elaborate crime wasn't enough to impress, Zaros made no secret of the fact it had been him, but made it in such a way that the authorities couldn't gather enough evidence to arrest him, let alone prosecute him. As for the extended family, they also proved to be intimidated and failed to respond. His unassailable reputation was made.

◆ ◆ ◆

Zsolt Meszaros's formal education, natural

charm and the huge amount of cash he'd accumulated from his illicit activities, meant he was also able to fit in with the more sophisticated end of Miami society. He became well established in the two most important and powerful Miami communities, and respected in both but for vastly different reasons.

To meet him in social circumstances, he was charm personified. He was feted in Miami's social circles. Considered a very successful businessman, a generous donor to charities, and a pillar of respect in the Miami community. His business interests were many and varied - restaurants, dry cleaners and casinos figured among his more respectable commercial activities, but other interests involved prostitution, blackmail, drugs and death.

Oh, and he also owned an Undertaker business. Not only a facilitating convenience to his darker business interests, but much to his surprise, also turned in a healthy profit every year from the legitimate disposal of the deceased. If healthy is the right term in the circumstances? He often joked with his friends. *'Who said that undertaking was a dying business?'* then would laugh fit to burst, as if it was the first time he'd heard the joke himself.

◆ ◆ ◆

PRESENT DAY

He was now on his third wife, a beautiful Argentinian woman named Valentina, some years younger than himself. She was tall, slim, raven-haired and elegant. He was particularly fond of this one, being also of Argentinian descent. That she had run away was hurtful and insulting.

When she was brought back, which he was confident she would be, he would ensure her life was unbearable, *for a while anyway - and prior to a tragic accident?* In his idle moments, Zaros would fantasize about her punishment. As for the man, or boy she'd run off with, he almost felt sorry for him, almost.

He thought about the body that had been pulled out of the sea. *The police thought it could be the man's business partner. So maybe Lenny found the three of them, killed this Jerry guy, and kept the other two intact as ordered? So why hasn't Lenny reported back?*

He shrugged, but couldn't stop wondering, *maybe Lenny found them, and they somehow got the better of him, killed him maybe? The only reasonable explanation of why Lenny hasn't called in. Shit, if that's the case, then it would drive them to hide somewhere even harder to find. Out of state maybe, or even out of the country?*

But then he knew running away wasn't as easy as most people think. He remembered the advice of an old cop he used to know. *'People never run away, they always run to something or somewhere.*

Once you look at it that way, you've got a better chance of finding them. In any event, he had an ace up his sleeve. *Her phone must be switched off or run out of battery.* But he knew Valentina couldn't live without her phone or talking to her sister. *As soon as she switches on her cell......*

CHAPTER 19

PRESENT – FLORIDA

29 MARCH 2017

The basement beneath Nelson's Boatyard measured 60 feet by 90 feet. It had sturdy wooden shelves along the right hand wall. The only way in or out was via some steep concrete steps then through a trapdoor, which was normally covered by some heavy boat lifting equipment. As far as Joe knew, apart from the people who installed the safe, only he and the old guy who sold him the yard back in 1999, knew the basement existed. Even Rudy, his manager, didn't know about it.

In one corner of the basement sat a huge high grade security safe. It had cost the best part of twenty five thousand dollars, including installation into a concrete base. He'd been assured it was thief proof, fireproof, everything proof.

'Hell, this safe could survive a nuke strike,' the

salesman had claimed. Joe wasn't sure if this last claim had any relevance in a post nuclear war scenario. Stored in the safe was some six million eight hundred thousand dollars. It had been a considerable logistical feat to get the money back to the USA. The original amount was nearer $40 million, but this had been seriously depleted by very inflated temporary storage costs, transportation and necessary expenses aka bribes. He looked at the safe and wondered. *Had it been worth the risks they'd taken, the effort, the planning, the stress. Only to end up with a load of cash, he was unable to spend comfortably, or leave to his nearest and dearest without fear of it all being confiscated?* He had finally hatched a plan to make it all work, but now...?

'Where the fuck are you Billy Ray?' he shouted out loud, then went to the stairway, turned off the light and walked up the concrete steps and through the big wooden trapdoor. His cell phone rang, he looked at the screen.

'Hey Frankie, how's it going?'

'Making progress of sorts Joe. Thought I'd call and give you an update. I met with Max, and he had some vaguely interesting things to say, tell you in more detail when I get back. I went to see the police Detective Sharkey, the detective handling Billy Ray's disappearance, then I met with Deanne, Billy Ray's old girlfriend. He shacks up at her place sometimes, when he isn't at his mother's place or staying on his boat that is.'

'Okay. So, are we any nearer to finding him, where he might be?'

'No, but, well looks like there's a woman involved.'

'With Billy Ray, there's always a woman involved, so what?'

'This might be different. Seems like he might have fallen for her big time, and there's a complication. She's married.'

'Don't tell me this is all about Billy Ray's joystick?'

'One way of putting it, but on the face of it, probably.'

'Unbelievable.'

'There's something Detective Sharkey told me in strict confidence, but I'm going to tell you as I think you need to know. A body's turned up, snagged by a couple of guys out fishing in the ocean.'

'What, they think it might be Billy Ray?'

'No Joe, least they very much doubt it. They can't be certain till they've done some more tests, DNA and all that sort of stuff, Detective Sharkey says it could be anyone. They get lots of bodies showing up in the ocean, so we shouldn't jump to any conclusions.'

'When do they think they'll get the results?'

'Well, that's the other thing. I sort of assumed the cops would collect DNA from Jerry's home, but when I went to look where Jerry lived, a trailer park in Fort Lauderdale. Jerry's trailer had been burnt down a couple of days previously.'

'Holy moly, what the fuck is going on?'

"I don't know Joe. Could be a coincidence, or could be Jerry's in the firing line as well, 'cos he's so closely associated with Billy Ray? Listen, can you think where Billy Ray might hole up, where he might hide? It would have to be somewhere three of them could live, although that might now be just Billy Ray and this woman.'

'I've been racking my brains about that Frankie but haven't come up with anything yet. Let me have another think. There's something at the back of my mind, but I can't quite get it.' Joe stopped speaking.

You still there Joe?'

'Yeah, it's just beginning to sink in, Jerry maybe being dead an all. I can't believe it, poor guy. We just got to find Billy Ray and soon.'

'Trying my best Joe. I'll probably drive back later today, so maybe see you tomorrow?'

'Sure thing Frankie,' Joe replied. Frankie decided to drive the one hundred miles back to Naples on the US41, the Tamiami Trail being the more scenic route through the Everglades. He'd been told that as he neared Naples, he'd probably get to see some of the gators that sunbathed on the banks of the canal running alongside the road. He left the suburbs behind and kept a steady speed along the two lane. Soon he was driving along the tree lined highway and once again he was awed by the sheer vastness of the sky, the light and the seemingly never ending grass lush, sturdy sawgrass prairies.

He passed by the Big Cyprus National Preserve, and then past the numerous Air Boat Ride companies, offering tours of the Everglade wetlands, past the Miccosukee Indian Village and wildlife parks with boardwalks. Alongside the road were huge black birds by the canal, flapping their wings, or just sitting with their wings out drying them in the warm Florida sunshine.

As he neared Naples, he saw his first alligator. He braked, amazed, then quickly looked in his rear mirror. Luckily there was no traffic behind him, so he pulled into a small parking area a little further up the road, put Charlie on his leash and walked back carefully along the narrow path by the side of the road. On the opposite side of the canal, not more than a few yards away, was a huge dark grey alligator lying on the bank, immobile, sunbathing. Charlie growled. The first time Frankie had heard an aggressive sound from him. He laughed.

'You'd make a very nice lunch for that monster Charlie.' Charlie didn't respond.

CHAPTER 20

PRESENT – FLORIDA

30 MARCH

Frankie woke up in his room at the Cove Inn. It took him a while to re-orient himself to his whereabouts. The sun was streaming through the curtains. Another beautiful Florida day. Charlie gave a little bark.

'I hear you Charlie. Come on.' After a walk around the block, they went back to the room, and Frankie showered shaved then went down for some breakfast. As usual, he brought something back for Charlie, and while the little dog was tucking in, he called Joe on his cell. Joe answered on the second ring. They made arrangements to meet at the boatyard at one o'clock. Joe said he could make it earlier, but Frankie declined, he needed time to think.

He spent the next hour doing his washing and chores, then took Charlie for another walk around the block, before leaving him in the room. Frankie changed into his shorts, got the small rucksack he'd bought and packed a towel in it along with a bottle of water, then left the condo and walked to Naples Pier. He watched the fishermen for a while before going down the wooden steps to the beach, found a space to put his towel down then went for a paddle in the crystal clear water watching shoals of small fish dart around his legs. He walked back up the beach, took his tee shirt off and lay down on his towel in the sun. He closed his eyes and dozed off.

When he opened his eyes, he noticed an attractive young woman unfolding a beach chair almost next to him. She wore a skimpy yellow bikini, had a deep tan, and wore her dark hair scraped up into a bun. She bent over to retrieve her beach towel which had slipped off the chair on to the sand. He couldn't help but take in her shapely figure. She turned quickly and caught him looking.

'You staring at my butt?' she said sternly.

'No, sorry I was...' She started laughing at his embarrassment.

'It's okay; I was teasing. You're the English guy with the little dog right?'

'Yes, how did you know?'

'I work behind the bar at the Dock pub. I served you a couple of times, and I've seen you walking your dog around the block. I made a big impression obviously.'

'No, I recognize you now. You look different.'

'Without any clothes on you mean?' They both laughed.

'You staying at the Cove Inn?'

'Yes, how did you know?'

'Just a guess. Lots of folks who come to the Dock pub stay there. Great little place ain't it?'

'Yes it is, really nice.' He wasn't sure if he was being picked up, or if she was just being friendly. He started to get up.

'Not scared you off have I?' she asked smiling

'No, I have to get back to make a call to someone back home?'

'Wife, girlfriend?'

'No, don't have either of those at the moment. It's a call to my business partner.'

'Right, Sounds like you're free to take me for a drink sometime then. My name's Mandy, yours?'

'Frankie, Frankie Armstrong and er yes, I'd love to take you for a drink.'

'Okay, well I'm on lunchtime duty this week, so call in the Dock any day, and we can make arrangements.'

'I look forward to that Mandy and very nice to meet you.'

'Back at ya,' which came out as backachya. Frankie looked nonplussed. 'Sorry, forgot you're a Brit, it means,' she put on a faux posh accent 'likewise I'm sure,' and did a little curtsy, then laughed. Frankie was captivated

'Okay, I get it now,' he said

'This date is going to be fun,' said Mandy and laughed some more.

'I'm sure it will be,' he replied, then bid her farewell and left the beach. As he made his way back to the Cove Inn, he smiled, *haven't lost the touch*, a spring in his step. Back in his room Frankie found his UK mobile and called Derek.

'Frankie, there you are, how you doing?'

'Okay Barnsie, you?'

'I am Frankie, I am. Is it true you've gone on holiday to Florida?'

'Not a holiday really. I'm helping a guy out with something. Remember the American soldier who shot the prisoner who was about to shoot me?'

'Yeah..'

'Well, he called me out of the blue last week and asked me to come out here and help find his nephew who's gone missing. He was calling in the promise I made at the time. Told him if ever there was anything I could do in return for saving my life, he wasn't to hesitate. You know the sort of thing you say when someone saves your bacon? Anyway, it's a long story, but things maybe aren't quite as straightforward as I was led to believe, so not sure how long I'll be staying.'

'Sounds intriguing Frankie. Tell me more.'

'Not now Barnsie, I need to find out a bit more

myself before I do.'

'Okay then, when you have the time. Email me first so I can be in the right place. Sounds like a long conversation. And... I'm not sure I should be saying this, but the grapevine, you know how it is? I heard why Penny left and just couldn't believe it. Never in a million would I have thought.... Anyway, I just thought I'd be straight with you and let you know I knew.

'That's okay Barnsie; it was bound to become common knowledge I guess.

'And, by the way Frankie, the same little birdie told me you've struck up a relationship over there, that true?' Frankie laughed.

'Not in the way you might be thinking, but don't tell anyone else I said that okay?'

'Okay, I think I get it.'

'Well get this as well. I was minding my own business, sunbathing on the beach just now, and a beautiful young woman, and I mean stunning, struck up a conversation with me and asked me to take her out for a drink.'

'Yeah right.'

'Honest, cross my heart.'

'All I can say is, if it's true, it would make a great Specsavers ad.'

'Cheeky bastard. Anyway change of subject, how's the nerd doing?'

'I assume you mean our senior IT operative, aka my nephew the nerd. He's actually doing great. Had to employ an assistant we've got so much work on. This cyber security thing was a great idea. It was me who thought it up wasn't it?'

'Of course it was, just after I'd suggested it to you. Anyway, I want him to look into something when he has a spare few minutes.'

'Okay, details.'

'Ask him to look for a website www. treasure for you.com, or maybe the four being the figure four, you know, instead of the word four? The people associated with it would be a Billy Ray Ballantyne and Jerry Keenen. Jerry Keenen might also be the guy who constructed the website. It's a website inviting investors to buy into a treasure hunt enterprise.

'Hold on there soldier, let me get a pen and a piece of paper. Okay, repeat.' Frankie did so. 'Got it,' said Derek, 'so what's this website for again?'

'It invites investors to help fund divers, and if they find treasure in a shipwreck, you share in the find. And before you say it, I know, barking, but they exist, and you'd be surprised at just what a big business this sort of thing is over here.' Derek laughed obviously thinking Frankie was exaggerating.

'If you say so Frankie. Leave it with me, and I'll get him on it.'

'Okay, thanks Barnsie. Call you later. Got to go now, see a man about a missing PI. Speak soon.

'Yeah, oh, and let me know how you go on with

Miss Florida.'

CHAPTER 21

PRESENT – FLORIDA

30 MARCH

Nelson's Boat Yard was located on Airport Pulling Road, surrounded by wire mesh fencing and full of boats on trailers. Boats of all sorts of sizes, ages, colors and condition. Frankie knew very little about the price of boats, but the size of Joe's inventory seemed to be at odds with his story of being broke. Joe appeared from an office located in the right hand back corner of the yard. It was a large wooden shed like construction painted black, with plenty of windows through which to see people entering the yard, or perusing boats.

Frankie had parked the bright green Mustang in a customer parking space and was now wandering around looking at the various boats for sale. He became fascinated with the variety on offer and began to idly imagine owning one and spending every day fishing in the blue waters of the Gulf of Mexico, getting a tan and swapping the one that got away stories over a few beers in a bar at night with other fishermen. A loud voice startled him out of his reverie.

'Hello Frankie.' Joe strolled over to greet him. Joe held out his hand and grinned. They shook, and Joe bent down to tickle Charlie under his chin. He straightened up and saw the look on Frankie's face.

''I know what you're thinking. How can this guy be broke when he has all these fancy boats, right?'

'It had crossed my mind I have to admit.' Frankie replied.

'Well see, most of these aren't mine. I sell 'em on consignment,' Frankie looked confused. 'Sorry I forgot you're a Brit. I don't buy them, I just sell 'em on behalf of the owners and take a cut, a kinda commission. So, unfortunately, I'm not as well-heeled as you might think looking at this lot.' He laughed and put his hand on Frankie's back to guide him back towards the office, Charlie in tow. Joe made some coffee then they sat down.

'Okay, shoot,' said Joe.

Frankie explained everything he'd found out, which was more or less what he'd already told Joe in the phone call the previous day. He had to repeat the details a number of times due to Joe's insistence on clarification of the smallest detail.

'Right, so good work to date Frankie. What's your next move?'

'I've got two things in mind, the second move depends on what you tell me.'

'Okay.'

'I need you to be straight with me Joe. I know you had a private investigator looking for Billy Ray so what's happened to him? And please explain why you didn't tell me?' Joe looked uncomfortable. Frankie kept his gaze on Joe's face looking him straight in the eye. Joe sighed.

'Okay, I did have a guy for a while, and he disappeared. I feel bad not sayin', but I thought if I did, you wouldn't agree to come and help.'

'You thought right Joe. Why the fuck would I get involved in looking for someone when the first guy who went looking has gone missing. Is he dead Joe?'

'I, I don't know.' Look he, the PI, Chuck Mainous, he found out that, well that a guy called Zsolt Meszaros was looking for Billy Ray. Chuck said that first impressions are that this guy Meszaros is a legitimate, respectable businessman in Miami, but when he looked under the covers, as he put it, he discovered that this guy, called Zaros for short, is a really bad actor. A hood, a genuine Miami gangster they say.'

'Who says?'

'Chuck's an ex Miami police detective and still

has plenty of contacts in the department, so he was able to get chapter and verse on this character. His legitimate businesses are profitable enough, said Chuck, but his other businesses are huge. Prostitution, porn, drugs, protection, you name it this guy's involved in it. Money laundering big time. Offshore accounts with hundreds of millions of dollars. The Feds have been trying to nail this guy for years, but he's been too clever for them, at least so far.'

'Okay, and...?'

'And well, Billy Ray might have run away with his wife. That was the last I heard from him.'

'What?! Jesus Christ Joe, so you thought you'd get me involved. Get me over here with a sob story then send me out searching for your nephew without telling me the risk I was taking?' By now Frankie was shouting. 'I could have been killed, murdered by some homicidal gangster for what Joe? A free vacation to Naples?' Is that how you treat people. I'm lost for words. Do the police know about this?'

'I don't know,' said Joe, looking grim. 'I don't know for sure that Chuck Mainous has been killed. He could have just had an accident, or maybe he'd been threatened and decided to disappear off the radar I....'

'Jesus Christ Joe. What were you thinking?'

'I guess I was thinking about Billy Ray.'

'You sure you weren't just thinking about getting your boat and your money back Joe?'

'No I swear it wasn't like that. Isn't like that. They were both silent for a while then Joe spoke.

'Will you still help me Frankie?'

'And why would I do that Joe?'

'Because I saved your life? You wouldn't be here today, wouldn't have been alive for all these years if it wasn't for me. I know I've been a jerk, irresponsible, not telling you the whole story but see, no other PI round here would help out after Mainous disappeared. Once they knew this Zaros person might be involved, they all took a pass.'

'I think I can understand why,' said Frankie.

'Is there any other way I can convince you to help?' I'll find a way to pay you, a lot of money.

'Thanks, but I don't need your money Joe. Is there anything else you haven't told me?'

'Yes. I kinda knew Billy Ray had met this woman.'

'So let me get this right Joe. Billy Ray's looking for a shipwreck, and you finance them so they can cash in on any treasure they find? Then he meets this woman, this mobster's moll and falls so hard, he gives up looking and goes into hiding, and the hunt for the treasure stops dead?"

'More or less, but a bit more complicated.'

'As in?'

'Well this romance, or whatever you want to call it, had been going on for a while and they were making plans. But according to Billy Ray, this Zaros guy finds out his wife is cheating on him and locks her up. Says he's going to kill her, but he's going to make her suffer first. Anyway, she manages to escape, breaks out with the help of some maid or somebody and makes a run for it.' No prizes for guessing where and who she runs to. So Billy Ray, Jerry and this woman get on the boat and hightail it. To where, who knows?'

'And you know all this how?'

'He called me.'

'He called you, Billy Ray called you. Now you tell me? Jesus Christ Joe.'

'He called me but wouldn't tell me where they were. I couldn't talk any sense to him over the phone. He's crazy about this woman and says his top priority is to protect her.' I tell him you can't protect her if you're broke. But he's not listening to sense. This woman has driven him crazy; he ain't thinking straight anymore. I tried calling him back a few times, but he won't pick up my calls'

'What about Jerry?'

'Same thing, no answer. Jerry's faithful, like an old dog who loves his master. He'll always do what Billy Ray asks of him.'

'So you send this PI to try to find Billy Ray?'

'Yup, I thought if the guy could find out where they were, I could go talk to Billy Ray face to face. I know I could get him to see sense if I could only get to talk to him in person.'

'And you knew about this Zaros guy, the mobster, but you didn't tell the PI Mainous or whatever his name was?'

'No and I'm ashamed I didn't. I thought if I did, he wouldn't take the job on.'

'So you lie to him, and then you lie to me? What about all that stuff about the fire in your boatyard, being broke? Was that all bullshit as well?'

'No that was all true, and I am broke. At least until I can get Billy Ray back on finding treasure.'

'Any more revelations Joe, or is that the whole truth now, any other surprises for me?'

'Nope, that's about it; nothing more to tell.' Joe had his fingers crossed behind his back. Frankie scratched his head wondering why he wasn't walking out of the door and finding the nearest travel agent to book his flight home. Then he realized. He didn't want to face going back home. 'Jesus Joe!'

'Does that mean you'll stay and help?' Frankie stood up and walked to the window looking out at the bright sunshine. A couple had just parked up and were looking at boats.

'You've got customers Joe.'

'Okay, I'll go see them when you give me your answer. Will you stay and help find Billy Ray, please?' Frankie sighed.

'For now, I guess. Look I need to go and find that boat. You say he wouldn't tell you where it was, where they were parked, sorry, moored or whatever the correct term is?'

'Moored is the right term and no, it's a Consort 45 Cruiser could go anywhere. Distance wouldn't be a problem. It's a big live on-board boat.'

'Boats like that, they don't have a tracker, like on a car?'

'Some do, but I don't know if that one does, and I sure ain't asking the owner.'

'Yes, I can appreciate the questions that might provoke. Okay well, what's the name of this boat and where was the last place you knew it was moored?

'It's called Falling Star, and the last place it was moored was Fort Pierce, but last time I checked, it wasn't there.'

'Well I've got to start somewhere,' said Frankie

CHAPTER 22

PRESENT – FLORIDA

31 MARCH

Frankie arranged to stop by Joe's boatyard early the following morning to drop Charlie off, rather than take him on another long drive across the state. This time he decided to use the faster route using the Interstate 75 to Fort Myers then crossing to the other coast via FL 80 and the US 27, but it was still a three hour drive. Frankie had learnt that Americans thought nothing of such distances and took long journeys in their stride. He'd talked to several people in Naples who drove thousands of miles from places such as Michigan, or Ohio, or New York without thinking it that big a deal.

And he had to admit, driving in Florida was a whole lot less stressful than doing the same length of journey in the UK or Europe. Here the drivers were much less aggressive, the roads wider and altogether a more pleasant experience. He reached Fort Pierce by lunchtime and followed the satnav instructions to Fort Pierce Docks. He was looking for the Pelican Yacht Club which was the last place that Joe understood Billy Ray to have moored Falling Star.

The Pelican Yacht Club was more than just a place to moor your boat. Spa, fitness center, swimming pool, restaurant, bar. *I could buy myself a boat and live here for the rest of my life* Thought Frankie as he got out of the car and made his way to the marina office. *Nothing stopping me.* He opened the office door.

'How can I help you sir? asked a smart middle-aged lady behind the counter.

'My name's Frankie Armstrong. I'm trying to find someone, well some people actually. The lady looked uncomfortable. 'It's nothing untoward,' he said, trying to reassure her, 'I'm just looking for someone who's gone missing, and they were on a boat that we think may have been moored here,' he got out his notepad, 'a Consort 45 Cruiser named Falling Star. The person who...'

'Yes, I remember it. Two nice young men, divers if I remember correctly, though I haven't seen them around in the last few days.' May I ask what your business is with this boat? We have to be careful you know.'

'Yes of course. The two young men you mentioned, Billy Ray and Jerry. They haven't been seen for a while, and Billy Ray's uncle Joe, who lent them the boat is very anxious to find them. I'm a family friend from the UK as you can probably tell by my accent. And I'm helping in trying to locate them.'

'Oh, I see, well I suppose there's no harm in you looking. Now let me see. She consulted her computer. 'Yes, berth 18. Just turn right at the boat ramp and follow your nose you can't miss it.

Frankie followed her instructions and found Falling Star. He wondered *why Joe had said it hadn't been there when he'd checked?* She was a very pretty looking boat, mostly white with lots of varnished wood and blue trimmings. Frankie clambered on board leaned down and tried to see through the side windows but couldn't see a thing. He went to the back of the boat and down into the well at the stern. There were two doors to one side which he presumed led down into the boat's main cabin. He tried the doors, and to his surprise, they weren't locked.

Making his way cautiously down the wooden stairway he descended into an open lounge area. All the blinds were closed, so only slivers of sunlight shone through. He opened the blinds and sunlight flooded in. He looked around carefully but couldn't see anything of particular interest.

'Are you down there?' came a stern voice from the upper deck. He went back to the bottom of the companionway and looked up. The lady from reception was standing there, looking anything but happy.

'You shouldn't be actually in the boat's cabin sir. We have strict rules about who can board a boat without the owners express permission.'

'Yes, I'm sorry, but the cabin doors weren't locked, and Billy Ray's uncle has reason to believe he might be in harm's way, so I really need to have a look around, see if there are any clues as to where he might have gone. You can come and watch me if you want, make sure I don't steal anything.'

'Well this is most unusual, I'm really not sure.'

'Look I can come back to the office, and you can call his uncle. It is his boat after all?'

'Hmm, I'm not sure that's necessary, I suppose you seem respectable enough.'

'Thanks, much appreciated and I won't be much longer I promise. Oh and by the way, would you keep records of boat movements, I mean would you know when a boat leaves and returns to its mooring?'

'No not really, only when people check in and check out, unless they overstay of course, in which case we have to take action...'

'Right,' said Frankie, 'I understand. But what about security cameras?'

'Well we do have CCTV security cameras, but looking for a boat movement would take forever. Maybe the boat owner on the next mooring might know something. He's a nice man, lives on board full time. I can almost guarantee he'll be in the bar right now. Regular as clockwork is Mr. Harper. Come on I'll introduce you. What's your name again?'

'Frankie Armstrong, yours?

'Delores.'

'Okay Delores, can I just have two minutes more for a quick look around, and I'll come straight to the bar.

'Okay Mr. Armstrong, two minutes.'

Delores was deep in conversation at the bar with a man of about seventy Frankie guessed. He had long silver hair brushed back and tied in a ponytail and looked for all the world like Spanish nobility. Delores saw Frankie approach and introduced him to Mr. Harper

'Dave please', he said, shaking hands with Frankie. Frankie dove straight in and asked him if he knew anything about his neighbor's boats recent movements.

'Well Falling Star was certainly away from her berth for a few days for sure,' he said in response to Frankie's question. 'Came back a week or so ago and strange to say I haven't seen Billy Ray or Jerry since.'

'Can you remember the exact date Dave?

'Er let me think.' Dave looked down at his hands and counted his fingers off. 'The 19th, Sunday the 19th. But they must have arrived back late because I didn't see or hear them arrive. I'd been for a few drinks in here as usual, and I wouldn't have got back to my boat until about nine, nine thirty, and they weren't back then, so must have been quite late when they moored up.

'Did you see them or talk to them the next day?' asked Frankie.

'No, pretty sure I didn't. Had my usual lie in. Got up about nine and went for some breakfast. I remember noticing that Falling Star was back in her berth and I had a peek through the windows as I walked past, see if they were there, say hello, welcome back, but couldn't see any sign of them. Haven't seen anything of them since. Most peculiar' Frankie turned to Delores.

'Would any of your CCTV cameras show Falling Star arriving on the 19th and who disembarked her the following morning?'

'I don't really know,' she replied.

'I think I can help there,' said Dave. 'The cameras covering this area are numbers five and six. Assuming they're working as normal, they would have captured those two events as a matter of course.' Frankie asked if he could watch the security camera recordings for the period in question, but Delores was reluctant to let Frankie see the CCTV footage.

'I mean you're not even a member, nor do you have any official status, I don't really see how I could.' Dave intervened.

'How about if I ask to see the footage and our new friend here can accompany me? I can't see what harm it can do? And from what you told me about his reasons for enquiring about Billy Ray and Jerry, I think we should try to help.' Delores reluctantly agreed and asked them to follow her to the office. The CCTV recording equipment was in a separate room behind the main reception. She showed them in, and they all gathered around the monitor while Delores set up the system to playback.

She set it to run from 6:00 p.m. on the 19th March at ten times the normal speed until an image of the Falling Star arriving at the mooring appeared on screen at 21:45 hrs. Delores slowed the recording down to normal, and they watched as the boat was slowly maneuvered into its berth then a man jumped off to tie the vessel up.

'That's Billy Ray,' said Dave. 'No sign of Jerry.' Delores put it back on to fast forward. She slowed it down again at 05:00 hrs. At 06:07 hrs. Billy Ray and a woman disembarked and walked quickly out of camera range. Delores let the playback run on medium fast until 09:00 hrs., but no one returned to the boat or emerged from it.

'No Jerry? Hmm, unusual,' said Dave, 'always together those two, thick as thieves. And the woman, I think she'd been here a while if it's the same one he introduced me to, can't remember her name. Don't really take much notice now, been a few female visitors in the past. No business of mine of course.'

'Any cameras covering the parking lot?' asked Frankie.

'Well yes there are, but it's quite a large parking lot, and I really haven't got time to playback all the cameras,' said Delores, 'I mean there aren't designated parking spaces so I wouldn't have a clue where to begin. And in the circumstances, I think I've done as much as I can to help. Now I'm afraid I have to get back to work gentlemen. So, it's been very nice meeting you Mr. Armstrong, and I do hope you find Billy Ray and his friends soon.'

Frankie thanked her, and they all vacated the room. Frankie thanked Dave for his help and went back to his car. He had some thinking to do, but first, he decided he'd better call Detective Sharkey to see if there'd been any progress on finding any matching DNA for the body.

He had to wait a while before being through to the Detective

'Mr. Armstrong, apologies for the delay, busy day today. You made any progress finding Billy Ray Ballantyne?'

'Fraid not Detective Sharkey. I just called to see if you'd identified the body yet? I went to the trailer park where Jerry Keenen lived in the hope

I could maybe get some sort of lead on where he might be, but his trailer was burnt down.'

'Yes it was, so no DNA there, but we got lucky. We found his car, parked in Fort Pierce marina parking lot, so that was enough to provide samples.'

'The body was that of Jerry Keenan then?

'Yup, it was.

'And the cause of death?

'Well the sharks had sure made a mess of his face and eaten away a good portion of it, but we were able to establish the likely cause of death. A bullet through the brain. The exit wound was clear enough. We're talking murder here Mr. Armstrong, so I should tread very carefully if I were you.' Frankie felt slightly nauseous. He was beginning to feel out of his depth.

'Thank you detective. I'll be sure to take your advice.'

'You be sure to do that Mr. Armstrong.'

'One more thing detective Sharkey. You said there are no known relatives for Jerry Keenan, so I guess you don't have a problem me telling Joe Nelson about this?'

'I guess not. We'll be releasing it to the media as a matter of course anyway. Anything else?'

'No, thanks again for your help.'

'Your very welcome Mr. Armstrong,' and with that, the detective cut the connection. Frankie sat for a while letting the information sink in.

Should I call Joe and let him know? Seems wrong somehow, better I tell him in person tomorrow. He set the satnav, followed the instructions, and was soon on his way west heading back to Naples. As he drove, he began to think about Penny. The great times they'd had. They'd always got along well he'd thought. Argued a bit from time to time, but nothing that serious. The sex seemed to be okay, from his side anyway. But she obviously hadn't been happy, o*therwise, why did she leave me for a woman? Is it worse that it's a woman and not a man?*

He found it just too depressing, so he put it out of his mind and tried to think about his next move. He'd lost trust in Joe. And he was certain there was more to all of this than Joe was admitting, *but the truth is I'm enjoying myself. A bit risky, maybe a lot risky but maybe that's why I'm still willing to play?* He looked at the time and realized he'd be back in time for a walk to the pier to check out the fishing, then maybe an hour on the beach before a few beers and dinner. Tomorrow he'd go and see Joe and bring him up to date, *see how he reacts to the news of Jerry's death.*

CHAPTER 23

PRESENT – FLORIDA

31 MARCH

Frankie called Joe the following morning to say he would meet him at the boatyard at ten. When he arrived and got out of the car, Charlie saw him and ran to Frankie leaping up. Frankie caught him in his arms.

'Boy, does that dog love you Frankie.' Said Joe, as he came ambling up. 'Come on. I got the coffee on.' They went and sat down in his wooden office, and he filled Joe in on his visit to the marina at Fort Pierce.

'So you found the boat?' Frankie explained about the boat being missing for a couple of days, then returning to the marina, with a woman on board but without Jerry. He told Joe about the CCTV footage showing Billy Ray leaving the boat in the early morning with the woman, but not Jerry.

'Shit, so what's happened to Jerry?'

'Sorry, Joe, no easy way to tell you this, but Jerry's dead. The body those fishermen pulled out of the ocean, the police confirmed, its Jerry.' The color drained from Joe's face. *No way he could fake that* thought Frankie, somewhat relieved.

'You sure?'

'They found a DNA match, so I'm sorry, but it's definite.'

'Do they know how he died, was he drowned or killed on purpose, murdered?'

'They think he was shot through the head.'

'Shot, my God.' Joe said then got up and walked around the small office then muttered something then walked out of the door. He returned a few minutes later and sat down.

'Jerry dead, I just can't believe it. And what does that mean for Billy Ray? I mean this guy, or the people who are working for him, they're obviously not out to teach Billy Ray a lesson. They're going to kill him.'

'Looks that way Joe, but at least we know Billy Ray and the woman were still alive when they left the boat. Hopefully, they've found somewhere safe to hide. We need to figure out where that might be. Get to them before this Zaros guy does. You need to think hard Joe, where might Billy Ray have gone to hide.

'I'm thinking Frankie, I really am.'

'In the meantime, what are you going to do

about the boat Joe? You going to leave it in the marina at Fort Pierce or bring it back here?'

'I'll leave it for now, let's concentrate on finding Billy Ray. If I could just think back... got it.'

'Got what Joe?'

'It's a bit of a long shot but...'

'Doesn't matter how tenuous it is Joe, we've got nothing so far, so anything you can think of? '

'Okay, well a few years ago, Billy Ray got into this doomer thing.

'Doomer thing, what on earth is doomer?

'Not is doomer. I mean as in being a doomer.' Frankie shook his head. 'They also call themselves Survivalists and other names too.'

'Sorry Joe, I'm none the wiser.'

'Well there's any number of these people, groups really I suppose. I'm not the best person to explain. They sorta believe the world's coming to an end, well not like the end of the world as such. But anyway, they go and live in camps, communes whatever. They're a bunch of nut jobs if you ask me, but Billy Ray got interested in 'em a few years ago, and I think his Mom, my sister you know, she told me one time he'd gone to live with one of these groups.

She was worried, wanted me to try and talk some sense into Billy Ray. I said I was willing to if she could tell me where to find him. Anyway, I think he came back of his own accord eventually. He never really talked about it that much afterwards.'

'So, you think that's where they've gone to hide?

'I just don't know. I guess it's a possibility, maybe? Like I say I'm not the best person to ask. That old girlfriend of his, Deanne, the girl you met, the one he stays with sometimes, I think she knows something about that all that kinda stuff. Leastwise that's who his Mom says put the crazy idea in his head in the first place.'

'Come on Joe, can you remember anything, any details at all, this could be crucial. When was this?'

'Two, maybe three years ago, I'd have to check with his mom to be more certain.'

'So, check with her Joe. In the meantime, I'll try to find out more from Deanne,'

'So, does this mean you're going to stay and help?' Frankie stood up and walked over to the window. *What's the alternative, go home to what?* He turned and looked at Joe

'God, I must need my head examining, but yes I'll stay for the time being.'

'Listen Frankie, you can't know how grateful I am for this. If we get, sorry, I mean if you find Billy Ray, and things get back on track, I'll be in a position to show my gratitude… and, well let's just say I'll make sure it's worth your while bigtime.'

'Money you mean Joe? Is there more to all this than you're saying?'

'No, no, just the treasure thing you know, things could turn out good maybe, and you could benefit an' all.' Frankie sensed there was more but decided it wasn't the time to press Joe. Lives were at stake.

'I'll go back to the condo and try to contact Deanne see what she can tell me about this doomer thing. I'll call you to let you know.' Joe thanked Frankie again, stood and shook him by the hand.

'Bye little fella', he said to Charlie as they walked away.

◆ ◆ ◆

Back at the condo, Frankie called the Floridian and asked to speak to Deanne; it sounded busy. Deanne came to the phone.

'Hi Deanne, it's me, Frankie Armstrong, remember I came to talk to you about Billy Ray?'

'Sure I remember, you found him already?'

'No, we haven't I'm afraid, but Joe, his uncle, thinks there's a chance he might have gone to hide away at some doomers, survivalist camp or whatever they're called. Seems to think it has something to do with you. Does that make any sense?'

'Hey, you know what,..., thinking about it, his uncle could be right. I mean what a perfect place to hide' *Great* thought Frankie, *a lead at last maybe?*

'So, Billy Ray did go and stay at one of these

camps?'

'He sure did, not sure how long he stayed though, quite a while I think.'

'So, do you know where this place is, an address, a location?'

She laughed.

'No, I'm sorry I don't. See the whole idea is that these survivalists, these doomers, they live in remote places, a bit secretive, mostly away from mainstream folks. They don't do conventional.'

'Oh right. Then any idea how I might find out, Joe says it was you who got him interested in the subject?'

'No, not me, it was my brother Leo, he's a journalist. Did a lot of work on these groups, knows a hell of a lot about the whole subject, the whys and wherefores. It was talking to him that got Billy Ray so interested. Billy Ray met him at my place, and they became friends, sort of. They talked for hours about survivalists and all that stuff.'

'How do I contact Leo, can you introduce me? I really need to get more information on this.'

'Yeah sure. Listen I'm really busy here right now, and I know that Leo wouldn't like that I just gave his contact details away without asking, so can you email me and I'll forward it on to him, and then he has all your contact details? You got a pen?' She gave him her email address. 'Email me now, and I'll email him on my break, so should have a reply soon. Bye.'

'Whoa, before you ring off Deanne, I need to tell you something. I don't want you hearing it on the news. They found Jerry's body in the ocean.' There was silence then a sob.

'When? Are they sure?'

'A few days ago, but they needed to get some DNA to be sure it was him, so yes it's Jerry, I'm sorry.'

'Okay, thanks for telling me. Email now and I'll send it on to Leo right away. I'll try calling him as well, tell him it's urgent he calls you, but he switches his cell off when he's working and might be away from his email, but I'll keep trying.' She rang off.

Frankie emailed Deanne, then making sure he had his cell and that it was charged up, he took Charlie for a long walk to try and shake the gloom he felt. They strolled up Ninth Street to Fifth Avenue and wandered down past the shops and restaurants. Charlie, as usual, attracted lots of admirers, and 'cute' was the adjective of choice for most of his fans. Charlie wasn't complaining about the attention.

Back at the Cove, Frankie checked his email, but there was nothing from Deanne, or her brother Leo. He paced the room, then made some coffee and sat down on the small balcony overlooking Naples docks. His cell rang.

'Hi, is that Frankie Armstrong? Leo Dvorak

here.'

'Hi Leo and thanks for calling. I imagine Deanne told you that Billy Ray's gone missing?'

'She did. She told me Billy Ray is probably on the run from some jealous husband and about his friend turning up dead. All sounds a bit crazy, but knowing Billy Ray... Anyway, not sure how much help, but if I can, I will. What is it you want to know?'

'Well, there's a suggestion he might have gone to hide in a survivalist camp, and it might be that we're clutching at straws. But in the absence of any other ideas about where he might go to hide, this camp seems the kind of place he might run to. We know he was hiding out on a boat, but I found the boat but no Billy Ray, or the woman he's run away with.'

'With Billy Ray, there's always a woman involved.'

'

'I'm beginning to realize that,' replied Frankie. 'So would you have any idea where this place is, this camp where Billy Ray may or may not be hiding?'

'Very sorry Mr. Armstrong, but I don't know where it is, other than somewhere in southern Florida. Billy Ray and I had many conversations about survivalists when he was dating my sis, but their relationship fizzled out, and it was only later that I found out he'd actually gone and joined one of the communes.'

'Please call me Frankie. And look, would you mind telling me about these doomers, or survivalists, or whatever they're called. If I understand a little more about them, maybe it could provide a lead. At the moment I've got nothing, and I understand you're an expert on the subject.'

'Expert is probably an exaggeration, but I did do quite a bit of research, so if you have the time, I'm happy to tell you what I know. The reason I was talking to Billy Ray about this survivalist stuff, was my editor had given it to me as a project. You know, a special interest piece for the Naples News where I worked back then.

'Well like I say, anything you can tell me would be a great help. If you have the time that is?

'Yeah, I can spare the time Frankie, no problem. And to be honest, it's still a subject that fascinates me. I've lived in Florida all my life yet didn't realize just how prevalent this is, not just Florida, but countrywide. So like I said, my editor told me to do some research on these various groups of people, who for want of a better description, have spurned conventional society, if there is such a thing as a conventional society these days. And it was fascinating stuff.'

'So when did this dropping out start?' asked Frankie.

'Forever... There have always been groups of people peeling off to find their own way. I mean look at the Amish?'

'Yes but they're a religious group aren't they? I mean the people you're talking about, what do you call them, survivalists, doomers, they're not religious are they....?'

'Some are some not. It's not easy to pin them down or pigeonhole them. There are so many variations and motivations behind each grouping and quite a few crossovers. White supremacists, not the least. Then you have groups who may have started out with good intentions, but then find it difficult to make ends meet, so they begin to indulge in a little thieving, then that becomes a way of making a living. But there are of course some communities who do manage to make it work, grow their own crops, raise livestock, hunt, fish and so on.'

'And you say these people are out of sight, off the radar? How does that happen, I mean surely the authorities know about these groups, where they are, who they are?'

'With respect, you're thinking like a guy from a small country Frankie. The USA is vast. You know, we could fit your little old UK into the state of Texas three times over. So there's plenty of room to hide away in the USA if that's what you want to do, especially if you're able to sustain yourself without needing to go to the supermarket every day.'

'Sort of dropouts from society?' Frankie asked.

'Not dropouts exactly. They call themselves by a few different names. Doomers, for instance, believe modern society is doomed. At least it is as presently constructed,' said Dvorak 'and you might have some sympathy for that point of view these days.'

'I know what you mean.' said Frankie, 'How about Survivalists, are they the same?'

'Well, the first time I heard them called that was when Deanne traded in her old Cherokee Jeep a few years ago. Later, the garage told her the mechanic who worked there bought it and that he was a survivalist. They said he had a bunker somewhere, where he was storing all sorts of stuff, fuel, food and all sort of supplies, and he wanted a Jeep to store there as well. I found it a bit hard to believe, to begin with.'

'A bunker and storing food and fuel. It does sound a bit far-fetched I have to admit Leo.'

'It might do, but go to any big magazine store, and you can pick up a copy of The Survivalist Magazine. Lots of adverts for remote locations with freshwater wells, fishing lakes, hunting and such. Some of them even say they have space for a helipad or a small runway. Places where communities can live, independent of the normal infrastructure the rest of us rely on every day and take for granted.

These people believe that the modern way of life is going to break down at some time in the not too distant future, maybe through another huge financial crash, worse than the last one. And this time, maybe so bad that normal commerce breaks down, the dollar and other currencies become worthless, and anarchy breaks out among the general population. Have you any idea what eighteen trillion dollars in debt means? It's as much as the USA produces in a whole year, an impossible debt mountain. And that's only the USA.

According to many economists, Europe's in a fine old mess as well, including the UK. Some very well respected financial experts believe that at some point in the future, the world's whole fiscal and economic structure could buckle under this huge unsustainable debt. Add in the instability in the Middle East, North Korean threat, China flexing its muscles etc., and you can understand why they think it a possibility. I don't know how true it all is, but people a lot cleverer than me claim it could be.

Then there are the terrorists, and we all know they're trying to develop weapons of mass destruction, just not the conventional kind,' he went on, 'a smuggled in nuclear device that blows Washington to smithereens and takes the government with it? Maybe an attack using germ warfare, smallpox, maybe poisoning the water supplies, nerve gas, or just plain old insurrection, political meltdown? If you think about it hard enough, you can come up with all sorts of doomsday scenarios? And the scary thing is, they could be right. Take that Ebola scare a few years ago for instance? It was stopped eventually, but for a while...?'

'When you put it like that, I can see they may have a point, quite scary.'

'Sorry, Frankie I get a bit carried away – journalistic license we call it.' He laughed, 'but as you say, they might prove us all to be complacent fools one day if or when their fears are proved to be sound. Let's hope that never happens.'

'I agree, and I appreciate the information Leo,' said Frankie, 'really fascinating stuff. Now I know what this doomer thing is all about, I really need something to help me find Billy Ray though. Can you remember anything he said that might give us a clue about the place he went to stay?'

'I understand, and I'll have a real good think, see if I can recall Billy Ray telling me anything that might provide a clue. If I remember anything useful, I'll be sure to give you a call as soon as.' Frankie thanked him and gave Leo his cell number and email address, then thanked him again and said goodbye. He looked at the time and called Derek.

'Hi Barnsie, how's cold and rainy Manchester?'

'Rainy and fucking cold. Don't tell me; you're just off to the beach?

'I wish. So, did Gareth have time to look into that website thing I asked about?

'Yes he did, and it got interesting. Let me put him on, and he can tell you better than me.'

'Hi Frankie. I found that website,' said Gareth, 'It wasn't difficult. The names of the two guys you mentioned were featured so easy to establish it was theirs all right.'

'And what did you think. Find out anything interesting?'

'Yes, I did. Like you said it's all about inviting people to invest in hunting for treasure. Crowdfunding in effect, but with an unusual goal. All sounds a bit fanciful, to begin with, but when you look at the stories they tell about people making fortunes, I can see the attraction. If I had any spare cash, I might be tempted myself.'

'So what was so interesting, I mean apart from the concept?'

'The investors. I tried a dummy run and got blocked. It wouldn't let me invest, said that particular opportunity was no longer open, but other opportunities would be offered in the future. It showed how much money they'd already generated and where it came from and showed a list of investors.'

'And?'

'I dug deeper, took some time and effort. It had been done very well by someone who knew their way around IT.'

'Come on Gareth, what had been done well?'

'Well it appeared there were all these individual investors, but when I went deep, I found a common link and eventually managed to establish the investments all came from the same source. The whole thing was dressed up to appear there were forty three investors I think I counted in the end. But, they were very well constructed fronts for the same investor. Whoever put this together was a serious techie. Walls and blind alleys, like IT snakes and ladders. Don't want to sound big headed or anything, but I don't know many people who could have worked it out. Correct that, I don't know anyone apart from me.'

'You're saying all the investors were the same person?'

'Probably, at least the money all came from the same offshore bank in Grand Cayman.' Frankie absorbed the information.

'Why would anyone do that?'

'Search me Frankie.'

'And who's behind it, you get a name?'

'Nah, different corporations, Bronco Island Investments was one I remember. Carlton Ridgeway was another, lots of names but all false fronts. I doubt you'd ever find out who was in the background.'

'Thanks Gareth I owe you a beer.'

'I'll take a raise instead if that's okay with you?'

'Cheeky bastard, but I'll think about it. Put your uncle back on will you?'

'Got what you wanted Frankie?' asked Derek

'I'm not sure Barnsie. Listen, thanks for that. He's a clever boy that nephew of yours.'

'Runs in the family.'

'Yeah right, call you back soon.' Frankie cut the line and sat there thinking about what Gareth had just told him. He smelled a rat, and the rat might be called Joe.

CHAPTER 24

PRESENT – MANCHESTER UK

31 MARCH

'You look a bit peaky Penny.'

'Yes, Jill I know, haven't been sleeping well lately.'

'You don't need to tell me that, tossing and turning all night. What is it?'

'Nothing, just feel, I don't know, unsettled. '

'Is this about Frankie, you beginning to regret leaving him?' Penny looked at Jill awkwardly. 'You can tell me Penny, you know, if you're having doubts. It's natural.'

'No I haven't, it's just we have a lot of history, and it's difficult not to remember, you know the good times.'

'You still love him?'

'Course I do, just not like that any more. I love you Jill, you know that. I, er, I spoke to him the other day.'

'Why didn't you tell me before?'

'I don't know, but he's met someone, in Florida.

'Florida? What on earth is Frankie doing in Florida?'

'Vacationing, and having a nice time by the sound of it. He was really lovely on the phone, very understanding, about us I mean. Seems he's got over the split, well certainly not bitter or angry anymore. Sent you his best wishes'

'Well that's good, maybe we can all move on now?'

'Yes, hope so, but the thing is the person he's met, well..., he's called Charlie.'

'He's called Charlie, a he?! You're not telling me...never, no, I don't believe it. Frankie in a gay relationship? You sure he's not just..., I don't know, winding you up, getting some twisted revenge in?'

'No, I don't think so. He said they met by accident. A friend introduced them and it just happened, they fell for each other.'

'Are you sure it's, how can I put this delicately, a close relationship, not just friends?'

'When he spoke to me, he told me they'd slept together for the first time the previous night.'

'He was lying.'

'No, he wasn't. I could tell he has genuine feelings for this Charlie. Frankie was never any good at lying, believe me, I can tell.' Jill looked at Penny, then gathered her coat up and handed Penny's coat to her.

'Come on. We'll both be late for work if we don't get a move on. We can talk tonight.'

CHAPTER 25

PRESENT – FLORIDA

1 APRIL

Frankie wasn't entirely convinced Mandy had been serious when they spoke on the beach, but when he went to the Dock Pub the day after meeting her, he found her washing glasses behind the bar, and she was just as friendly. She seemed genuinely attracted to him even though she was obviously a lot younger than him, maybe too young? But what the heck it's just a meal and a couple of drinks...

He wasn't looking forward to the date as much as he might have. He kept playing the conversation with Leo over in his mind and became more convinced of the possibility of Billy Ray hiding out at the camp. *Got to be the most likely place he'd run to* he thought, as he dressed for his date. He put on some casual clothes, chinos and a blue linen shirt and sandals. He made sure he had his

American cell in his pocket in case Leo called.

The evening temperature was still in the low eighties. They'd agreed to meet in the Cove Inn reception area, from where they could stroll down to Third where he'd made a reservation at Campiello's Italian restaurant. He made sure Charlie had enough water then patted him on the head.

'See you later little fella,' then he went out of his room and along the walkway, down the stairs and headed for reception to meet his date.

They arrived at Campiello's and were guided to an outside table. The restaurant was busy. Mandy looked stunning, dressed in a light khaki shirt over a white top and cream jeans. Her dark lustrous hair hung down in ringlets. Beers were ordered and served, then the menu presented by the waiter who mostly ignored Frankie. Frankie didn't blame him. Mandy went for the Shrimp al Forno starter, Frankie plumped for the Beef Carpaccio. They agreed to share a large pepperoni and Italian sausage pizza as their main course.

'Okay, who's first?' She said when the waiter had left to put in their order.'

'First?' asked Frankie

'Life story to date in five minutes.' She took a sip of beer. 'I vote you first.'

'Okay,' said Frankie, and he gave her a brief description of his life to date, starting with where he was born and ending with Penny leaving him.'

'Wow, you've done so much. So sorry about your wife leaving you. Must have been really tough, all the more so, I mean it being a woman an' all.'

'It's okay I'm over it now, now come on, your turn.'

'Whoa, more information required. Like what are you doing here and what's your birth sign, I'd guess Pisces? I'm all into the astrological thing.'

'Nope wrong Aquarius, January 30th.'

'And the year?'

'You mean the year I was born?'

'Yes, let me guess. 1970?'

'I'm flattered, no 1963.'

'Gosh, you look so much younger.'

'Yeah right. Now enough with the flattery and enough about me. Come on, your turn.'

'Just a minute buster, you haven't said why you're here in Naples? Explain.'

'Came to visit an old army friend. Someone I met in the gulf war, that's all. After the thing with my wife, I felt I needed to get away. Now come on, no more about me, your turn.'

'Okay, but your story is going to make my life seem so boring. Well, here we go. I was born to second generation Russian immigrants. My grandfather and grandmother fled the revolution to escape the Bolsheviks. They were referred to as the White Émigré at the time. Anyway, I was born in Wisconsin in 1982 and lived a fairly typical American life. After I graduated, I decided I wanted to see the world, intending to go back to my studies after a couple of years wandering the globe. That was some seventeen years ago. Still, I just might go back in the next year or so.

I've been to most countries, Middle East, Far East, even back to Russia for a couple of years. I've done every kind of job you might imagine and some you might not. The last couple of years I worked the Celebrity Cruises line. Last May one of the stops was Key West. I jumped ship, made my way up the Keys, working in hotels mostly. Got to Naples four months ago, and here I am having dinner with you. Told you it was boring compared to your life.'

The waiter arrived with their first course. Frankie ordered more beer and Mandy had a glass of the house white. They carried on chatting throughout the meal. Frankie remembering some funny stories about his life, Mandy telling him about some of the more interesting jobs she'd had, which included rounding up cattle on a South American ranch. The beer and wine flowed as did the conversation. When they'd finished their meal, Frankie ordered an Uber and asked Mandy where she'd like to be dropped off.

'You mean you're not going to invite me back to your Condo?' she said laughing. Frankie wasn't sure if she was serious, but though he might as well go for it.

'My apologies, would you like to come back to my place for a nightcap?'

'Sounds good to me,' she said giggling. The Uber arrived, and they got in.

◆ ◆ ◆

Frankie woke to the sensation of his face being licked. He smiled, *so nice*. Then he moved and felt as if his head would fall off. He slowly opened his eyes and saw Charlie standing on the bed looking straight at him. He woofed, obviously desperate to go out.

'Okay, just give me a minute Charlie.' *Oh, my head, Jesus Christ how much did I drink last night?* He made his way to the bathroom. After he'd finished, he went to the sink and looked in the mirror, moaned and splashed water on his face, then dragged on a pair of shorts and a tee shirt. He found his keys and the dog leash and took Charlie out for a walk. The fresh air helped. He got back to his room, put some food out for Charlie, made sure he had water and went back to lie on the bed. Ten minutes later his brain started to function. He tried to remember what had happened the previous evening. The last thing he recalled was getting out of the Uber with Mandy. *Where is she, presumably she left after... after what?* He remembered her asking him to invite her back, getting out of the Uber and looking forward to a night of unbridled sex. He couldn't remember. *Surely I'd remember that?*

He got up and looked around the room. Then he saw his notebook by the coffee machine; a page ripped out. He went over and picked it up. Thanks for a lovely evening X Mandy

He shrugged, and it hurt his head. He looked for his wallet and found it. *Surely I didn't spend all the cash I had? I definitely paid the bill with my credit card. Where's the cash?* 'Oh shit,' he said out loud and emptied the contents of his wallet onto the little desktop. Much to his relief, his driving licence was there, as were some business cards, but no cash and no credit card. He tried to think. *Oh Christ, where are my phones?* He found his UK mobile on the dresser, but couldn't find his America cell phone, then membered *I took it out with me last night, where are my trousers?* He found his trousers on the floor by the bed and found his cell.

He went and sat down on the bed. *Fallen for the oldest trick in the book. Me Frankie Armstrong, security specialist and first-rate gold plated mug. Shit shit shit! Better cancel the card.* His laptop was still there. He Googled NatWest black card UK, got hold of his UK mobile phone and called.

He eventually got through to the security team and reported his card stolen but fudged the circumstances. She'd managed to make two AMT withdrawals of the dollar equivalent of £2,000. In total $2,673, plus there was a list of purchases from the 24 hour Walmart store in North Naples. Amongst other stuff, she'd bought a TV, a laptop computer, electronic games and other easily sellable items. The cost of which amounted to another $3,547, at which point the card system pulled the plug, the algorithm software noting the unusual activity and automatically suspending the card until cleared by an operative.

The details of the withdrawals and purchases were told to him by a weary NatWest security operative, who obviously held in disdain, all people careless enough to let their card get stolen. She went on to ask Frankie how the thief could have obtained the details necessary for the withdrawal and illicit purchases. Frankie said he didn't know and thanked her for her help.

He felt sick again, made his way to the bathroom where he threw up. He switched on the cold water and washed his face with the flannel, then swilled some water round his mouth spat it out and went back to lie on the bed. Charlie joined him and snuggled up. After another ten minutes or so he felt a bit better and started trying to figure out what had happened and wondered if he should report the events to the police. He decided to delay that decision until he'd got a clearer picture in his mind.

He thought through the details of the night

before and realized Mandy had got his date of birth out of him by pretending to be interested in his birth sign. *Clever bitch... But how about the PIN number for the card, surely she'd need that?* He thought for a few minutes more. *Oh fuck, she watched me pay for the meal last night and clocked the number.....* He sat up on the edge of the bed and felt dizzy again. He took deep breaths and recovered. Then it dawned on him. *She drugged me, Jesus, the fucking bitch spiked my drink when I went to the bathroom... I thought the beer tasted a bit funny when I came back.* He couldn't help laughing. *That must be a first, a date rape drug being used to achieve the opposite effect*

The credit card people told him they would normally issue a new card, but as he was in America that was going to be a problem. They also said he might be able to claim some or all of his money back from the bank, but he'd have to contact them with all the details and see what they said. He told them he'd do that, but not just now. The lack of money was a temporary inconvenience. He would ask Derek to wire some money over somehow. *If that's not possible, I'll just have I'll have to borrow some money from Joe*, he thought.

He went back to the subject of whether he should report the theft to the police but decided he'd wait until lunchtime then go visit the Dock pub and see what they had to say about their glamorous employee. In the meantime he decided another hour in bed was called for. He woke later, and his head hurt less. He dragged on his shorts and walked the short distance to the Dock Pub. Mandy wasn't anywhere to be seen. He wasn't surprised. He walked over to a man who seemed to be in charge.

'Hi, I'm inquiring about an employee of yours, Mandy, don't recall her surname, but she works behind the bar.'

'And you are?' asked the man. His badge had the name Vance and Bar Manager on it. Frankie thought the quickest way to get an answer, was to be honest.

'A victim I'm afraid. We went out on a date; I suppose you'd call it. I'm staying at the Cove Inn, and I met Mandy when I was walking my dog, then we bumped into each other on the beach, and well...It looks like she stole my credit card.' Vance, the manager, looked sympathetically at Frankie.

'That so? Well, I obviously can't comment on your allegations, but I can tell you she hasn't shown up for work today and isn't answering her cell, so..?'

'I don't suppose you could give me her address and or her phone number?

'No I don't suppose I could. You'd have to get the cops involved for me to hand over that sort of information.'

'Okay, I understand. I'll leave you my details

and phone number then, and if by any chance you find out anything you can tell me, perhaps you'd call me?'

'Sure thing.' He said. Frankie took out his pad, wrote his details down and handed them to Vance.

'Could you tell me how long she's worked here?'

'Not long, a few weeks. Came and said she'd work for minimum wage, and tips. No brainer to have a good looking chick like that behind the bar.'

'Did she make any friends while she was here?'

'Not that I know of, but she could have. Look I don't want to seem unhelpful but I've got a pub to run, and you're going to have to excuse me. And I'd really appreciate it if you wouldn't go interrogating any of my staff. They also have a job to do. You've been taken for a ride buddy. It happens. My advice, put it down to experience and move on.'

'Okay Vance, thanks, you're probably right.'

'No probs, mind how you go.'

'Thanks,' said Frankie as he made for the door.

'Hey buddy,' shouted Vance. Frankie turned round. 'You do realize what day it was yesterday?'

'Sorry?' said Frankie, wondering what Vance was talking about, 'what day?'

'Look at the date,' said Vance before laughing

and walking off to attend to a customer at the bar. Frankie looked at his watch, 2nd April.

'Shit,' said Frankie as he walked out of the door.

♦ ♦ ♦

Frankie spent the afternoon, researching the survivalist phenomena. Trying to pinpoint any known survivalist camps in Florida but came up with nothing useful. There were some statistics, but nothing that indicated any locations of any survivalist camps. Waiting for Leo's call was getting to him, so he took Charlie for a long walk. He got back to the Cove and decided a run along the beach would help get him back to something normal in both mind and body.

Apart from one or two other nighttime joggers, the shoreline was mostly deserted, and he ran along in silence with just the noise of the waves lapping up onto the beach. As he ran further along the shore towards the Gordon Pass where the Gordon River spills into the Gulf of Mexico, he came across four fishermen. By the amount of effort being expended, one of them was fighting a fish of considerable strength. He stopped to look.

'Big fish?' he asked one of the men.

'Yeah, big fuckin shark man.' The fisherman was trying hard to reel the shark in, his friends looked on making encouraging noises, whooping and jumping up and down when the shark took off, the fisherman's reel emitting a high pitched zinging noise as the line was stripped off. The fisherman fought to get the fish under control adjusting the drag on the reel to tire the shark out. The fish fought back again and again, then made one final run, then ran out of fight. The fisherman reeled it, and this time there was little resistance.

As the fish neared the shore, it turned and ran again briefly, then once again ran out of steam and was reeled in yet again. The fishermen were all so engrossed as to be completely oblivious to the little crowd that stood watching, fascinated. Eventually, the shark gave up the fight completely and was hauled up on to the beach, where it was admired and photographed by the fishermen and the passers-by who'd stopped to watch the spectacle. It was a magnificent creature of some seven feet in length, all black and silver in the half moonlight.

Frankie wanted to move on but felt the need to wait until he saw the fish safely returned to the sea. Silly he thought, but nevertheless, he waited. The fishermen took some more photographs, their flashes accentuating the dark blue and silver contrast along its sleek body. Then after carefully removing the hook, the four of them cautiously waded in carrying the shark supporting its weight in a large wet towel, hammock style. As soon as they were a few feet in, the shark started to flex. They took the towel away and raced back on to the beach. It was almost comical. Frankie laughed, congratulated the men on their catch, then resumed his run.

The episode had completely absorbed him for a while and given his brain a rest, but he still couldn't come up with anything, any ideas of how to get a steer on where the survivalist camp was that Billy Ray and his girl may or may not have fled to. He parked the problem, and as he started to run back along the beach, his mind switched to Penny. He turned things over in his mind again and tried to recall any warning signs, any clues that she'd been so unhappy as to leave him.

She obviously had been unhappy, he accepted that, but what was it? *If she changed her mind and wanted to come back, would I forgive her? Could things ever be the same if we did get back together?* He decided there was little point in such speculation. She was gone, and he had the rest of his life to live. He got back to the Cove, showered and suddenly felt exhausted. He took Charlie for a late turn around the block, then came back switched on the TV, watched for a few minutes, turned it off and went to bed. Checked his cell phone again. He thought about the Mandy situation and decided not to report it to the police; then sleep took over.

CHAPTER 26

PRESENT – FLORIDA

3 APRIL

He woke to the sound of rain hammering on the balcony windows. Instead of the usual light show splitting the room into rays of bright sunshine and shadow, the room was dull and dark. He called reception to ask if he could borrow an umbrella so he could take Charlie out for his morning walk. They offered him a rain slicker. He discovered that Charlie didn't like rain. His tail was almost dragging along the ground as they walked around the block. He got back from the walk, dried Charlie off then called Joe. Frankie had decided not to say anything about the website and mystery investors, for now anyway. Joe picked up on the third ring.

'Just going down for breakfast Joe, so I thought I'd give you a call.' Joe asked if there was anything new to report. 'No nothing relating to Billy Ray, but I do have a personal problem in that my credit card was stolen, so I'm a bit stuck for cash. I'll get some wired to me, but I'd be grateful if you could help out in the meantime Joe.'

'Wow stolen you say, how'd that happen?'

'My own fault really, I'll tell you next time we meet, but no big deal.'

'Okay and sure, no problem for the cash, a thousand dollars okay?

'More than enough Joe thanks. Have you spoken with Billy Ray's mother yet about the survivalist camp thing?'

'I did, and she remembers Billy Ray saying something about the subject, but she really doesn't know when it was. Billy Ray's a bit of a gipsy, so she's got used to not knowing where he is and gave up trying to keep tabs on his movements years ago. As long as he regularly calls to talk to her, she's fine. Obviously, he hasn't called her for a while, and she's worried sick. Did his old girlfriend know anything?'

'Not directly, but Deanne put me in touch with her brother Leo. He's a journalist who did a lot of research on survivalist groups for a feature article he was writing. It was Leo who got Billy Ray interested in these survivalists, not on purpose, but Billy Ray got very taken with the idea, and as you said, went to stay with one of these groups for a while. Problem is, Leo didn't know which one or where it was other than somewhere in south Florida, so we're no closer to getting a fix on where he might be.'

'Is that a dead end then?'

'Not necessarily, Leo's looking into it some more and will let me know if he finds anything useful. In the meantime, I'll stay here and do some more research on the internet. Not that it's been very productive so far but got to keep trying. I'll let you know if I find anything useful. If you can rack your brains Joe, and call me if you think of anywhere else he might have gone to hide, anywhere, doesn't matter how unlikely.'

'Okay Frankie, I'll try my best. Good luck with your research and let me know the minute you find out anything.' Frankie assured him he would.

Breakfast was the usual 'heart attack on a plate' feast. Frankie had started jogging more often to run off the extra weight and had limited himself to three of these breakfasts a week. After he'd eaten, he took some coffee back to his room along with some smuggled sausage for Charlie, then worked on Google for an hour, researching doomers and survivalist groups. But he made no real progress. The rain had stopped, so he took Charlie for a long walk. Stopping at the 7-11, he bought some milk, teabags and a copy of the Naples Daily News.

Back in the condo, he read the paper, skimming the news reports. A coffin had slipped out of the back of a hearse on the Tamiami Trail on its way to the burial ground, spilling the body out on to the road and caused a five mile tailback while the police tried to decide the most appropriate way of dealing with the issue. A famous pop star had said that some of his best songs had been written while staying in Naples.

A Florida man had been sentenced to death for the brutal murder of his wife and her lover. He put the newspaper down and went to sit on the little balcony overlooking the Naples Dock. The weather had much improved, and once again the sun was shining. Charlie came and sat under his chair.

'So what am I doing here now? Looking for a person I've never met, why? Oh yeah, because I owe Joe my life. But Joe isn't being straight with me. I'm sure he's being economical with the truth by some measure. And then there's at least one person who could have been killed by a Miami mobster, a missing PI who could also be dead and the distinct possibility that I might somehow get tangled up with these hoodlums.

Added to which, no leads, nothing to go on.

'Bollocks' he said out loud. 'Come on Leo.' The absence of any other potential lead was frustrating. *Maybe I'm setting too much store by the doomer camp thing? I need some distraction.'* He decided to go and watch the fisherman on the pier, get some tips on how to fish there. He couldn't take Charlie, who looked forlorn when he left the room without him. He walked up 9th then took a left and walked down towards the pier. He loved Naples and began to rethink his decision to abandon the search for Billy Ray. *Truth is I'm enjoying the craic* as his Irish friend would say.

He got to the pier just in time to witness a fantastic run of Spanish mackerel. The fishermen on the pier were having the time of their lives. There were whoops and yells as they landed the fish, whipping them over the rails where the hapless creatures flapped around on the wooden decking. The run went on intermittently for nearly an hour. Frankie was mesmerized. Eventually, as the fishing passed its dizzy heights, a fisherman to his left spoke.

'Wow, I wouldn't have missed this for the world. Shoulda left an hour ago and be sitting in the dentist's chair by now, but I wasn't gonna let a simple thing like a dental appointment make me miss such a great run of fish.' He high fived Frankie who'd seen it done loads of times on TV but had never actually high fived before in his life. He made his way back to the Cove trying to rationalize. *I should stay because I love it here and I'm enjoying the excitement of looking for Billy Ray, but I should go home because that's where I live, that's where my real life is, or was. I'll compromise, give it a few more days, maybe a week and then I'll reconsider.*

Charlie gave him his usual enthusiastic welcome as he walked through the door of his condo room. He made some tea, sat down at the small desk and opened up his laptop. He scrolled through his emails, deleting the various rubbish messages. He stopped, an email from Leo Dvorak. He opened it. Call me, was all it said. He called.

'Hi it's Frankie Armstrong, you just emailed?'

'Hi Frankie, thanks for calling back. I think I might have something. I've been looking over all the stuff I researched on survivalists back then. For quite a long time after the article was published, I kept an eye out for any news on these sorts of people. I guess I was just fascinated with the whole idea, why people did it and so on? Anyway, I found some notes I'd made about an outbreak of dengue fever in one of the doomer's camps, an abandoned old logging camp in the Everglades that these people had taken over. I've thought back, and my feeling is that this was around the time Billy Ray went to stay with one of the groups,

'Dengue Fever, what's that?

'Pretty serious is the short answer. Not surprising in some ways. The virus is transmitted by mosquitos, and that's one sort of critter there's no shortage of in the Everglades. From what I know, dengue's rarely fatal but it can be if people aren't treated, and it's very contagious. Been occasional outbreaks in Florida before.'

'So how does this relate to finding Billy Ray?'

'Well you know, like they say on those corny TV detective shows, no such thing as a coincidence. So, I wondered. Did Billy Ray leave his survivalist camp around the same time as an outbreak of dengue fever in one of them? See where I'm going?'

'I do, and from your tone, do I assume there's more?'

'There is. I called Deanne, and she said she remembers Billy Ray saying something about having to leave the camp because of some sort of infestation or serious hygiene problem, something like that. She thought it was something to do with contaminated water, but she now thinks about it, that was just her assumption. She's sure he mentioned people being ill with some sort of fever. He also said he was getting bored anyway, not enough to do and he was missing his home comforts and the sea.'

'Right, said Frankie, 'and you know the location of this camp?'

'I do, well not precisely, I know the general area, but I think I know how to find it.'

'But we still don't know for certain that it's the camp Billy Ray stayed in?'

'No, but in the absence of any other lead, you might want to consider this has serious potential?'

'I do Leo, don't get me wrong. This is great. Certainly has possibilities. What's your next move?'

'I need to check with a couple of people who might know a bit more about the outbreak, see if I can get a more precise location. Leave it with me, and I'll get back to you, okay?'

'Leo, if you give me the dates of the outbreak, maybe I could do some research as well?'

'Not sure that would help Frankie, I know the people to contact and can get to them quicker than you would. Anyway, I might need to call in a Favor or two to get the info without going through the normal channels.'

'Understood Leo but let me know as soon as possible. I need to get to Billy Ray before anyone else does.'

'Got it Frankie. I promise to call you as soon as I know anything useful. Frankie gave him his cell number again just to be sure, 'and thanks, thanks a lot. Look forward to hearing from you soon.'

'You bet,' Leo said and broke the connection.

Frankie was excited by Leo's call. The prospect of a seriously good lead had him buzzing. For whatever reason, and in defiance of any sensible logic he thought, *I'm on the hook and I've got to stay and see this through.* This unexpected interruption had given him purpose, just at the moment when he felt he wasn't getting anywhere. He needed to succeed, to prove something to himself. Penny leaving had knocked him sideways and devastated him. He had never before experienced such utter desolation and despair. When he realized she'd really gone, it seemed the future held nothing for him. He could never have imagined the crushing impact such an event would have on him.

That he still loved her surprised him. He still felt great anger but no bitterness now. In those first dark hours, when he'd finally accepted she'd really left, he'd been so depressed, he'd genuinely contemplated ending it all. He'd called to try one last time but got her voicemail. Asked her to call him as soon as she got his message, but Penny hadn't called back, so he'd made the decision. He had absolutely no doubt that without that unexpected call from Joe he would have taken those pills, washed them down with booze and gone to sleep never to wake up. So, if Joe but knew it, he owed him two lives, not just the one.

Now, with the passage of time, he could only wonder how he could have possibly contemplated taking his own life. *How stupid do you have to be to let anything drive you to that level of despair?*

'Shit happens,' he said out loud, and Charlie suddenly appeared at his feet and looked up at him. 'I said shit happens, not, would you like to go for a walk?' Then he laughed 'Come on, I need some distraction until Leo calls back.' He slipped his cell phone into his pocket, then took Charlie for a walk down Broad Avenue to Old Naples then turned left on to Gordon Drive, which ran south, parallel to the beach. Frankie wore just a tee shirt, shorts and sandals. There was a tangy warm breeze wafting off the ocean. He reckoned the temperature to be in the low eighties. The sun hung high in the soft blue sky, a few wispy clouds as a backdrop. A large Osprey glided over him with a fish in its talons, flying back to its perch to sit and eat its catch.

There was no sidewalk as such. No one expected anyone to actually walk down Gordon Drive. But the wide sculptured grass lawns along the side of the road provided a reasonable alternative. Palm trees of all sizes and shapes adorned the lawns alongside the road. The trees casting deep shadows across grassy areas with neatly trimmed bushes, under which beds of rich soil were cut out of the sod and adorned with flowers of every type, color and hue. These grass islands were interspersed with impressive sweeping driveways of grand dwellings which were rarely lived in. Variously high and low hedges were planted in front of the houses, low ones showing off the palatial mansions, high hedges providing privacy. The houses and gardens along Gordon Drive were simply stunning thought Frankie. *What kind of money do you have to have to own one of these piles – and, it probably isn't even their main residence!*

He knew from his walks along the beach that the reverse side of the houses on the right had gardens that backed on to the beautiful beaches providing the owners with stunning views over the Gulf of Mexico and spectacular sunsets. The further south he walked, the more elaborate and impressive the houses became.

He eventually came to a dead end, where the Gordon River flowed out into the Gulf. He turned around and began to walk back. At the top of Gordon Drive, he had the option to turn right and go back to the Cove Inn, but he was too wound up waiting for Leo's call, so he continued along Gulf Shore Boulevard then turned right on towards Fifth Avenue.

Fifth was the very essence of opulence. Fancy restaurants with terraces spilling out on to the wide sidewalk, realtors, top-notch gift shops, elegant clothes shops, cigar shops. He walked up the avenue, passing The Inn on Fifth where flunkies stood around the hotel entrance waiting to welcome the next well-heeled visitor, then stopped at the window of a jewellers to admire the glittering display of necklaces, diamond rings, exclusive watches and assorted high-end bangles and baubles. He looked through the shop window where a salesman was attending to a wealthy looking couple, he in his seventies at least, and his glamorous blond companion no more than early thirties he guessed.

The jewelry salesman reminded him of Uriah Heap as he stood there talking clasping his hands together. *Obsequiousness personified* thought

Frankie and smiled. He was just about to walk on when something about the woman caught his attention. She detached herself from her companion's arm to pick up the item of jewelry being discussed.

She looked different, blond hair, different hairstyle, *but it's her, Mandy!* At the same time as he recognized her, she put the necklace down on the counter and looked towards the window. her eyes flickered in recognition, then she recovered and returned her attention to the old man, stroking his arm affectionately

Frankie kept staring, willing her to look at him again. Charlie had seen another dog and was mewling and straining at the leash. He ignored him and continued to stare. After a long minute, she looked up and almost imperceptibly, no doubt to see if he'd moved on. She shook her head at him, then turned to her companion took a pack of cigarettes out of her purse, held them up to her companion who frowned, then she whispered in his ear.

The old man smiled, nodded and carried on talking to the salesman, then took out a small wallet from his pocket and handed over a credit card. The woman came out of the shop, pack of cigarettes in her hand. She took a cigarette out, produced a small silver lighter, lit it, inhaled the smoke and blew it out slowly. She turned towards Frankie and nodded for him to follow her.

She walked a few yards up Fifth, well out of sight of the shop stopped and turned to Frankie.

'So what are you going to do now? Did you report me to the cops?'

'As it happens I haven't yet no,' said Frankie.

'Why not?'

'I didn't see much point. I thought you'd be miles away by the time I told them, in another state probably. I assume Mandy isn't your real name and that's all I had. So apart from telling them I got suckered by a beautiful girl, who said her name was Mandy, who worked as a barmaid in a pub, but no longer works there. And I took her out to dinner, and afterwards she hinted at sex, then likely drugged me and stole my credit card.

I think all I'd really get would be pity, and a report reference number. Although thinking about it, I guess I should, then maybe I can claim the stolen money back from the bank, unless you're going to give it back of course?' Frankie had worked himself up, his voice raised and loud.

'Look, please calm down. I know you're mad at me, but I can explain.'

'Of course you can. We could invite your sugar daddy in there to join us? I'm sure he'd find it interesting.'

'Look, there's a Starbucks up the street on the other side of the road. I'll meet you there in ten minutes and after you've heard me out, if you still want to report me and tell my friend what happened, then so be it.' Frankie hesitated.

'I've been taken for a sucker by you once, why should I believe you? I'll be sitting in Starbucks twiddling my thumbs while you do a runner.'

'No I won't. Think about it. You saw my friend give the jeweler his credit card, so if I do a runner, as you call it, then go to the cops, they can demand the jeweler tells them who the guy is and you can get to me through him, okay?' Frankie's cell rang. He kept looking at the girl but answered his phone.

'Leo?'

'It is Frankie, can you talk?'

'Not right now, I'm on Fifth walking the dog. Can I call you back when I can talk properly, won't be long, I'll find a coffee shop and call you back in about five minutes.'

'Sure thing Frankie, I'll be here.' He turned back to Mandy

'Ten minutes, Starbucks, and if you don't turn up, I will find you and bring you a heap of trouble.'

'I'll be there.' She said and went back into the jewelers. Frankie wondered if he was being naïve, but walked up Fifth, Charlie in tow, found an outside table at Starbucks. He tied Charlie's leash to the chair, ordered a white coffee, took out his cell phone and dialed.

'Leo, it's Frankie, sorry you were saying?'

'Yeah, well I managed to locate a guy who knew a guy and eventually I spoke with a Doctor Blaga at the University of Miami hospital. They handled the dengue outbreak in question. Most of the sick people at the camp were well enough to travel to the hospital, but they had to send a small team out to the camp to attend to one particular lady who was in a bad way. Anyhows, it took the guy a while to look up his old notes, but eventually, he called me back with a sort of general location.'

'Leo, that's fantastic. Great work.'

'That's not the best of it Frankie, the guy was also able to give me the GPS coordinates for the camp.'

'GPS coordinates. Leo, you're a star, can you email them over?'

'Already done Frankie. I assume you're not at your laptop?'

'No, sitting in Starbucks waiting for someone, but I'll be back in front of my laptop in about twenty minutes or so. I'll get right on it then. Listen, thanks again. I owe you big time.'

'No, you don't Frankie. Happy to help. Let me know how it goes won't you?'

'I certainly will,' Frankie replied and cut the connection. He found Joe's number on speed dial and called. It was Joe's voicemail. He left a message.

'Hi Joe, some good news maybe. Call me back,'

then he put the phone away and sipped his coffee. He idly picked up the bill the waiter had left on the table and suddenly remembered, *Shit! I've got no money to pay for it.* He sat there getting angry with himself. *If she doesn't turn up, I'm going to feel a complete fucking idiot, in more ways than one.*

He looked at his watch, nearly fifteen minutes, then started trying to figure out how to explain to the waiter that he had no money, when she suddenly appeared and sat down opposite him. She leaned down and stroked Charlie's head and got a big tail wag in return.

'Hello Charlie.'

'You remembered his name?' said Frankie. The waiter arrived.

'Coffee black,' she said. 'Frankie?'

'Another white one please.' The waiter disappeared into the back. 'Course you'll have to pay,' he said, 'as I realized after I'd ordered the first coffee, that I had no money to pay for it. Someone stole it all.'

She took out three twenties and passed them over. 'Thanks very much, I'm sure,' he said and pocketed the money, then said. 'Okay let's have it.'

She took a deep breath, then began.

'Clayton, that's the guy you just saw me with, he's gone to make some calls, and I don't have much time. So, I'm going to give you the abbreviated version. Please don't ask any questions until

I've finished okay?' Frankie nodded, the waiter arrived and put their coffee's down. She sipped.

'My younger brother has valvular heart disease. He's ten years younger than me. It was only diagnosed a year ago, and he needs an operation. My folks can't afford the cost and, they couldn't afford to pay health insurance, so it's a problem.

We don't have any relations here or back in Russia who can help, so we tried other ways to raise the money, crowdfunding all that sort of stuff, but all we got was just a few hundred dollars. So I made a decision a few months ago that I would get the money any way I could. I know I'm attractive, great body.

Men have always lusted after me, so I thought why not? Why not use the asset God gave me, even though he might not approve of how I use it.'

She took another sip of her coffee.

'I go for jobs like the one in the Dock pub where I know I'll meet wealthy guys. You were one of my victims, if you like. Don't know if you can get the money I stole back from the bank but I hope you can. Anyway, one way or another, I've managed to raise $78,000 so far, but I'm still well short. I need to raise about $200,000 minimum. Clayton is a find, wife back in the Hamptons. She doesn't like it down here, he does, and he likes me.

He's offered to put me up in a condo in Venetian Bay, and I'm going to take him up on it, take him for as much as I can. You're shocked, but Clayton is a billionaire. A hundred K is chump change to him.' Frankie opened his mouth to speak, but she motioned for him to wait and took another sip of her coffee before carrying on.

'Now I know you're thinking this another bullshit story, and you're not going to fall for it this time. So, I've written down these details. My real name, the name of my father and mother and their address. My cell phone number, and each of their cell phone numbers. You can call them and ask them about my brother Nikita or Nick as he mostly gets called. After that, if you want to report me to the police, then be my guest, but I'd ask you to think if you could live with the knowledge that you'd denied my brother a chance to live. There that's it. Now you can ask your questions.' Frankie was trying to absorb what he'd just heard.

'You sleep with people to get the money?'

'Yes, but not like a prostitute, well not in my mind anyway. But I will use my looks to develop a relationship that enables me to get my hands on a significant amount of cash, and if that means sleeping with some guy, then yes I will, and I have.'

'So, you're sleeping with Clayton?'

'I can cope without the euphemism. What you mean is am I letting him fuck me. Yes of course I am. Every opportunity is different, so I play them as best I can. If I don't have to have sex to get the money I won't but if it's the only way, then I will. I was tempted to have sex with you 'cos for once I found someone I genuinely liked, but I thought it would be better if I slipped you some Rophy instead.'

'That sounds a bit contradictory, should I be insulted or flattered?'

'Not sure, but it was obvious to me you're still in love with your wife, despite what happened. Didn't seem right somehow.' Frankie took a swig of his now cold coffee.

'Natalya Petrov. Did I pronounce that correctly?'

'You did. Listen I hate to rush,' She stood, 'but if I don't get back to Clayton right now, he's going to wonder where I am. He can be a bit possessive, so I'll have to go.'

'Okay, well I'll think about what you've told me. Will I see you again?'

'Maybe? I live each day as it comes and try not to plan too far ahead.' She was standing next to Frankie now. 'Bye Charlie, bye Frankie.' Then she bent over and kissed Frankie full on the lips and walked quickly down Fifth Avenue without looking back.

◆ ◆ ◆

Joe called back just after he'd arrived back in his room at The Cove.

'Good news you said. I could do with some of that.'

'Could be Joe. Leo Dvorak, Deanne's brother, the journalist guy I told you about.'

'Yeah, the guy who knows about these survivalists and stuff.'

'Right, well, long story short, he's been able to give me a location that might be the place where Billy Ray stayed. Some old logging camp in the Everglades. Reckons Billy Ray left 'cos of a dengue fever outbreak, so he was able to trace the camp through some medical records at Miami hospital. This Leo guy said the dates are around the same time Deanne says Billy Ray left the camp.'

'That's great. When do we go?'

'We?'

'Yeah, I think a trip into the Everglades on your own might be a bit too..., not dangerous exactly, but off the beaten track it can get a bit tricky out there. I think two would be better than one, don't you Frankie? Anyway, Billy Ray doesn't know you from Adam so he might shoot first and ask who you were later.'

'Shoot?'

'Turn of phrase Frankie, but he won't know who you are will he, so he might well get spooked?'

'Yes, you're right. So how soon can you be

ready to go.'

'You got good directions?' Not easy to find stuff once you leave the main highway.'

'I'm just looking at the email from Leo with the directions on it. He says he got the first part of the directions from Google, some place called Pahay-okee Trailhead, if I'm pronouncing it right that is? Then to get to the camp itself, he's given me some GPS coordinates.'

'Great stuff, email 'em over. I've got plenty of GPS units here. Standard stuff on boats. Finding this place should be a breeze. How about we make an early start tomorrow. You can drop Charlie off here. Don't want him eaten a by a gator, do we? Melinda can look after him. We'll go in my truck. Six a.m. sound good to you?'

'I'll be there.'

'Oh, and Frankie, best wear some long trousers and a shirt with sleeves. Maybe get a hat too. Those mosquitoes can be vicious varmints. Walmart's the best bet if you haven't got any of that sort of stuff.'

'Okay Joe, I'll go to Walmart later. See you at six.'

CHAPTER 27

PRESENT – FLORIDA

4 APRIL

Traffic was heavy on the US41 out of Naples. Joe had rigged up a separate GPS in the big silver truck he'd chosen for the journey. He explained that some satnavs used GPS, but the integral one in the truck didn't. Frankie had brought along the map and directions printout of the initial part of the journey which Joe had fed into the truck's satnav system.

'A hundred and thirty five miles, that right?' asked Joe.

'Yes correct, two hours and forty seven minutes it says.'

'Okay well, we got plenty of time to think about how we handle this situation when and if we find Billy Ray and this girl. You had any thoughts on that?'

'Yes. We have at least one death attributable

to this situation, maybe two? The missing PI you hired may well be dead, at least based on what happened to Jerry. If we assume that Billy Ray was involved somehow, not in the actual killings, but witnessed them or whatever, then he's not only fleeing a jealous husband who happens to be a Miami mobster, but is in fear for his life, and that of the woman. By the way, I found out her name. It's Valentina. Looked her husband up on the internet. Like you said, he comes over as a respectable businessman. Involved in charities and all sorts of community projects. Are you sure this PI Mainous was right about him being a gangster?'

'Chuck Mainous was certain of it. And as I said, he is, or he was, an ex-Miami police detective, I think he'd know. And as you just pointed out, Jerry was murdered, and Mainous is missing, so if this Zaros character didn't kill them, who did? And not forgetting, Billy Ray has stolen his wife.'

'You're right. So back to his wife, as I said, she's called Valentina. Saw a picture of her and she is a stunner.'

'Am I surprised? That Billy Ray.... So, let's assume,' said Joe, 'that they're at his camp we're going to. Cos if they are there, how are we going to find out? I mean Billy Ray will have told them not to tell anyone, won't he?'

'I suppose he would have. Well, we tell them you're his uncle and...hmm?'

'Exactly, how can they deliver a message to

someone they deny is there?'

'How about you write a note to Billy Ray, show it to them so they can see what it says, and ask them to give the note to Billy Ray if he should turn up. Then we say we believe them if they claim Billy Ray isn't there, but we'll hang around for half an hour anyway. That gives them a chance to give the note to Billy Ray and once he knows it is really you, why wouldn't he show himself and at least listen to what you've got to say?'

'Good idea, you got any paper?'

'I've got my notebook. When we stop for petrol, sorry gas, you can write it out.'

'And what am I going to say?'

'Something only he and you would know, so he knows it's definitely you. Could be something inconsequential from his childhood or a family matter that no one else would know about.'

'Okay, got that. Looking ahead, I've been thinking about where he can hide them while we help him get this fixed. Another boat seems the obvious answer.'

'Good short term solution Joe, but if Zaros is the sort of man we think he is, then he's not going to cool down after a few days, change his mind and let Billy Ray off the hook. He'll most certainly put a contract out on him, and that could be in place forever.'

'You're right Frankie. We need a long term solution. Otherwise Billy Ray's going to spend the rest of his life going from one hiding place to another and always looking over his shoulder.'

'Okay, we're agreed on that Joe, so any suggestions?'

'Well, initially we give this Zaros guy time to calm down a little. Maybe I could also persuade Billy Ray to see sense, convince him there's no future in this relationship. Maybe we try to persuade this guy's wife to go back to her husband? Then if we can't get Billy Ray or the woman to see sense, we try to negotiate. I mean if the guy likes money, maybe we can buy him off?'

'Okay, but where are you going to get enough money to pay off a guy like that Joe? I don't know what sort of sum you had in mind, but from what you said about him before, already having lots of millions, doesn't sound like he'd be interested in a few thousand dollars?' Joe looked conflicted.

'I can get my hands on more if necessary. Let's just leave it at that for the moment, okay?' But Frankie didn't think it was okay and wanted to know how Joe could find the sort of money they were discussing. He decided now might not be the right time to ask. They drove on in silence for a while.

'We need to fill up,' said Joe as they passed a sign indicating a gas station ahead. They pulled into the gas station forecourt, and Frankie went to the restrooms while Joe fueled up the truck. When Frankie came back, he sat in the cab while

Joe went to pay and use the restrooms. Joe returned, drove away from the gas pumps and parked at the far end of the gas station. 'Let's write this note. I thought of something only he, and I would know. When he was about eleven, Billy Ray was shooting at tins in the yard with a .22 rifle when he accidentally shot next door's cat. He came to me crying, and I knew it was an accident 'cos he was so fond of that cat, always getting told off for bringing it up to his bedroom.

He was also sweet on the girl next door, similar age. Said she would never talk or play with him again if she knew he'd killed Kipper, name of her cat. So rightly or wrongly, I helped him bury it and told him it was our secret. Far as I know, no one else ever knew. I remember when he was much older, after a few beers, reminiscing about this and that, he told me he still felt bad about it. Funny how things like that stay with you ain't it?' Frankie passed his notebook and a pen to Joe. He wrote the note, folded it in two and put it in the glove compartment.

Joe started the engine, and they drove out of the gas station and back on to the highway. After a couple of miles, they encountered a traffic jam and had to slow down to a crawling pace. Joe looked at his watch.

'Just what we need, hopefully, this will clear soon enough,' he said. After a frustrating ten minutes crawling along, they came to the source of the problem. A huge lorry transporting oranges had somehow left the highway and had spilt the contents of its load across both lanes. Joe laughed

'Whole new meaning to the expression orange squash,' he said and laughed at his own joke as they passed the police cars and emergency vehicles dealing with the accident.

'That was my family's business way back when,' said Joe as he pressed down on the accelerator and they resumed driving at seventy miles an hour. Frankie looked at his watch.

'Don't worry Frankie; we'll be there soon enough.'

'The sooner, the better Joe. So, tell me about this family business?'

'You really want to know?'

'It would be interesting, and we've got time to kill. My own family lived in the same area in the north of England since the beginning of time,' said Frankie.

Joe laughed.

'Okay, well my dad used to tell us kids all about our ancestor Hubert Nelson. He'd been a farmer in Sussex England, and for whatever reason, he got married and left England for a new start in America. They survived the crossing and eventually made their way to Florida. Seems they were able to raise enough money to buy a small orange farm in St. Augustine.

'Great place to grow oranges,' said Frankie

'Yeah it is, but strange to say, oranges aren't native to Florida, a guy called Ponce De Leon is said to have brought the original seeds over here.'

'That name rings a bell. I think I've seen a statue to him in Naples?'

'You have, on the 41, outside the First National Bank. Where was I, oh yeah, so five generations later, I came along. There were four of us kids in the family, my three sisters and me. My dad assumed that being the only other male in the family that I'd take on the farm when I left college. But I hated farming. My dad eventually admitted that my sister

Beth was a much better farmer, and she loved it. I, on the other hand, loved boats, anything to do with water, and fishing and all that, so when I was eighteen, that would be in 87, I moved south to Naples Florida and never went back, apart from family visits, funerals and all that sort of stuff. My sis, that would be Billy Ray's mom. She followed me down here, met a guy called Ballantyne settled down.

I'd got myself a job in Bill Kenwood's Boatyard. I did everything, cleaned boats, repaired and delivered 'em and sold 'em. Then when 9/11 happened things changed. I got really angry. One of my childhood buddies was killed in the Twin Towers attack, and that made it personal. Bill, the owner of the boatyard, had passed two years earlier and he had no kids, no relatives he liked, so he left the yard to me. I renamed it Nelsons Boatyard in 2002.

Anyway, even though I'd married Belinda by then, I got all these noble patriotic feelings and felt I had to defend my country, so I joined the army. Belinda was distraught, but to quote John Wayne,' and assuming a very realistic John Wayne drawl said, 'a man's goddadoo what a man's goddadoo.' They both laughed. 'Anyways, I left the business with my manager Rudy and ended up serving three years in the army, including a two year stint in the Iraq war where we met. So now you know.'

'Really interesting Joe. Look that sign said five miles to the Pa-hay-okee Trailhead.' They reached the turnoff and stopped while Joe switched on the GPS and punched in the coordinates. A map appeared on the screen showing their destination via a narrow trail off highway 9336. Joe turned the truck around and back on to the highway, then took a left down the trail shown on the map. There were signs of recent traffic along the bumpy old logging track, with broken branches and leaves littering the floor of the trail.

Joe looked at Frankie and raised his eyebrows. Hardwood tree hammocks grew at intervals. The vegetation on both sides was thick and impenetrable. Large birds flew out of the undergrowth on occasion, and in a heart stopping moment, a tiny deer leapt across their path. Joe braked just in time and managed to miss the delicate looking creature and swore under his breath as he concentrated on avoiding the larger bumps and root growths in his path.

As the truck trundled along, low branches of mangrove trees occasionally swatted the windscreen then sprang back to partially screen the area behind them. As they drove deeper into the wetlands, Frankie could feel the increase in humidity and once again wondered at the craziness of people wanting to live in such an inhospitable wilderness. Joe tapped his finger on the GPS.

'Nearly there,' he said and turned a corner. The scene in front of them wasn't exactly what they expected. The flashing blue and red lights of the two vehicles, one a police car the other a police truck, took them both by surprise.

'What the fuck...?' said Joe as he braked and brought the truck to a shuddering halt. Two policemen standing by their car turned around, looked at the truck, then both drew their side arms, pointed their guns at them and shouted.

'Get out of the truck and put your hands on the roof, legs apart. Now!' Joe and Frankie obeyed the officer's instructions. One policeman approached, the other remained where he was. Frankie was the first to be patted down. He attempted to speak as the officer approached but was told to shut up.

'Clean,' he shouted back to the other cop when he'd finished. Then he went round to Joe and gave him the same treatment. 'Clean also,' he shouted. 'You can take your hands down now,' he said to them both. The other officer lowered his gun and came to join them. In a more relaxed voice, the first policeman spoke.

'Okay, explain why you're here.' He appeared to be the one in charge. Frankie left it to Joe to talk. He explained they were here to find his nephew Billy Ray Ballantyne, who'd gone missing some weeks ago.

'Missing you say?'

'Yeah, missing, as in we don't know where he is.'

'Okay, cut the sarcasm' said the first officer, then the other policeman spoke.

'So why do you think your nephew would be staying at this camp?'

'It's a long story, but Billy Ray, he stayed here some years ago. Recently he got mixed up with a woman; she'd run away from her husband and they, she and Billy Ray that is, were trying to hide from him. They'd originally hidden out on a boat I'd lent them, but somehow the husband found out where they were, so they hightailed it, and we thought this was a place Billy Ray might think would be a good place to hole up.'

'So you came here to check?'

'That's about it, yes. Look what's happened,

why are you here?' asked Joe.

'All in good time. So, you are?' he asked Frankie. Frankie told them he was a friend of Joe's. That they'd met in the gulf war and he was helping Joe look for Billy Ray. The officer turned back to Joe. 'You report him missing?'

'Yeah, a while ago, to Detective Sharkey at the Fort Pierce police department.'

'Okay, your full name address and the full name of this nephew you say's gone missing.' Joe provided the information which the officer wrote down on a pad. The policeman then went back to his car, sat in the driver's seat and began talking on his radio. The three of them stood waiting in an awkward silence until he came back. 'Okay, your story checks out.

'Can you answer my question now?' said Joe, 'why are you here?'

'Sure,' said the officer, 'we were called here by the, not sure what to call him, let's just say, the boss man of this here group of survivalists or whatever. So, we got a call to say that two men came to the gates of this place this morning, shot the gatekeeper dead, a guy called Jeb. Then they smashed through the gates with their vehicle, waved guns about, grabbed one of the women in the camp and demanded she tell them if a man and a woman had arrived at the camp in the last few days.

Said they'd shoot her if she didn't say. So she

told them she knew a couple had arrived a few days ago and told them which trailer the couple were staying in. We've interviewed the guy in charge,' the policeman looked at his notes, 'a Joshua Cooper, and he said the couple's names were Billy Ray Ballantyne and a woman called Lola, but he said he wasn't entirely convinced Lola was her real name. The raiders, if that's the correct term, went to the trailer and manhandled the couple out, put 'em in the back of their car and lit out. Nobody lifted a finger stop them. Not unusual, people were in shock, still are. Said the attack only lasted a few minutes. They were in and out like professionals. So, can you shed any light on who these people, these kidnappers were?' Joe shook his head.

'No idea,' said Joe. 'Didn't anyone get their plate?' he asked.

'They did and guess what, it was a false one. You know who the broad is, this Lola, the one your nephew ran off with, who her husband is?'

'Fraid not,' Joe replied, 'the last time my nephew called was just after he'd disappeared. Wouldn't tell me where he was, only that he'd got involved with some married woman and they were hiding out from the husband.'

'You?' said the cop looking at Frankie. 'Same questions, any idea who these people were, who the woman was?' Joe looked at Frankie and gave the slightest shake of his head.

'No, no idea,' said Frankie, 'but when I spoke with Detective Sharkey after Joe here had reported his nephew missing, Mr. Sharkey indicated there was someone else looking for Billy Ray. Said something along the lines of not being the sort of people you'd want to have looking for you.' The officer looked at his partner, then said to Joe.

'You forgot to mention your nephew's buddy. According to the Fort Pierce police department, he was shot dead and dumped in the ocean. I assume you know all about that?'

'Yes we do,' said Joe, 'which is why we're so worried about Billy Ray.'

'And you have no idea who shot and killed your nephew's buddy?'

'No, we don't officer,' replied Joe. The man gave Joe a hard look, then sighed

'Okay, you can go now. But be aware, there's a couple of vehicles likely to be coming down the opposite way down this track, paramedics and a meat wagon for the deceased. Wouldn't want another incident out here in the middle of nowhere, would we?'

They got back in the truck, and Joe turned it around then drove away back along the track. Neither one of them said anything until they were back on highway 9336. After about a mile, Joe pulled into a picnic area. He opened the glove compartment, took the note out and ripped it into little pieces, then threw it through the open window.

'Fuck,' he said angrily.

'You think it was wise not to mention this Meszaros character?' said Frankie

'Don't know is the truth. All we got is speculation from a missing PI. The minute we mention Chuck Mainous and start to tell them he's missing, we get ourselves into a whole heap of shit trouble. They'd have us back to headquarters, and we'd be tied up for who knows how long?'

'So what do we do now Joe?'

We go back to Naples, and along the way, we try to figure out a plan to get them back.'

They drove along in silence for quite a while, each lost in their own thoughts, processing what had just happened. Then Joe turned the radio on and chose a country music channel. Frankie lost himself in the lyrics, listening to the folksy renditions, love found, love lost, love unrequited and so on. Then there were the livelier versions of country, with the fiddles, woops, yeehaws and banjo plucking. *Made you want to get up and dance around.* Joe turned the volume down a little.

'So any thoughts Frankie? We know who's got them but what can we do about it? Can't prove it's this Zaros guy. We go to the cops and say what? Tell 'em this missing PI said it was Meszaros's wife that Billy Ray ran off with and that he's found 'em, had them kidnapped and more than likely will kill them both, 'cos he's a ruthless murdering bastard.'

'Well the right thing to do would be to report what we know, or what we think we know to the authorities,' said Frankie, 'but you're right, it's mostly supposition, unsubstantiated information from a source no longer available. By the way, I've been thinking about that. I assume Mainous's wife or his employer has reported him as missing to the police?'

'Yeah, I got a call from the agency I hired him through, just after he went missing. They said they'd report him as missing, but not sure there was a wife in the picture. Anyway, don't see where that gets us.'

'No, just wondered. The police didn't come to see you, ask any details about what he was doing for you?'

They called me and asked a few questions, and I told them the truth. After all, they already had a record of Billy Ray missing, so it all kinda made sense. They asked me about any places he might have gone to find Billy Ray and again I told them the truth about Billy Ray and the boat. I never heard from them again.'

'Okay, here's what we do Joe. We negotiate with this Meszaros character. No other choice. You said you could raise a significant amount of money if necessary. Is that true? I don't want to know where from. You can tell me after this is all over, depending, but I obviously have some problems with things you've said that contradict each other. One minute you're broke, the next, you're not quite as broke as you first claimed, then you say you can get your hands on what, a million dollars?'

'It's complicated, but yeah, if push came to shove and it was a matter of life and death for Billy Ray, I could raise that sort of money. What do you have in mind, just buying his freedom? What about the woman?'

'I don't want to say exactly what I have in mind, but I do have the germ of an idea. Not sure if I'm being a bit fanciful? I need to talk to someone else to see if what I'm considering is feasible. But for the moment, let's hold that. I'll go and see this Meszaros guy, see if he'd be willing to let Billy Ray go in exchange for money. His wife, I don't know about. We'd have to play that one by ear.'

'You said you'd go see him; not we'd go.'

'Yes Joe, you're too close to Billy Ray, emotionally I mean, and emotion isn't a good basis for negotiation, especially when there's also emotion involved on the side we're negotiating with. Don't forget the insult this guy feels about someone stealing his wife. Believe me, it's a powerful force.'

'You sound like you have personal experience on the subject?'

'You could say that, but let's not go there okay?'

'Okay Frankie, didn't mean to intrude. So how do we play things with this thug?'

'I'll call him to set up a meeting. He's hardly going to admit he's kidnapped them of course, so it's going to have to be handled carefully.'

'This other idea, can you give me a clue what it is?'

'I'd rather not just yet. I might just be overestimating things I don't know about.' He looked at Joe who shrugged his shoulders.

'Well, I sure don't have any ideas, so...'

'I have to talk to someone first, but subject to him confirming certain things. I may have an alternative method of applying the pressure to get this Zaros guy to release Billy Ray. But if my idea isn't feasible, then we'll have to go with plan A which is to buy him off. You okay with that Joe?'

'Yeah, I am.'

'And I have to ask you this, but what's the maximum amount you can put up to get Billy Ray back?'

'Can we just see how the guy goes with the one million dollar offer and take it from there?'

'Okay, leave it with me. I'll need to make contact with Meszaros first thing tomorrow, hopefully before he's done anything drastic. It's a bit late to be calling my people in the UK to check out my other idea, but I'll try as soon as I get back to the Cove. In the circumstances, I'm going to leave Charlie with you, okay?'

'Sure thing, and keep me in the loop. Can't wait to hear what this other idea is.'

CHAPTER 28

PRESENT – FLORIDA

4 APRIL

Billy Ray and Valentina sat side by side in the back of a large Cadillac limousine with blacked out windows, speeding towards Miami. Tape across their mouths and hands taped up in front of them. Valentina started to wriggle violently, eyes pleading with Billy Ray, who realized she was having problems breathing and was panicking. Her face turned red. He managed to get the attention of their two captors by kicking the seat in front of him.

The man in the front passenger seat, a large dark haired bearded individual, turned around and also realized what was happening. He grinned, then reached over and ripped the tape from Valentina's mouth. She coughed and spluttered, coughed some more, then breathed in deeply. Eventually her breathing and face color returned to something like normal.

'Why do you have to tape up our mouths for Christ's sake? I mean who the fuck is going to hear us if we shout?' she screamed.

The man turned toward the driver. A pale faced cadaverous looking man.

'She got a point there partner.'

'Yeah okay, so take the tape off the guy's mouth,' said the driver, 'But you two, just keep quiet, or the tape goes back on, got it?' Valentina didn't bother replying. The man in the passenger seat stretched over again and ripped the tape off Billy Ray's mouth.

'We don't want to damage the goods before we deliver them, do we Seth?' said the large man to the driver. They both laughed. After a while, Billy Ray plucked up the courage to speak.

'Where are you taking us?'

'Oh come on boy, figure it out. Mr. Meszaros would like to have a little chat with you about stealing his wife.' They both laughed again, louder this time. Billy Ray was silent for a while then spoke again.

'How did you find us?' he asked. The big guy delved into his pocket and brought out the phone he'd confiscated from Valentina.

'This little baby.'

Billy Ray looked at Valentina.

'You didn't?' She looked back confused.

'I didn't call anyone. I saw some of those other

people using their cell phones, and I put the battery in and switched it on. I was going to call my sister. You weren't there. You were out hunting or whatever, so I couldn't use yours. She'd have been worried sick Billy Ray. You know I usually call her every day. But then I remembered what you said, so I didn't call, honest.' Billy Ray looked at her, his expression a mixture of disbelief and anger.

'I told you not to put the fucking battery in, not to switch it on. What didn't you understand Valentina? Phones can be traced even if you don't make a call, you stupid...Jesus Christ.' Valentina broke into tears.

'Don't call me stupid. I hate you,' she sobbed and turned away. The two men in front found the exchange hilarious and began laughing again. When they'd calmed down, the bearded man took out his cell and tapped in a number.

'Hi Seth, we're about twenty minutes away, what does the boss want us to do with them?' He got his instructions from Seth and finished the call.

'Okay partner, they want us to drop the guy off at the warehouse. Seth will take care of him, then take madam here directly to the boss.' Valentina looked at Billy Ray and leaned into him.

'Billy Ray, I'm really scared,' she said. Billy Ray nodded, then spoke to the men in front.

'Hey fellas, look, my uncle's a very wealthy

guy, he'll pay you plenty to let us go. Why don't we give him a call? You could have enough to get well away from here; live like kings.' The bearded man turned round.

'Well that's very considerate of you,' he said smiling, 'live like kings eh?' He turned to the driver. 'How much do we want to let them go partner?' The driver laughed. The bearded man turned back to Billy Ray.

'You really have no idea who you're dealing with do you boy? There isn't enough money in the world to make it worth double crossing Zaros. He would find us wherever we ran to. We could change our identities, have plastic surgery, go live in Bolivia, the North Pole, Timbuktu, and he'd still find us and rip our throats out. You stole the wife of the most ruthless guy on the planet. Enjoy the ride you two, the rest of your short lives is gonna be hell on earth.' Billy Ray looked at Valentina; her face resembled faded parchment.

CHAPTER 29

PRESENT – FLORIDA

4 APRIL

Frankie checked the time, calculated the difference and called. Derek often stayed late at the office.

'Derek, glad I caught you.'

'Hey, it's the cowboy Casanova from Florida. How's things over there, weather good? It's pissing down here, you won't be surprised to learn.'

'The weather's great, but the situation I've got involved with has gone a bit grim.'

'Oh yeah, Miami Vice, sex, drugs, rock n roll. Go on, tell all.' Frankie briefly explained what had happened since they last spoke. 'Jesus Frankie, I'd get out of there if I were you, you're going to end up on a slab.'

'Can't do Barnsie, got to see this through. I know it sounds crazy, but I'm hooked, never felt so alive, especially since Penny left. I can't tell you how hard that hit. This, whatever it is has helped me get over it. Listen, I need to speak to your nerdy nephew, he still around?'

'I assume you're referring to our senior technical operative? He is, in fact, he's so enthusiastic these days, I have to kick him out of the office. Otherwise he'd be here all night. I'll go get him, but what are you up to?'

'I'll explain another time, or ask the nerd to tell you, but this has to be kept tight okay?'

'Bloody hell Frankie, you're beginning to sound like we're really in Miami Vice. Hang on.' A couple of minutes later Gareth came on the line.

'What's the haps Frankie?

'What's the what?'

'It's what the cool Americans say; it means what's happening. Come on Frankie you're the one in America, I just yearn to be there.'

'Listen, you help me out on this and get a result. I'll buy you a trip here, all expenses paid.'

'You serious?'

'Never been more serious in my life Gareth. Now forgive my naïve questions and concentrate on the objective. I might be asking you the wrong way to go about this, but someone's life might depend on if we can pull this off.

'Wow Frankie fire away, I'm in, whatever it is.'

'Okay, get a pad and pen, I don't want to do this by email, nothing written down and this is extremely confidential, no boasting to friends, you tell no one, understand, well other than your uncle Derek okay?'

'Yep understand and got my pad and pen.'

'Okay, well there's this businessman based in Miami he's called Zsolt Meszaros,' Frankie spelt his name out, 'he has legit businesses, and to all intents and purposes is a respectable member of the Miami community, involved in charitable works and so on. But he also has other businesses. He's a very very wealthy individual but he's, to put it bluntly, a gangster, and from all accounts a ruthless killer, okay, you understand?'

'I understand what you just told me, but I'm not sure where this is going.'

'I'll explain. Meszaros has a legitimate trading company called Miamisun Holdings Inc. I've checked it out online, and it's an umbrella company that owns four other companies. You can look up details yourself when we've finished. But they list their various trading activities as restaurants, dry cleaners, casinos, and undertakers, plus some other similar types of businesses. His other less legitimate business interests are said to include, money laundering, prostitution, protection rackets, drug dealing etc. etc. You get the picture?'

'Yep.'

'Okay, so this man is holding some people. I won't bother you with the details, but he's kidnapped two people, and in all likelihood, he'll kill them unless I'm able to persuade him not to. And don't bother suggesting I go to the police. With this guy, it won't work, probably make things worse if anything. So I'm going to try and negotiate with him and offer him a shitload of money to release these people. But he might not bite. Seemingly he has so much money, it might not be enough to persuade him to cooperate, so I need another method of convincing him to do what I ask.'

'You want me to hack into his computer system, right?

'Got it in one.'

'Jesus Frankie, this is scary.'

'Is it possible, could you hack in?'

'Maybe, maybe not. If he's half as clever as you say he is, he's going to have the mother of all security systems protecting his data. By the sound of it, this guy would have thought very seriously about protecting his data, not just from hackers, but the authorities as well.'

'Yes, I realize that. I didn't assume it would be a walk in the park. Reasonable to assume he'd want to protect himself from any chance of his system being hacked into by the IRS or whoever. So, are you saying you don't think it can be done Mr. Genius hacker?'

'No not saying that. Remember Gary McKinnon?

'Yes, I do as it happens, wasn't he the one who hacked into America's military system or something?

'That's the man, he hacked into NASA's computer system as well, and I reckon I'm at least as good as him. But it won't be easy. So, let's say I did get in; what would you want me to do?'

'I'd like to be able to hold him to ransom in some way. I mean I've read about these Russian hackers who get into computer systems and lift money, or data or threaten to wipe data out if people don't pay up. So, I suppose I was thinking along those lines, but you're the expert, so I'm looking for ideas, but if you can't get in then it's a non-starter.'

'Let me do some research, find out what I can about his companies, see if there's any chance but my guess is I won't be able to breach his security, at least not in the, shall we say, in the normal way.'

'There's another way?'

'Well not normally, but you said you were going to negotiate with him, didn't you?'

'I did Gareth. What difference does that make?'

'Let me do some thinking. I have an idea.'

'Okay, but we need to act fast. I intend to try to talk to him tomorrow morning to arrange a meet. I'll begin trying at eight a.m., which is one o'clock in the afternoon your time. Any chance we can get this worked out tonight?'

'If I drop everything I'm doing and work through the night I can.'

'Do it and tell your Uncle Derek it's a matter of life and death, literally. Easier if I call you back. Does two hours give you enough time?'

'A couple of hours should be enough to make an assessment. If it's sooner, I'll email you to call me back.' He broke the connection. Frankie was desperate for a beer, or something stronger, but resisted. He needed a clear head. An hour and twenty minutes later he got an email from Gareth. *Ready to talk, call me.* He sat on the bed and called.

'Bad news is I've looked at their system, and it's very unlikely I can get in. Security is tight as a proverbial duck's arse. The good news is, I've thought of a way round the problem, but it's not without some drawbacks and would maybe put you in danger.'

'Tell me your alternative plan, and I'll worry about the danger bit.'

'Okay, well you have your laptop there don't you? And you'll need a good internet connection. And I'll need you to have a memory stick, a USB memory stick.'

'Right, well I think I have all those, in fact, I have a couple of memory sticks in my bag, one full of photos, the other has some company stuff on, but it's all old stuff now.'

'Well the memory sticks you already have are

probably okay, but for what I have in mind you might want to go and buy as small a memory stick as possible, preferably 64 gigabyte capacity.'

'Sounds intriguing. Okay, I think there's an Office Depot not far from here.'

'Okay, then this is the plan. You download some software from the internet. I'll tell you how to get it. Once it's installed, you can give me access, and that will enable me to take over your laptop. Then I'll download some bespoke software I'll be creating, and I'll load it on to your memory stick, which, unless you get a new one, I'll need to wipe beforehand, so all the original stuff will be deleted okay?'

'Okay, no problem.'

'The stuff I load on to your memory stick will be automated to download itself when inserted into the USB port of any computer. Now, this is a one-time download, and once it's finished transferring this software on to its new host, it will wipe itself clean, so one shot is all you'll have.'

'Wait, are you saying I've somehow got to get this USB memory stick into this gangster's computer system?'

'Basically, yes. But it can be any PC or laptop connected to his system. Doesn't matter as long as it's on his system. I can almost guarantee that even his own laptop or personal office PC will be connected to their main system somehow.'

And this will work?'

'No reason why not. See, imagine their system is this big house with a front door, locked and bolted with guards protecting it night and day, plus it's surrounded by a wall with barbed wire that prevents anyone gaining access to the garden, but there's a back door which no outsider could get to, which is basically left unlocked, so if someone could get around the back of the house.'

'Okay, you don't have to paint the pretty picture. I might not be technical, but I think I can work out what you've got in mind, at least in principle.'

'Yes, sorry about that, used to talking to clients that way, some of them are just so dumb.'

'Thanks Gareth.'

'No Frankie I didn't mean....' Frankie laughed.

'It's okay Gareth no offence taken. So go on, what will this software of yours do, assuming I can get it plugged in to one of their PCs that is?'

'Well, it'll sort of infect their system. One of the first things my software will do is make a call out, to me.

'Don't firewalls and such prevent that sort of thing?'

'They do, but they're a sort of one way barrier, designed to stop things getting in, not getting out.'

'Right, hadn't realized that, carry on.'

That will give me direct access to their systems. From there I can work on getting access to their entire network, all their servers and data, in a way that just wouldn't be possible via the internet. And it will be fast, permanent and untraceable. It will enable me to access all their files. What I suggest is that once I have complete access, I take a mirror image of all their data and load it on to a server somewhere. Somewhere secure, but not here. Again, somewhere they won't be able to trace. Then you tell me what you want me to do.'

'Such as? I mean what could you do?'

'Where do I start? I could wipe their system completely afterwards, and then we'd be the only people with all their data. A bit drastic, but that's the nuclear option. If you want to show them an example of what I could do, I could remove funds from one of their bank accounts. You indicated they had lots of dodgy money in offshore bank accounts didn't you?'

'Yes.'

'Well we could steal it and who could they complain to? Not the authorities, that's for sure. Or we could just transfer funds from one of their accounts to another of their accounts, demonstrate what we're capable of. Or we could release their entire data to the IRS and the FBI?' Frankie, who'd been standing, went to sit on the bed.

'Jesus Gareth, you could do all that? Surely

once they know you're in their system, or been in their system and copied their data, they could do something, change everything, transfer stuff, move their funds to new bank accounts, all that kind of thing?'

'It's possible in theory, but a mammoth task that would take them forever. And anyway we'd have a copy of the original data, which they could render out of date in terms of us being able to access bank accounts, but we'd still have all the historical incriminating stuff, assuming you're right about this guy's business interests being as you described?'

'I er..., just give me a minute to absorb all this.' Frankie went over in his mind all he'd just been told. 'How long would it take for the software on the memory stick to download, infect I think you said? How long would that part of the process take?'

'Hard to say precisely, anything from two, to seven minutes at a guess.'

'Could you test it so you could be sure of the time it would take?'

'Yes, once it's completed and ready to go. But Frankie, I can't do this on my own, I'd need the rest of the team in tonight, well Terry and Bill at least, if they're sober. I'm going to have to offer them some serious overtime pay Frankie.'

'Do it, whatever it takes Gareth, I'd prefer it if they didn't know the full details.'

'No worries, I won't have to tell them specifically what this is for. I could say we're doing it as a security test for a new potential client, see how robust their system is. And it's urgent. They won't care as long as they're getting paid, double time?'

'Double time it is Gareth. A question, what if I did get the thing into a USB port, then someone spotted it and took it out.'

'Yeah, well that would be a problem if they removed it before it had completed its task.' Gareth replied

'Right, and I've just had another thought. Without a doubt, this guy will have security guards, and I'm very likely to be patted down, made to empty my pockets. If they do, then I've blown it?'

'Memory sticks are only small, so maybe tape it under your armpit or some other more intimate part of your body. Surely they're only going to be checking for guns? But then again, they might think wire, a mic if he's as bad as you say. So, they'll make you lift your shirt up to check, maybe make you take your shirt off, underpants even? You could tape it to the inside of your leg, or in your crack maybe?'

'Jesus Gareth, can we stop talking about my intimate body parts. I'll figure something out. So, the way I see it, I've nothing to lose by having this as plan B, maybe plan A, but whatever. I use the meeting to negotiate their release on the basis of paying him a load of money, and I try to get this memory stick in play. If I do succeed, then I'll have him by the short and curlies, for want of a better expression, and I won't have to pay him a penny to boot.'

'A better expression might be blackmail Frankie.'

'You know Gareth, you're as subtle as your uncle, and that's no compliment.' They both laughed.

'Okay spade a spade, said Frankie, 'As a consequence of being blackmailed, he obviously forfeits the money I offered him. I think we could call that a win-win?'

Gareth called his team in to ask them to come in, with the promise of double time pay. No one refused. Frankie drove to Office Depot in the mall and bought two of the smallest memory sticks he'd ever seen. He'd been thinking about Gareth's suggestion, so he drove north up the I41 to Walgreens and bought three different types of tape for keeping wound dressings attached to your body. Then he went back to The Cove and waited. He suddenly felt lonely, sitting in his room watching the television and he realized how much he was missing Charlie.

He got up, went to the bathroom stripped off all his clothes and stood in front of the mirror and tried taping one of the memory sticks to various parts of his anatomy. His UK mobile rang.

'Okay I think we're ready for stage one,' said Gareth, 'you got your laptop ready?'

'I have, plugged in and connected to the hotel's wireless network. And I've bought two new tiny USB memory sticks 64 gigabytes.' Gareth told him to stick one of the memory sticks in the laptop.'

'Just a silly thing,' he said, 'but better mark one of the memory sticks. You don't want to get them mixed up?'

'Right will do. But hang on, any problem programming both memory sticks? Back up, I'm a great believer in back up.'

'No problem, just take a few minutes longer, but a good idea.' Gareth told him how to download the program to enable him to take over his laptop, and Frankie watched the screen as Gareth took control, the cursor moving around at lightning speed compared to his own pedestrian efforts. Oblong boxes with a series of colored bands appeared on the screen, sliding to nothing as the software was dumped on to the first memory stick, then the second.

'Just going to test this last memory stick to make sure it's taken it all, yep that looks good,' said Gareth. 'Okay, over to you Frankie, I've done the hard bit…. Ha ha.'

'Yeah right, said Frankie. 'I'm going to try and get some sleep now, some hopes. Then I'll try to get a meeting with this guy tomorrow as soon as poss. So, if he does agree to meet me, I might have to call you late evening maybe very late. You okay with that?'

'Yes Frankie. I'll keep my mobile charged up and by my side all the time, so just call me when you know the time you're meeting is and I'll be on standby. You know what you have to do, so good luck.'

'Thanks, I'll need a bucket load of that stuff.' They said their goodbyes and finished the call.

CHAPTER 30

PRESENT – FLORIDA

5 APRIL

'I trust you didn't sleep well last night?' Billy Ray hadn't ever seen Zsolt Meszaros in the flesh. He'd taken a look on the web, so he knew who was talking to him. He said nothing in response. When he and Valentina arrived at wherever they were now, they'd been separated, and he'd been thrown into a small dark, windowless room, with no air conditioning. It was reminiscent of the third world jail cells he'd seen on the TV or in the movies.

They'd chained him by the wrist to a steel bed secured to the wall, with just enough length to get to a metal lavatory with no seat. They'd left him a metal jug with some lukewarm water. A small recessed light was permanently lit. He'd tried to sleep on the thin mattress, but the heat had been unbearable. He felt exhausted and scared.

When the door had opened, Meszaros and another man stepped through it and closed the door behind them. Meszaros walked around the small cell as if in deep thought. The other man took up a stance in front of the door, hands together in front of him, guard like. After his initial remark about sleeping, Valentina's husband leaned against the wall, arms folded, looking at his prisoner.

The mobster was dressed in a very sharp expensive looking suit. Medium height, not thin, but not overweight. Well groomed, dark hair slicked back with grey wings. Slightly swarthy complexion. An old scar down his right cheek. The stern brown eyes and thin hawk-like nose completed the overall look of a sharp, intelligent man you wouldn't want to mess with. Eventually, Billy Ray spoke.

'What have you done with Valentina?'

'Ah, you're asking about my wife's welfare? How kind, how considerate you are. And to be fair to Valentina, you're not the ugliest man on the planet. I can see the attraction, in a way. A bit of rough I think the correct term is? As for my wife, she's had a change of heart it seems. Asked for my forgiveness, claims she made a big mistake, got carried away; literally I suppose you could say,' he laughed briefly.

'No, my wife stealing friend, it's yourself you

should be concerned about. Valentina, well she has certainly offended me, hurt my ego, badly. I don't know if I can forgive her, but she's a beautiful woman and repentance in her case is something I can contemplate. But you, you have nothing to offer me at all. My only consideration in your case is how much pain to inflict on you before you die. Or perhaps I might let you live but punish you in a way so that life will have little meaning for you, other than years of pain and misery.

You'll certainly never enjoy a woman again by the time I've finished with you.' His cold, unemotional delivery was all the more terrifying for its apparent lack of anger. 'Now I have a question. I sent my man Lenny to find you, and I've heard nothing from him since the day after he left here, I assume he did find you. So what happened to him, I assume he's dead?' Billy Ray looked at the floor. 'Tell me.

'Go fuck yourself,' muttered Billy Ray in reply.

Meszaros turned to the man guarding the door and nodded. The man moved from the door over to where Billy Ray sat on the bed. Billy Ray stood up, and the man delivered a terrific blow to his solar plexus. He fell to the floor his left arm extended at an upwards angle constrained by the chain. He lay there gasping for air, then felt the man take his other arm under his own arm bending it backwards against the elbow bone, then extending his hand. He felt a hard object against his little finger, then excruciating pain. He screamed. The man let him go.

He sobbed in pain and opened his eyes. On the floor in front of him was his little finger. The man kicked it away and told him to get back on the bed. He crawled back on to the bed, his hand bleeding profusely. The man threw the bolt cutters over into the corner, well out of reach.

'Put your hand out.' Billy Ray tucked it under his other armpit. 'Hold out your fucking hand or lose another finger,' said the man. He held out his injured hand, and the man wrapped a large handkerchief round it and tied it with a tight knot. 'Sit up', said the man. He sat up.

'Okay, so, what I asked you before,' said Valentina's husband.

'Yes, he's dead,' replied Billy Ray.

'Who killed him? Don't lie, I'll know if you do I'll know, and this time it won't be your finger, capiche?'

'I did. Had no choice, he would've killed me, so it was him or me. Anyway, he killed my best friend Jerry, shot him in the head. The bastard deserved to die. And he shot the PI my uncle sent to find me, just killed him in cold blood.'

'I don't care about your friend, or any PI. What did you do with Lenny, with his body?'

'It happened on the boat, while we are out in the ocean, so we dumped it, him, over the side.

He'll never be found. We wrapped him in chains.'

'We, by we you mean...?' Billy Ray said nothing. The man stood there looking at Billy Ray, then seemed to make his mind up about something. Suddenly he spoke to the other man. 'Let's go,' he said, and they left, bolting the door behind them.

❖ ❖ ❖

Zaros went back to his office still thinking about the man he'd just spoken to and decided to put the matter off until later when he felt calmer. He'd learnt that acting in anger or in any state of heightened emotion often led to mistakes. He wasn't in the mistakes business. He sat down at his desk to begin his usual morning task of checking reports from the managers of his various businesses. These reports were printed off by his secretary and put into individual files. He opened the first file. The phone on his desk buzzed. He answered.

'This had better be important, you know I don't take any calls till noon.'

'Yes sorry I really am Mr. Meszaros,' said his secretary, 'but this man insists on talking to you, and he said his next call would be to the police. Something about people being kidnapped. I thought he was some sort of crazy person, a crank, so I talked to Bob and asked him what I should do. He said maybe tell you, but....'

'Okay put him on. Does he have a name?'

'Yes, Francis Armstrong, he's British I think.'

Ah, the man working for the uncle... 'Put him through.' The phone bleeped twice. 'What can I do for you, Mr. Armstrong?'

'Meet me so we can all avoid any further problems.'

'I'm not sure I have any problems that you can solve. Would you care to explain what you're talking about, but make it quick I'm a busy man.'

'Billy Ray Ballantyne. I won't bother with the details, you know all about it, so I'd like to meet and negotiate his release.'

'You're kidding me, right?'

'No, I'm not. Look, can we cut the crap Mr. Meszaros? I can offer you a lot of money to let him go. I know you're a very wealthy man already, but who doesn't want more right?'

'That would normally be a reasonable assumption, but in my case, it may not apply.' While he was talking, he was calculating *it would be unwise not to meet this man, if only to be able to assess what he knows.* 'However,' he continued, 'you amuse me Mr. Armstrong. And although I haven't got the least idea of what you're talking about, it would be churlish of me to refuse to meet a man offering me money for nothing.'

'It's okay Mr. Meszaros, no need to be coy, I'm not recording this conversation so you can relax.

This isn't a trap. I wouldn't insult your intelligence. Can we meet later today, say one p.m. at your Miamisun offices. I looked up the address on Google, Premier House 33056 56th Avenue 3319, is that correct, above the Sun Casino?'

'One p.m. it is Mr. Armstrong. I look forward to meeting you, goodbye.' Frankie cut the connection and fell backwards on to the bed. He was shaking; then he was laughing.

'Jesus Christ,' he said out loud *I'm going to get myself killed if I carry on like this. Who the fuck do I think I am, Bruce Willis?'*

CHAPTER 31

PRESENT – FLORIDA

5 APRIL

Frankie called Joe.

'So, you're going to see this Zaros guy today?'

'I am Joe, so I need to know about the money. How quickly can you get your hands on it? And if we do get to the point where he might agree, he's going to want to know when we can pay him, that I'm sure of.'

'Well, depends on how much we're talking about. How much do you intend to offer him?'

'I thought I'd try half a million to begin with. Say that's the maximum we can offer, then go from there. Is one mill the maximum for you Joe?'

''Sort of, maybe. I could go more, but if he won't take million, I mean? You know, supposing he said ten million dollars, well I just can't do that, and anyway, with a guy like this, in this situation, surely the money is more a token, a matter of pride? Billy Ray's made a fool of him, humiliated him, and a powerful man like that has to have a very good reason to justify letting Billy Ray go.

This guy has employees, friends, and enemies, who he daren't show weakness to. His sort know they have to be seen as tough and ruthless, otherwise they're finished. It's tricky Frankie, and I have to be honest, I think this is probably a waste of time, but we've got to try for Billy Ray's sake.'

'Hang on in there Joe. If the money doesn't do it, which I agree is unlikely, I do have another plan.'

'And that is?'

'Rather not say at this stage Joe, but if you're a praying man, then I suggest you ask the man upstairs for some serious help.'

'I am and I will. Frankie, I know I haven't been entirely honest with you about certain things, so I'm all the more grateful for what you're doing now.'

'You should be Joe, and after this is over you've got some explaining to do, but for now, let's focus on getting your nephew back in one piece.'

'What about the woman?' said Joe.

'That's a bit more complicated. It is his wife after all, so I don't know. I'll have to play that one by ear, but let's concentrate on getting Billy Ray free first if we can.'

'You're right Frankie. We need to stay focused. And like I say, I'm sorry I wasn't more, err, accurate about things.'

'Accurate! that's bullshit Joe, and you know it. What you mean is, you lied to me, plain and simple. But now's not the time to deal with that. For reasons I'm finding hard to explain to myself even, this has turned into something I just feel I have to see this through to the end. When it's over, I'm going to expect a full explanation from you about the money and everything else. Assuming I get through all this in one piece that is?'

'Yeah I know Frankie, I promise to tell all, cross my heart.' Joe crossed his heart with his right hand. Frankie raised his eyes, then looked down at his watch.

'Got to go Joe, wish me luck.' He wanted to allow himself plenty of time to get to Miami.

He made good time across Alligator Alley and with the invaluable help of the satnav, made his way through the city of Miami to Miamisun's offices. He parked the bright green Mustang in the underground parking lot opposite, then sat in the car for a while and composed himself. As small as it was, the USB memory stick taped under his arm felt like a brick.

The previous night he'd donned the blue lightweight cotton jacket and button down shirt he planned to wear for the meeting. In anticipation of being patted down for a handgun or wire, he practiced raising his arms then unbuttoning his shirt for inspection, without revealing the memory stick taped under his armpit. He'd also practiced taking the memory stick from under his armpit, by effecting to causally scratch in the immediate area, then taking the memory stick in his fingers and palming it into his trouser pocket. He practiced for an hour until he'd perfected the technique to his satisfaction, then gone to bed and slept fitfully, waking before dawn.

Walking across the road, he couldn't help but be impressed by the elaborate 'porte-cochere' the grand facade of the sun casino. Romanesque columns on either side of the huge ornate gold doors, provided an imposing impression of opulent grandeur and indulgent decadence. A huge sun symbol hung over the main entrance lighted in such a way as to give a Catherine wheel effect. An overdressed flunky in a fancy red frockcoat plus top hat and two blond bimbos in skimpy gold dresses completed the grand ensemble.

Frankie found the more modest business-like entrance to Miamisun Inc's offices a few doors down from the grand casino entrance. He was ten minutes early. There was a keypad and intercom to the right of the door. He pressed the button and a metallic voice asked for his name and who he was coming to see. He complied. The voice told him to check in at reception. He was buzzed in and walking through the doors, found himself in a hallway with a lift either side.

A list of the company's offices hung on the wall. Miamisun's reception was on the 7th floor. He gulped, checked the lump under his armpit and pressed the lift button. On the way up he practiced in his mind what he was going to say, tried to assume a calm, cool, indifferent persona, and took deep breaths to try to bring his heartbeat rate down to something like normal.

As the lift opened on the 7th floor, a large man stood there. He signaled him to approach him.

'Arms up please. I'm sure you won't mind me conducting a security search Mr. Armstrong?' he said amiably enough.

'No, not at all,' said Franke,' raising his arms and parting his legs while the man patted him down.

'Pockets please,' said the man. Frankie took out his keys, phone and wallet. The man took his phone. 'If you don't mind, I'll keep this and return it to you on your way out.'

'And if I do mind?' asked Frankie. The man looked at him. 'It was a joke, sorry,' said Frankie.

'Huh,' said the man, 'very funny I'm sure,' and slipped the phone into his pocket. 'Follow me.' They walked down a corridor; walls painted pale cream, large pictures of various Miamiscapes adorned the walls. They turned a corner. The man knocked on a pale green door, opened it and leaned in.

'Clean,' he said, then nodded, held the door open and motioned with his head for Frankie to enter.

'Come in sit down. I won't offer you coffee, you won't be here that long,' said the exquisitely dressed blue suited man. *I've never looked that smart, well-groomed and well dressed in my life* thought Frankie, *not even on my wedding day.* There was no handshake. The man remained sitting in his luxurious looking office chair behind a large ornate wooden desk the size of a ping pong table. Frankie sat and looked around for the presence of a computer, a laptop, or another adjoining room with a secretary using a computer, nothing... *shit* thought Frankie.

'Tell me who you are, and why you're here?' Zaros rested his elbows on the arms of his chair, steepled his fingers and assumed a look of patience as if waiting for a child to explain how he'd broken a window with his football. Frankie took a deep breath. He explained how his old friend Joe, who he'd met in the Gulf war had called him to ask for his help finding his missing nephew. Then he fast forwarded to the day before yesterday when they'd gone to the survivalist camp.

'We'd good reason to believe that Billy Ray, and his..., sorry, your wife Valentina, had fled to the camp to hide' Zaros smiled briefly, Frankie continued. 'Anyway, as you know, we were right, but they'd gone, taken away by your thugs, who shot an innocent man in the process. Did they really have to do that?'

'As I have absolutely no idea what you're talking about Mr. Armstrong, I really can't answer that. Now you said you wanted to give me some money, is that correct?'

'Half a million dollars to release Billy Ray.'

'Goodbye Mr. Armstrong, please close the door on your way out.'

'A million dollars, but that's it. There isn't any more Mr. Meszaros. Look I appreciate your angst, your anger at this young man who, well who stole your wife, I've also recently been....' Zsolt Meszaros held his hand up. Frankie stopped speaking.

'Get out Mr. Armstrong, get out now, before I decide to punish you for your impertinence. My stolen wife, as you describe her, is presently relaxing in our apartment and preparing for a very important Veteran's charity dinner this evening. As for your missing friend, I'm afraid I can't help you, but I know that a lot of missing people turn up in the most dreadful state, often as a dead body floating in the river for instance, and sometimes showing signs of the most dreadful torture before they took that last breath.

In fact, I believe that for such people, death is often a blessed relief. Goodbye Mr. Armstrong.'

He pressed a button on his desk, and the large man entered the room. 'Mr. Armstrong is leaving now.' The man stood back to let Frankie out of the door, then escorted him down the corridor. He went with him in the lift down to the ground floor, then returned Frankie's phone and keys and saw him out through the front door on to the street. Frankie looked back through the plate glass window. The man smiled, waved and mouthed bye bye.

Frankie turned and walked back across the road and leaned against the low wall. *There goes my master plan, big clever idea. Shit for brains me!* He couldn't bring himself to call Joe. He looked at his watch and called Gareth to tell him the bad news.'

'What's the haps Frankie?'

'The haps as you put it, are shit. Just got thrown out on my ear. He wouldn't consider the money I offered, turned down a million dollars. Can you imagine just how wealthy you'd have to be, to do that?'

'I assume you couldn't get the stick into a machine?'

'Not a prayer. Didn't see a laptop, or any kind of computer, let alone one to get the memory stick into. Me and my great ideas. Maybe I've watched too many James Bond films?'

No Frankie, it was a sound plan, don't beat yourself up about it.'

'Nice of you to say, Gareth, but the guy is obviously completely ruthless, so the chances of Joe's nephew getting out alive now are just about zero. Maybe I just have to go to the cops and see if they can do something? Can't really see someone like him being intimidated though.'

'You tried Frankie, and it was a good idea, I mean it, a really good idea. It's not your fault it didn't work.' As Frankie was listening to Gareth, a limousine pulled up outside the casino. Two men got out and went in through the ornate entrance. Then a couple walked off the street and went inside, the doorman holding open the door for them.

'Gareth, is it likely that the company's other businesses would be connected to the same main computer network system?'

'It would be normal practice, yes. If they're remote, I mean as in another physical location, they'd more than likely to be on a company VPN, a virtual private network.'

And would there be a problem trying to get into the main system via this VPN, as difficult as via the internet?'

'Probably not. IT security people tend to focus on an exterior threat from the internet. They usually consider a threat from within their own network as maybe less likely, and give it a lower priority. They probably have internal firewalls, might not, but if they do I can almost guarantee they won't be anywhere near as well configured, as the ones to protect them from a breach via the internet. What are you thinking Frankie, I can almost hear your brain whizzing round?'

'Well, I'm looking at a casino owned by Miamisun Inc. It's located on the ground floor of the same building as their head office.'

'Right, well if it's in part of the same building, it might even be on the same physical network. You going gambling Frankie?'

'I am Gareth, in more ways than one.'

◆ ◆ ◆

Frankie crossed the road again and made for the casino entrance. He was greeted with a smile and a 'welcome Sir' from the doorman who held the door open for him. He also got a cheeky wink from one of the Barbie dolls by the door. Once inside Frankie was horrified to see a notice apologizing for the inconvenience, saying recent events had forced the management to install metal detectors. He saw a man with a wand stopping someone at the interior entrance which you had to pass through to enter the casino proper.

The security man made the customer empty his pockets and put his stuff in a plastic container, airport security style, swished the wand around him and in between his legs, then waved him through. To Frankie's surprise, the security man then waved the next three people through without examination. *Random searches.* Frankie waited for the next person to be examined then pushed his way gently into the loose queue, so he was next in line. He got through without hindrance and began to breathe normally again.

Once inside the foyer, he was treated to an array of color and bright lights. A huge fountain with water shooting up into the domed ceiling provided the centerpiece, the water appearing to change color as it shot up into the air, then cascaded down a central column back into the reservoir beneath. Behind the fountain was a huge array of slot machines, the air busy with the noise of handles being pulled, the reels spinning and whoops when one of the machines cashed out and gave forth.

Behind the slot machine area, were the gaming tables, roulette wheels, rolling dice crap games and many well attended card tables. Dark suited floor managers roamed around the gambling floor, with earpieces, some speaking into their wrists. Frankie stood taking it all in, then wandered around trying to remain casual and inconspicuous. *One way or another I've got to get into some sort of admin area.* He spotted the bureau manned by a scary looking pofaced lady in a dark business style suit. Obviously, a position where brains and not beauty was the priority he thought. There was a small queue of people buying chips or cashing in their winnings.

He watched for a while and couldn't see how he could possibly get into that office. He wandered around looking for the manager's office. There was no obvious manager's office, but there was a door towards the back of the room, marked Strictly Private. An idea popped into his mind

'*Okay Frankie*, he said to himself, *Showtime.* He walked back to the booth issuing chips and asked for two hundred dollars' worth, in ten-dollar denominations, *last of the big gamblers...*

'There you go honey,' said the stern lady behind the counter, cracking a smile and changing her whole appearance in the process. Best of luck.' *She has no idea just how much luck I'm going to need to pull this off.* He took tens and walked round to find a blackjack table with a vacant seat near to the door marked Strictly Private. He sat down next to a large brightly yellow jacketed man complete with a bright red shirt and a bolo tie. The man turned as Frankie sat down.

'Welcome stranger. Hope you can change my luck,' he said in a loud and heavy southern accent. Then he laughed and slapped Frankie on the back nearly unseating him.
Frankie said he'd do his best.

'Hey, you a Brit, no maybe an Aussie?' Frankie told him he was British and tried to concentrate on placing his chips on the table. The cards were dealt face up. Frank got an Ace and a Queen. *Typ-*

ical he thought. The croupier paid everyone out, having dealt himself three cards adding up to twenty two. The loud man guffawed.

'I knew you'd change my luck,' he said. Frankie smiled and turned towards him to avoid another friendly slap on the back. Frankie wanted to get this over with. He tried to be patient and played another two hands, then stood up, put his hand to his chest, screwed his face up as though in excruciating pain and spoke in a croaky voice

'Oh, shit no,' he said, then slumped back on to his seat and collapsed forwards, letting his upper body fall across the table.'

'Jesus Christ, the man's having a heart attack' said his new friend and turned to the croupier. 'Call someone for Christ's sake, call the medics, the emergency services.' The man leaned over Frankie. Hold on buddy, you'll be alright, we'll get some help.' Frankie looked across the top of the table and saw the croupier stand up craning his neck, looking for help, his hand under the table. Frankie hoped he was summoning a manager. A man in a dark suit arrived and took charge. His new friend quickly told the floor manager what had happened. Frankie made an effort to stand up, then sat back down, his right hand clasped to his chest face still winced with pain.

'Please don't call the medics, he said in a weak pleading voice, 'I'll be okay if I can just lie down somewhere quiet for ten minutes. It happens to me every now and then, long term heart problem, nothing they can do about it, I just need to rest and recover, then I'll be okay really, then I can get out of your hair. I'm really sorry to cause a fuss.' He winced a bit more, took a deep breath and swallowed. 'If you could just help me get to somewhere quiet, where I can lie down, I'll be okay. It's always the same, ten minutes or so and I'll be right as rain.'

The floor manager looked around for support; none came. By now the situation was drawing the attention of some nearby gamblers. Frankie knew they hated stuff like this in a casino, least he was betting they did. *Get the distraction out of the way and let people get back to throwing their money away.*

'Okay bud, if you can stand up and lean on me, you can go lie down in the office. You sure you don't want the medics?'

'No honestly, just a lie down.' Frankie got to his feet feigning unsteadiness. He leaned heavily on the floor manager who clasped a firm arm around Frankie's waist to support him. They slowly walked the short distance across the room to the door marked 'Strictly Private'. Still holding on to Frankie, the manager knocked on the door and waited briefly. There was no response. He talked into his wrist.

'Hey Bill, this is Danny. I have a guy who collapsed in the casino, and I need to get him into Velma's office to lie down.' There was a pause, then Danny continued. 'No, she must be on a bathroom break or something. The guy says he'll be okay if he can just lie down somewhere quiet for a few minutes, ticker problem,' another pause, then he continued, 'yeah, but I have to get him out of the way. It's causing a big distraction, people rubber necking, stopped gambling to see what's going on, and you know how much the boss would like that?

Look, just give me the access code would you? My arm's nearly breaking holding this guy up.' He was given the code and began tapping it into the keypad, then turned the doorknob and the door opened. 'Thanks buddy,' he continued, 'yeah, ten minutes max then I call the paramedics if he don't recover,' pause, 'yeah I know back entrance, bye.' Frankie wasn't particularly a religious man, but at that moment, he closed his eyes and said a silent prayer of thanks.

In the left hand corner of the room were five modern square upholstered chairs joined together, reception room style forming an L shape around a coffee table, There was a door and a glass partition to an adjoining room, a small office with a desk and a PC monitor on it. *Please let the interconnecting door be unlocked,* thought Frankie, as he tried to concentrate on how to play out his next couple of moves.

'Lie down you said, these chairs okay?'

'Perfect,' said Frankie, 'if you can just help me.' The man helped Frankie to lie down along three of the chairs then went through the connecting door into the office, looked around and came back with a cushion to put under Frankie's head.

'You okay now bud?' said the man

'Yes thanks, feeling a bit better already. Sorry, but would it be possible to have a glass of water please?'

'Sure thing,' said the man, 'You gonna be okay on your own for a minute? Frankie said he would be. 'I'll go get a waitress, hold on pal.' The man went back out through the door. *Now or never he said to himself*. Frankie jumped up ripped the memory stick from under his arm, went through the door. He looked at the desk and underneath was a small computer tower, the back exposed to show a number of different shaped ports. There were two spare USB ports.

The memory stick was slippery with sweat from his armpit, and he nearly dropped it as he knelt down under the desk. He tried to insert it in the right hand USB port, but it was the wrong way round. He turned it over and successfully slotted it into the port, then quickly moved back through the interconnecting door just as the door from the casino opened. He fell on the floor full length, and a woman shrieked. Frankie rolled over blinking his eyes rapidly as though having some sort of fit; then he closed them. The manager followed closely behind the woman.

'What's this man doing in the office, what's going on?' The manager knelt down and slapped Frankie gently on his face. Frankie feigned waking up.

'Sorry Velma, the guy had some sort of attack out there said he just needed to lie down somewhere quiet, and he'd be okay, but he don't look too good does he?' Frankie opened his eyes and feigned trying to sit up. There was a knock on the door which was still ajar. A waitress came in with a glass of water on a small tray.

'This for him?' she said, 'what's wrong with him?'

'He kinda collapsed out there, so I brought him in here. I laid him down on the chairs but looks like he fell off.'

'You want me to look at him, I used to be a nurse?' said the waitress

'Sure thing,' the man said obviously relieved and stood up. The waitress kneeled down and put her hand behind Frankie's neck to support his head, then asked the manager to pass her the glass of water and put it to Frankie's lips. He sipped. The floor manager passed the cushion to the nurse to rest Frankie's head on.

'Is that my seat cushion?' said the discombobulated Velma, 'you've been in my personal office?'

'Just to get something to put under his head,

don't get your panties in a twist.' Thelma fumed, Frankie spoke in a weak voice.

'Sorry, tried to get up too soon and I think I fainted. Feeling much better now. If you can just help me back on the chairs. The waitress helped him up, and he could smell her perfume. Frankie said he'd rather sit than lie down and asked for another sip of water. The waitress obliged, then insisted on taking his pulse. She sat next to him, took his wrist in her hand, pressing her thumb to monitor his pulse, while the others looked on.

'I'm really feeling much better now,' he said 'so thanks for all your help and I'm sorry to have caused you any problems, but just give me a couple of minutes, and I think I'll be okay to go.' The waitress let go of his wrist.

'Well his pulse is certainly fast, and he's sweating a lot, but he doesn't seem as if he's dying. Maybe you should go see a doctor just to be on the safe side?' she said to him.

'I will, as soon as I get back to my hotel. I'll get them to arrange it for me. Frankie saw that Velma was in her office looking around, picking up files, putting them down again. She came back into the reception room.

'You sure this guy didn't go into my office?' she said to the floor manager.'

'Why, something wrong, something missin'?' he replied

'No, but you shouldn't let strangers come in

here. That door's marked private for a reason,' she said pointedly. Frank made to stand up slowly, allowing the waitress to help him. He straightened up and tried to ignore Velma's steely stare. She obviously had her suspicions.

'There', he said 'I'm feeling better already.' The waitress said she'd better get back to her work. She smiled at Frankie and left.

'Can I call you a cab?' asked the floor manager.

'No thanks, the fresh air will do me good, and thanks again for all your help, I'm really sorry to have caused any trouble.'

'No trouble, no trouble at all buddy' said the manager, as he opened the door to let Frankie out. 'You sure you're okay now?' the manager asked again

'I am now thanks. Bye,' said Frankie.

'Yeah sure, bye' said the manager and closed the office door behind them. Frankie was conscious of the manager watching him as he made his way towards the casino entrance. As he walked, he imagined Velma searching her office for any irregularities and just hoped enough time had passed for the memory stick to do its job before she found it. He was sure she would, she was that sort of woman. *But even if she does find the memory stick, there'll be nothing on it, assuming Gareth knows what he's doing.* It took an enormous effort for Frankie to walk slowly when all he wanted to do was run like hell and get out of the place. Then he heard the floor manager shout.

'Hey there buddy, wait up.' Frankie stopped and turned. The man was striding towards him purposefully. Frankie didn't know whether to run but decided he didn't stand a chance of getting out the door without being stopped.

'What is it?' he said, trying his best to remain calm.

'Your winnings, you won, that last hand' he said, 'I cashed in your chips for you,' and he handed Frankie a thin wad of dollars.

'Oh yes, thanks, very kind of you,' said Frankie, 'well bye again,' he said putting the money in his pocket, then turned and carried on walking to the entrance.

'Yeah, sure thing, have a good one,' said the floor manager as Frankie walked away.

CHAPTER 32

PRESENT – FLORIDA

5 APRIL

Zsolt Meszaros had maintained his calm air of indifference until Frankie had left, and his henchman out of earshot. Then stood up, walked the short distance to the sideboard, picked up a valuable antique vase, stood back then hurled it at the wall with all his strength, shouting a curse in Spanish as he did so. The vase smashed into smithereens. He went back behind the desk, sat in his chair and brooded. Conflicted wasn't a state of mind he liked or was used to. He was always sure of his next move, never had doubts, no matter what the situation. His ruthless decisiveness was one of his greatest assets. He doodled on a piece of paper, then had an idea.

Taking the lift to his penthouse on the 24th floor, he tapped the code into the keypad and entered his spacious penthouse apartment. Huge floor to ceiling windows afforded an impressive vista, the cityscape of Miami with a view of the Atlantic Ocean in the distance. Some calming music was required. He chose nocturne in E, sat down on the sumptuous sofa, leaned back, closed his eyes and let the music wash over him. Ten minutes later he got up walked to the bedroom, inserted the key and opened the door. Valentina lay on her back on the Grand King size bed, eyes closed. He walked over sat on the bed and smoothed her brow. She woke, looked at him, terror in her eyes. He took her bound hands in his and taking a key from his pocket, he undid the handcuffs. She rubbed her wrists looking warily at him.

'What shall I do with you, my lovely little wife? I should kill you, you know. I've killed lots of people for much less. Not that I've ever had a wife run away before.' Valentina was now sitting upright on the bed.

'I told you, I made a big big mistake Zsolt honey, and I'm so so sorry. I just don't know what I saw in that man, he's horrible, and I hate him. I'll make it up to you, please just give me another chance I'm begging you.' She sobbed.

'But do I believe you? And can such an act of treachery go unpunished?' I have my pride and my reputation. What would my friends and enemies make of it if I simply let you live without paying a price?'

'Tell me what to do Zsolt? I'll do anything to make it right between us, anything.'

'Okay my beautiful Valentina, I may have a solution. You'll do anything to show me how sorry you are, right?'

'Yes, anything, anything at all, just tell me.'

'Okay, well tonight there's a big charity ball. I want you to get yourself down to the beauticians or whatever those places are called, get your hair done, have a massage, relax and tonight get dolled up in your finest dress, buy a new dress if you wish. And we'll have a lovely evening. I'm the guest of honor, which is just a way of acknowledging I'm the largest donor. They've asked me to make a speech, and I'd like you by my side when I do, looking your stunning best.'

'Is that it, is that all you want me to do?'

'Yes, well just one other thing. Tomorrow morning, we're going to take a little trip on my Beechcraft. Geoff will be flying us, but maybe you can have a little go at flying it for a while on the way back?' You'd like that wouldn't you?'

'Yes, I would, sounds exciting. Where are we going?'

'Oh, I don't know, somewhere over the Everglades, somewhere nice and remote. We'll have another passenger, at least we will on the outward part of the trip.'

'Sorry, are we going to land in the Everglades?'

'No, we're not, but our passenger is. We're taking your boyfriend with us, and you're going to push him out at 12,000 feet.' The color drained from her face.

'No Zaros I couldn't do that,' she said, 'I couldn't kill anyone.'

'See that's not true is it? I know you helped your boyfriend kill my man Lenny. I liked Lenny, unlike you, he was faithful. So no more lies my sweet innocent Valentina, I know you can kill when it suits, we all can. 'He looked her straight in the eyes. She held his gaze then looked down at the floor. He put his hand under her chin to raise her face so she had to look at him. 'Anyway my lovely, it's either him or both of you, understand?' His voice had hardened. She nodded. 'Now off you go and get pampered, I want you looking your very best for my big night tonight. We'll have a great time.'

CHAPTER 33

PRESENT – FLORIDA

5 APRIL

Frankie sat in his car in the parking lot, closed his eyes and did some deep breathing. He felt drained. The adrenaline and nervous tension had left him, and he felt weak, completely drained. Gradually he began to feel better. He took out his UK mobile and called Gareth.

'Yo bud' said Gareth, 'well done my man. How'd you do it?' Frankie wasn't sure about how this new relationship was developing. Far removed from when Gareth referred to him as Uncle Frankie. *Still got to accept, without Gareth, things would be looking seriously grim now.*

'Oh., You know already?' He said.

'Sure, I know. Just had an incoming from their system, got the guys on it already.'

'It worked that fast? Jesus Gareth you're a genius!'

'You only just realized? The firewalls we've come up against so far don't appear to be that problematic, so we're worming our way through.'

'How long will it take?'

'Don't know; it's not really like that. Depends how it goes. With luck, we could have access to most of their data within a few hours. I have to say Frankie, it's looking good, but at this stage, I can't promise it'll go like clockwork. No guarantees, there's plenty of unknowns here. So, like I say, looks promising, but we're not there yet. So come on Frankie, tell me how you did it, how did you get that stick into one of their computers?'

'Luck mostly combined with, if I say so myself, a not inconsiderable amount of bottle. I went into their casino on the ground floor of the building their head office is in. Then I got some chips and had a game of blackjack then feigned a heart attack. Truth is I was so scared I nearly had a real heart attack.'

'And how did that help you get near to a computer?'

'I chose a blackjack table near the door to some sort of admin office, assuming it might have a computer in it, and it did. I played a couple of hands, then did my acting bit and had my heart attack, fell across the table. I don't think I've ever been so scared in my life, not even in Iraq.'

'Wow awesome,' said Gareth, 'go on.'

'Well, I managed to stop them sending for medics, asked if I could just lie down somewhere quiet for a while, said I'd be okay. I knew they'd want to get me out of the way, so they took me into the office. I lay down then asked them for a drink of water, and while the guy went to get some, I managed to slip the memory stick into a slot in the back of a PC in the next room. I nearly didn't make it though. The woman whose office it was nearly walked in on me while I was doing the dirty deed.

'Unbelievable man, so you didn't need the second stick?'

'No, what should I do with it?'

'Take a hammer to it or flush it down the loo.'

'Will do as soon as I get the chance. So when can I put the arm on this guy?'

'I'll call or email you as soon as I think we have the lot, or enough. If it all works out, I guess you'll want to demonstrate to him just what we can do?'

'I do and believe me I can't wait. Anyway, we need to do this as soon as possible. God only knows what he'll do to Billy Ray, and when.'

'Working on it now Frankie, be in touch soon.' Gareth cut the connection. Frankie was about to call Joe, then thought better of it, deciding to wait till he had something concrete to say. He started the car set the satnav for the Cove Inn's address in Naples and began his journey back, grateful for the distraction of driving.

◆ ◆ ◆

During the drive back, Frankie's mind once more turned to Penny. He missed her, missed talking to her. Wanted to tell her about Naples, about what he'd got involved in, although he knew she'd tell him he was crazy and to leave it alone. They'd always talked quite a lot, which was partly why he'd been so shocked. Like she'd been living another life outside theirs, some parallel existence. How could he have not suspected? How come he didn't pick up on anything?

The time had passed quickly, and he was nearly back in Naples. His UK mobile rang, he answered driving one handed. There were no laws in Florida banning speaking on a phone and driving.

'Gareth.'

'Just to let you know Frankie, we're making serious progress, should have a fuller picture in another hour or so, but looking good.'

'When you have this full picture, what will you be able to do?'

'Potentially some quite interesting stuff, but we're working on some tricky encryption at the moment. If and when we crack that we might be into some really good stuff. What I can tell you is this guy is rich, man, like seriously rich, and that's just his legit stuff. Why he needs to be involved in the other stuff, I mean why would you take the risk?'

'It's called greed Gareth. Call me back as soon as you can. I'm nearly back at the motel.'

'Okay, but before you go, I also looked up his name, you know Meszaros?'

'And?'

'It means butcher, the name Meszaros means butcher.'

'Oh great. Thanks Gareth, just what I needed to hear.'

'No probs Frankie, just thought you'd like to know, bye.'

Frankie got back to the Cove and took a shower. Rather than wait around twiddling his thumbs he took an early evening walk down to Third Street and sat in a coffee shop watching the people go by and lusting after some of the exotic cars that variously drove slowly along, occasionally parking and disgorging their passengers to eat at one of the many restaurants lining the street.

He got up and strolled around the corner to the pier. Some people were already going down to the beach to prepare for the sunset. Invariably spectacular, the setting sun slowly dipping below the horizon turning the sky shades of deep red, orange, yellow and beaten copper against a blue backdrop with wispy clouds hanging over the sea. He sighed and started to walk back to the Cove Inn.

Back in his room, he took a beer out of the fridge and stood on the small balcony overlooking Naples docks. He missed Charlie's company. His mobile rang.

'Okay Frankie, you want the good news or the really good news?'

'I'll take the good news first please.'

'Okay, well as I said before, the guy is seriously rich. We ignored all the other data, HR, management issues etc. etc. and concentrated purely on financial data. The legit business accounts and bank details were easy to get at, but I assumed you wouldn't be all that interested in that stuff. So, we looked around for the real meat and came across a load of encrypted data. This is where we had to put in some serious work. But as you know, I'm a genius, and so eventually we cracked it. There's a whole slew of offshore bank accounts with regular and semi-regular deposits recorded. The totals in some of these accounts are eye watering. I counted thirty four offshore accounts, Grand Cayman, St Lucia, Brunei-Darussalam, Seychelles, Vanuatu, Samoa and others. You get the picture?'

'I do, but how does the money get into these accounts?'

'Back in the days when I considered using my

hacking talents for, shall we say, more nefarious purposes? I used to fantasize about how much money I could extract from the unfortunate targets and then studied how and where I could squirrel it away. No point in making loads of dosh then wondering what to do with it. You have to have a plan. So I did a bit of research on how to get cash money into offshore banks, and it's fairly easy. Some people take suitcases full of the stuff on private yachts. Some launder it through false companies, shuttle the money from pillar to post, country to country making the trail next to impossible to trace. In my fantasy, I'd have been rich enough to charter a plane and fly the cash out from a private airfield.

Official bodies just don't have enough resources to stop this sort of activity and rely on tip offs, but if your organization is tight, no leaks, it's not an issue. So, hiding it is not that problematic, but getting it back to the UK or anywhere else, and legitimizing it, is entirely another matter. So if I'd carried on with my plan, I'd have had to spend the rest of my life cruising around the Caribbean, gorgeous women draped over the deck of my yacht.'

'Okay I've got the picture Gareth, let's get back to planet earth now. What can we do with this data?'

'Well, I've taken digital copies of all these accounts, locations, deposit records and balances.

Now, these will alter over time, money in or out, maybe some accounts closed, new ones opened. But even if the data is out of date, it would be dynamite if the IRS were to get their hands on it.'

'Yup, I get that, so if this is the good news...?'

'Okay, the really good news, we eventually found all the passwords and codes for these accounts. The techies had hidden them in three separate encrypted files, but we managed to crack them, so in theory, we now have the ability to do all sorts of things. We could empty an account, maybe empty them all. Certainly, we could transfer monies from one account to another as we wish.'

'You're pulling my leg?'

'I'm deadly serious. We could probably only do it once. That's to say, once they know we've got the passwords, they'd change them, no doubt about that, but even then, maybe we could find the new ones?'

'Can they lock you out once they know you've hacked into their system?'

'Depends but not easily, and if they could, it would take them a while. We could probably leave some sleeper software in there, and they'd think they'd got rid of us, then we could re-activate it later or set it to re-activate itself on a specific date in the future.'

'So we've well and truly got them by the short hairs?'

'That would be fair to say Frankie.'

'You're a fucking genius Gareth a gold-plated fucking genius.'

'That would also be a fair description.' They both burst out laughing.

'Right, this is what I want you to do. Set up a transfer of say ten million dollars from one account to another. Is that sort of money available in any of the accounts?'

'They're all well over that Frankie, ten mill is pocket change for our Mr. Meszaros.'

'Right, well you need to tell me which account you're taking it out of numbers and name of the bank. Could we make it ten million?'

'Yeah no problem, give me ten fifteen minutes, and I'll come back to you.'

Frankie looked at his watch, nearly six p.m. The man said he was taking his wife to a charity dinner. Would he have left by now? Frankie suddenly realized it could all be too late anyway - *might all be a complete waste of time, maybe Billy Ray's already been killed? If he's done it, killed him, I'll screw the bastard every which way I can.* He got up and paced around, looked at his watch again and suddenly realized he had no method of contacting Zsolt Meszaros now. His offices would be closed.

'Shit,' he said out loud. *Tomorrow might be too late.* He had the feeling that his visit today, far from preventing Billy Ray's demise, might have served to hasten it, assuming he wasn't dead already. Something in the mobster's demeanor that afternoon made him think that Billy Ray might be still alive. But, having refused the money he'd been offered, he might reasonably assume that Frankie would go to the police to report his suspicions, try to get them to at least go and see him. There would be a record of the incident at the survivalist's camp which would give some credibility to his story, albeit no proof that Meszaros was involved. The obvious way for the thug to prevent any chance of the police finding Billy Ray, was to kill him and get rid of the body.

'Shit, shit, shit,' said Frankie repeatedly as he paced around his room. Then he remembered, stopped *the man said he was going to a charity dinner, what was it he said, a Veterans Charity Dinner?* Frankie went to his laptop, typed Veteran's Charity Dinner Miami into Google and added today's date. Bingo! The Faena Hotel Miami Beach. Attendees included senators and showbiz celebs the glitterati of Miami and beyond. A plan hatched in his mind, *might even be better than trying to get hold of him at his offices?* He made himself a coffee and sat outside on the balcony. His phone rang.

'Okay Frankie, we have lift off. All prepped and ready to go. All you have to do is call or text me. Just say do it, and I'll press the button on a wire transfer from one of his bank accounts to another. I did think it might be a better idea to transfer the funds to my account over here, they're badly in need of some replenishment, but I guess that's out of the question?'

'It is if you want to avoid a ruthless killer on your tail for the rest of your natural. Let me get a pen, and I can take down details. Okay, go.'

'I'll be taking ten million dollars out of Palma Telford Inc., account number 4928461 Carib International Bank St. Lucia and transferring it to account number 4569870 in the name of Triton Holdings Inc at the Cayman International Bank.'

'How long will it take?'

'The funds should come out of the account almost immediately, not sure how long it will take for them to land in the other bank, but I can make it an overnight request, or urgent. Which one do you want?'

'Make it overnight, let him sweat. And thinking about it, do the transfer now. I need it already done when I speak to him.'

'Your wish is my command boss.' And Gareth laughed

'Frankie got back on to his laptop and took down the number of the Faena Hotel, then dialed.

'Faena Hotel, how may I direct your call?'

'First, I need to know when the charity dinner, the Veteran's charity dinner that is, what time does it start?'

'I'll transfer you to banqueting; please hold.'

'Hello banqueting, Haley speaking how may I help?' Frankie established the pre-dinner cocktail party had already begun.

'Okay Haley, I need to speak with the manager now, and it's urgent.'

'Yes sir. May I say who's calling and the nature of your call this evening?'

'The name's Armstrong, and I have a very important message for your manager. This is a matter of extreme urgency, a matter of life and death.'

'Putting you through to his office now, please hold.' Sickly music played on the line.

'Duty manager Gonzales Picking speaking, how can I help?'

'Mr. Picking, I can't stress the importance of this enough, but you have to get a message to one of your guests at the Veteran's charity dinner. I have to speak with him right away, a matter of life and death.' He could imagine the manager's thought process trying to judge if he was talking to some sort of head case.

'May I have your name sir and the nature of the emergency? Have you tried calling the police?'

'My name is Armstrong, and a person may die in the next couple of hours if I don't speak urgently to one of your guests, a Mr. Zsolt Meszaros.'

'Mr. Meszaros is one of the guest speakers at this evening's dinner, and I believe he's currently preparing to make his speech, I couldn't possibly interrupt him.' Frankie desperately tried to think of a way to cut through this. He took the piece of paper out of his pocket.

'You have a pen and some paper?'

'Yes,' said Picking.

'Then take down these details and show them to Mr. Meszaros. Can you do that at least?'

'I guess I can, but if he won't come to the phone then I'm afraid I'll have to hang up, and you'll just have to try to contact Mr. Meszaros some other way, maybe call him at his office tomorrow?'

'Okay, I'll do that, but show him the details I'm going to dictate to you now.' Frankie reeled off the name of one of the companies, the name of the bank and the account number. One should be enough he thought. The manager asked him to spell the company name again and checked the numbers.

'Also, please tell him ten million dollars will disappear from the account in ten minutes if he doesn't come to the phone right away.'

'Ten million?' said the manager, 'are you some sort of nut?'

'Put it this way Mr. Picking, are you willing to risk your job by not giving Mr. Meszaros that message. You really want to take the risk of him losing ten million dollars because you think I might be a nutjob?'

'Hold the line,' said Picking and disappeared. There was the noise of a door closing, then muffled voices. Frankie heard Meszaros's voice asking the manager to give him some privacy and close the office door. The phone was picked up.

'You've almost certainly just committed suicide Mr. Armstrong, may be delayed by a day or two until I find you, but find you I will. You obviously have no idea just who you're dealing with. So, you have details of one of my companies and a bank account number big deal. As for stealing ten million dollars of my money, don't be utterly ridiculous.'

'Oh, I'm not going to steal any of your dirty money Mr. Meszaros, but I am going to use it to demonstrate the hold I have over you. Funds will be transferred to another of your offshore accounts just so you know.'

'Hold, what hold?' Meszaros said in a mocking tone.

'I have the lot, your entire financial data,' said Frankie, 'down to the last dollar, no sorry, the last cent. Both the legit stuff and the other stuff.'

'Who do you think you're kidding, you fucking moron? Exactly how would you have got hold of this data? And please don't tell me you hacked into my system. My IT security people are the best in the business, and I don't believe anyone could breach the internet security they installed. They even employed some of the most notorious Russian hackers to try to get in and they failed. So nice try Mr. Armstrong, but your claims are pathetic, you're pathetic. Now I'm going to get back to my dinner, and I'll deal with you in the morning. When my people catch up with you, and they will, expect a very slow and painful death.'

'Check with Velma in your Casino office.'

'What on earth are you talking about? I've had just about enough of this nonsense.' Meszaros's voice had lost some of its confident tone.

'We didn't access your system via the Internet. Let's just say we got into your IT system via the back door so to speak.'

'What do you mean back door, what the fuck are you talking about?'

'I'll leave you to work it out. In the meantime, as we say in the UK, you're stuffed. So, if you're interested in staying out of jail, you'll shut up and listen. In case you want proof I'm not lying, check your bank account in Grand Cayman, the one the banqueting manager there just passed you details of. You'll find that ten million dollars left it a short while ago.' There was a long silence. 'Mr. Meszaros?

'What do you want?' came the reply.

'That's a much better attitude. Is Billy Ray still alive?'

'Yes.'

'Is he okay or have you damaged him?'

'He's okay.'

'Be more specific.'

'The boys got a little carried away.'

'Again, be more specific.'

'He got a little roughed up, and, he lost a little finger.'

'What?'

'An accident.'

'No, it wasn't. A man like you doesn't do accidents. What were you going to do, chop him up a piece at a time?' There was no answer.

'Let's get on with this Mr. Armstrong, you have the advantage for the moment, but this is temporary. You might be able to mess around with my bank accounts for a while, steal some of my money maybe, but not for long. I'll soon have them back under control, and when I do, you're dead.'

Time to press home the threat thought Frankie.

'You don't seem to understand Mr. Meszaros, so let me make it clear for you. I have a copy of all your financial details, income from any and every source. Bank accounts, onshore offshore, legitimate and otherwise. Records of all deposits, transfers, the lot, for the last however many years you've been in business. I'll have continuing access to your entire computer systems and will have for the foreseeable future. Your technical people may try to lock us out, and they may be partially successful, who knows?

But whatever the future holds, we have copies of enough historical material to send to the

FBI and or the IRS at any time. Illegal financial dealings that will ensure you'll be locked up for the rest of your life, or at best, you'll spend the next however many years in Court. So, Mr. Zsolt Meszaros, you are going to do what I tell you and release Billy Ray.' Meszaros didn't reply. Frankie waited, then Meszaros spoke.

'Where do you want him delivered to?'

'I'll let you know tomorrow morning. And he'd better have had that finger wound attended to properly.

'I'll get it seen to. Is that it?'

'No, there's one more thing, the delicate matter of your wife?'

'You're going too far now Armstrong. She stays. I told you, said she made a mistake and wants to stay.'

'I find that hard to believe. I'll talk to Billy Ray about that once he's free. But you will agree to let him speak to her as part of this deal.' Meszaros didn't respond. 'That wasn't a question,' said Frankie.

Meszaros laughed then said.

'Okay, but you might want to tell him that she was willing to kill him. We'd planned to take him on a little trip over the Everglades on my Beechcraft tomorrow morning, and Valentina agreed to push him out of the aircraft, once we were high enough to ensure he couldn't survive the fall of course.' Meszaros laughed again. 'Like I said, she accepted she'd made a big mistake, didn't know what she saw in the man. She asked for my forgiveness, begged. I told her that shoving him out of the plane would be the price she had to pay to earn my forgiveness.'

'So she was coerced, agreed under pressure? What would you have done to her if she'd refused?'

'It's not important now, is it? She agreed to do it, and she would have done it. That's all he needs to know. Valentina realized just what she was giving up, running away with that loser. She had her little adventure now and wants to come back. The bottom line is Mr. Armstrong; she was prepared to trade his life in return for getting her life of luxury back.' Frankie couldn't help but believe Zsolt Meszaros was telling the truth, so he didn't respond other than to say,

'I'll call you in the morning to tell you where to bring Billy Ray,' then he ended the call and redialed. Joe's phone rang out then went to voicemail.

'Frankie here. Result, Billy Ray will be brought back tomorrow morning, all in one piece, more or less. A little damage but nothing too serious. Talk later.' He put his phone down on the table went out on to the balcony, lay down on the sun lounger, closed his eyes and listened to the seagulls crying and boat mast's rigging clinking in the breeze.

❖ ❖ ❖

Frankie fell into deep sleep and was woken by the chirruping of his cell phone. He was momentarily disoriented then looked at the screen. He answered.

'Hi Joe.'

'Hi Frankie, I got your message, that's fantastic news Frankie. Sorry I couldn't answer. Had an emergency, one of my customers in trouble out in the gulf. His engine failed just as he was bringing it in to store in my yard.'

'Not to worry Joe.'

'I can't believe you pulled it off Frankie, tell me more.'

'Billy Ray will be dropped off in Naples tomorrow. We need to tell Meszaros where to bring him.'

'Fantastic. You said damaged in your message, how do you mean, is Billy Ray hurt bad?'

'I think he's okay. The thug said he'd been roughed up a bit and that they cut off his little finger.'

'Jesus Frankie, what a fucking monster.'

'He is Joe, but it could've been much worse. I think we got to him just in time.'

'Frankie, I can't tell you...' Frankie interrupted.

'Let's just get this finished Joe, then we can all

sit down and talk, but it's not quite over yet. I don't trust this Meszaros any more than I would a rattlesnake.'

'How much did you have to offer him?'

'He wouldn't take money. I never thought he would. I had to use something else to persuade him to cooperate, but I'll tell you more when we meet tomorrow, right now I'm feeling a bit bushed. So where do we want Billy Ray delivered to, your boatyard?'

'Yeah, what time are you thinking?'

'Said I'd call him in the morning, so let's say I call at eight, so ten thirty a.m. at your yard, okay?'

'Sounds good. Wait, what about the woman, she coming as well?'

'No she's not, and I need to talk to Billy Ray about that when we get him back.

'Okay, sounds a bit mysterious, but it can wait. And thanks again buddy, you've been....' Joe's voice began to break.

'It's okay Joe, see you tomorrow.'

◆ ◆ ◆

Frankie dialed Gareth's number.

'You brace the man?' asked Gareth

'I did, and he caved. He's agreed to release Billy Ray tomorrow.'

'You okay, you sound a bit funny?'

'I'm good thanks, just a bit knackered, this acting business, not as easy as it looks.' They both laughed. 'So we're solid on what you said? He can't all of a sudden kick you out of his system, can't reverse what you've done?'

'Nope, it's all like I said. Eventually, they might be able to clean it up some, but they'd find it next to impossible to get us out of there altogether, anyway I've planted the sleeper software I mentioned before. In theory, I could activate in the future and start the process all over again. The only way they could be sure to have us out completely would be to install a new parallel system and start to transfer their data across, but we still have a copy of the incriminating historical stuff don't we?'

'We do, Gareth, just wanted to be sure. This guy is trickier than a boatload of monkeys and vicious and ruthless to boot.'

CHAPTER 34

PRESENT – FLORIDA

6 APRIL

Frankie called Meszaros's office at eight a.m. and was put straight through. It rang once and was answered
'Meszaros,'
'Frankie Armstrong. I'll keep it brief,' and Frankie gave him the time and location of the boatyard. The mobster grunted and cut the connection before Frankie could ask about Billy Ray.

Frankie and Joe waited just inside the gates of the boatyard. At 1020 a black Cadillac Escalade swept through the gates and parked in the middle of the yard. Two suited heavies got out, one older, one younger. They nodded briefly to Joe and Frankie, then walked around the yard, looking behind boats, checking the roof out. One walked towards the office and started to open the door. Joe started to move and was about to shout at the man when Frankie grabbed his arm.

'Leave them Joe; they're just checking security.'

'Yeah okay, I suppose,' said Joe frowning. The men came back together by the side of their vehicle and talked briefly with each other. Then the older one of the two took his cell out of his pocket, pressed a single button and put the phone to his ear. He spoke and nodded. Two minutes later another black Escalade drove into the yard. This one had darkened windows. The passenger door opened and another suit got out and opened the rear door. Out stepped a young man, his arm bandaged and in a sling. He looked dazed by the bright sunlight.

Joe rushed over and hugged him. Frankie stayed where he was. Joe and Billy Ray spoke briefly then Joe took him by the arm and led him towards his office. Frankie was about to go to join them when a silver Lincoln Town Car with darkened windows drove into the yard. The driver got out and opened the rear door and out stepped Zsolt Meszaros, adjusting the cuffs of his shirt sleeves. He walked over to Frankie. All his men stayed where they were.

'I've delivered the goods as agreed,' he said. Frankie was about to speak, but Meszaros held his hand up and continued. 'I checked my bank accounts, and as you said, the money was transferred to another of my accounts, so you've proved your point.'

'Yes,' said Frankie 'I have.' Meszaros spoke again.

'Here's a number the punk can call Valentina on.' He handed Frankie a piece of paper. 'It's available for twenty four hours. One call then the phone will be destroyed. I've kept my end of the bargain.' Frankie tried to speak, but Meszaros hadn't finished. 'Now I know you think you have me over a barrel', he continued, 'but this is not a one way street. I'll make it crystal, so there's no misunderstanding Mr. Armstrong.

If you ever use the data against me in any way, there are instructions left with certain people who will hunt you down and kill you, and kill anyone associated with you, family, friends, business associates whomever. Doesn't matter where you are in the world, my guys will find you.'

'You finished with the threats now?' said Frankie. 'Well, the same goes for you, scumbag. If I think you've harmed Billy Ray, his uncle or anyone associated in the future, I'll make sure the data gets to the authorities and the media, and you'll spend the rest of your life in jail, threat or no threat.' Meszaros smiled.

'You've got some balls I'll say that,' he said. Then turned, walked towards his car waved to his people. They all got into their respective vehicles and drove out of the yard like a presidential convoy.

Frankie stood and watched them go, then walked towards Joe's office, knocked and opened the door. The wooden office wasn't huge, but big enough to accommodate a business desk, three chairs and a small sofa along the wall under the window. Billy Ray was slumped on the sofa. He started to get up as Frankie entered.

'Don't get up please; you must be shattered. But nice to meet you at last.' Frankie walked over and shook Billy Ray by his good hand.

'Likewise,' said Billy Ray smiling, 'I owe you a big thank you Frankie. Joe here's been telling me all about you and what you did to find me at the camp, then get me freed. I guess I owe Deanne and Leo a big thanks as well?'

'I'm sure they'll be relieved to know you're okay,' said Frankie.

'Hey,' said Joe, I'm still waiting to find out some of the details myself, so come on Frankie, how'd you do it, how'd you get that motherfucker to let Billy Ray go?'

'Before we get into that, I have to give this to you,' he handed Billy Ray the piece of paper with the phone number on. 'This is a number you can call Valentina on, anytime in the next twenty four hours. One call only then the phone will be destroyed, okay?' Billy Ray took it and nodded. 'But before you call her, I need to tell you something. Meszaros claims she'd agreed to kill you, push you out of his plane over the Everglades.'

'Jesus Christ,' said Joe.

'What!?' said Billy Ray, straightening up on the sofa, his face drained of color. 'Valentina do that to me? She wouldn't?'

Frankie spoke.

'I don't know how true it is, but he said she'd agreed to do that so she could stay with him and get her life of luxury back. Now I'm no expert on women, believe me Billy Ray, but that guy Meszaros, well, he seemed to me to be telling the truth.' Billy Ray put his good hand up to his face and covered it briefly then slumped backwards.

'I believe him,' said Billy Ray in a small voice. Joe intervened.

'What, you believe that hoodlum, that gangster, why would you believe a guy like that?'

'Because Valentina and me, we weren't really getting along that well towards the end, I think she missed her stuff, the material things, the lifestyle. She did love me, for a while anyway, but maybe it's for the best. New start, no complications. I've had just about enough of complications. Jesus, throw me out of a plane, unbelievable. Frankie I can't thank you enough,' said Billy Ray his voice breaking.' Frankie held his hand up.

'It's okay Billy Ray.'

'Borrow your cell uncle Joe? Let's get this over with.' Joe walked out from behind his desk and handed Billy Ray the phone, then went back and sat down.

'You want some privacy?' Asked Joe

'Nah,' said Billy Ray, looked at the piece of paper and dialled. 'Hi me,' Frankie could hear the faint female voice speaking ten to the dozen, Billy Ray replied, 'Yeah I'm okay. You're staying?' he listened to her reply. 'Yeah I understand, yeah, and no I didn't believe you would've. So long Valentina, have a good life.' He pressed the red button to cut the connection and tossed the phone back to Joe. 'Okay, what now?'

'Well I was going to suggest we wait until tomorrow to talk this thing out, 'said Frankie, ' I have a lot of questions I want answers to, but it depends. Do you feel okay to talk now Billy Ray or shall we do this tomorrow? That hand must be giving you some pain.'

'Do you want to see a doctor Billy Ray? I can get you to one right away,' said Joe.'

'No, I'll be okay, they took me to some doctor before we left and he dressed it and gave me some painkillers. So, providing there's a continuous supply of good hot coffee, I'm happy to talk all day. Make up for all that time in solitary confinement. I'll let you know if I start to fade.'

◆ ◆ ◆

Frankie moved one of the chairs so he could

face both Joe and Billy Ray, sat down and made himself comfortable.

'Wait,' said Joe 'I'll go make us a big pot of coffee.' He opened the door into a small kitchen and left the door open. They could hear him pouring the water and messing with the coffee machine.

'By the way Joe,' Frankie shouted, 'where's Charlie?'. Billy Ray looked at Frankie a little confused. 'Been looking after him while you were away,' said Frankie

'Oh right. Nice little fella, ain't he?' Frankie nodded. 'Great dog.'

'He's with my wife Melinda, she's looking after him,' shouted Joe from the kitchen. 'Coffee coming up.' He came out with a tray with cups milk and sugar, went back in and brought out the coffee percolator, poured three cups and returned it to the kitchen. Billy Ray said he'd take his black, so Frankie took a cup over to him, carefully pointing the handle round so he could hold it in his good hand. He poured some milk in his own coffee. Joe came back and sat behind the desk, took a slurp of coffee.

'Okay Frankie, how d'you do it?' asked Joe. Frankie put his cup down on the floor.

'Not yet Joe, you've got some explaining to do first. And I want the whole story this time, no bullshit, understand? I assume Billy Ray here knows it all, but I don't really care. I want it from the day we met in Iraq, the day you saved my life. I think I've earned the right to be told the truth, all of it. Before you start, let me help you a little bit. I don't believe for one minute that you hadn't checked up on me before you called. You knew I was involved in security, had my own security outfit, so like I say Joe, no crap, the truth, the whole truth and all that stuff.' Frankie bent down picked up his cup again and took a swig. Joe drew in a large breath, puffed his cheeks up then blew it out. He looked at Billy Ray.

'Like he says, Uncle Joe, he's earned the truth,' said Billy Ray.

'Okay, well if you want the whole story, I guess the best place to start is, before you and I met,' said Joe, 'See I got fiercely patriotic after the twin towers attack in 2001. I was before that too, but don't think I would have volunteered for the army, but that attack left me feeling helpless. A good old friend of mine Jimmy Ricchiuto died in the attack on the Twin Towers that day and that just piled on the agony. Anyways, like a lot of other guys feeling the same way, I eventually decided I just had to do something so in September 2002 I enlisted. They asked for volunteers to join the bomb squad, to train in unexploded ordinance and such. It sounded interesting. In March the following year, we invaded Iraq, and then it got really interesting. They thought I had some leadership potential, so was promoted to corporal.

You know as much about war as I do Frankie, it ain't no walk in the park. I was kinda looking forward to it in some ways, doing something positive, but it isn't quite the way it worked out. Not really. There was the initial invasion. We went in just after the 101st airborne division. Big adrenalin rush, but that soon wears off after you're targeted by those Katyusha Rockets and realize your life hangs in the balance, especially when you see some of your buddies blown to pieces. I can still hear the noise of those launchers in my nightmares. Then there were the long days of inaction, boredom, tedious fucking boredom, and then up and at 'em, adrenalin, fear, all that.' Joe stopped talking and took a big swig of his coffee.

'So what I'm saying is, you start to reassess. Your life, your values, you think about what's important. Sometimes you get angry, your ass hangin' out on the line, putting yourself in harm's way defending what? There I was out in the fuckin' desert killing people I didn't want to. Most of the Iraqi soldiers I saw looked pitiful. Sure there were the ones who enjoyed fighting, hated us, hated America, but the others...? And then you get to thinking about the guys on Wall Street and the politicians sitting in their big air-conditioned offices making fortunes and, well, like I say, you reassess. So when this opportunity came along, I thought why not, why don't I get my nose in the trough as well?' He stopped again and drank some more coffee.

'In May 2004 the fighting had been over a while, but my unit was still there, but one particular day we were ordered to escort a shipment from Bagdad Airport to some of the old Iraqi ministry offices. When we got the shipment there, we had to unload the pallets, then break up the packages and carry them to a room with a huge vault. There was a funny sort of atmosphere about the whole thing. The Iraqi guys who were helping, telling us where to put the stuff and so on, looked sorta furtive.

So I did some asking around, what was this stuff? But no one knew, or said they didn't. I smelt a rat. We were billeted in the center of Baghdad for the next couple of weeks, waiting on orders for the next assignment. One night a couple of us were out having a drink in one of the illicit bars that sprang up. Alcohol was officially banned, but you know the army? I recognized the sergeant who'd been in charge of the offloading of the stuff when we delivered the boxes to the storage vault. So I went over and chatted to him, waited till he was nice and mellow then managed to finagle out of him just what was going on, what was in the boxes.

When he told me I thought the guy was pulling my pisser. Dollars he says, millions of dollars.

Said it'd been going on for months, once, twice a month. Shipments of shrink wrapped dollars from the good ole USA. What the fuck for? I ask him. Bribes, he says, keeping certain people sweet, who the fuck knows? Then he tells me something that made me re-think my entire attitude to the war. He said,

'Don't know about you buddy, but when I get back, I'm gonna retire in the lap of luxury.'

'You are?' I ask.

'Darn tootin I am, I've earned it buddy,' and winked.

'He was well in the bag by then. I ask him, are you saying you helped yourself to some of this money? He laughed fit to bust.

'Why not,' he says, 'plenty to go round. No one seems to have the least fuckin idea where it goes. In fact, a little birdie told me the US don't care 'cos it's Iraqi oil money, not US tax dollars. See, I wouldn't steal a dime from a fellow American, but Iraqi oil money, why the fuck not? Spoils of war my good buddy, spoils of war.' Then he fell off his stool.

Then fate, or lady luck, whatever, took a hand. Two days later my unit was ordered to go back to the same place we'd taken the stuff to. We arrived and were told to load some crates on to a truck and take it to another facility in a place called Sabaa Al Bour. There were other army details loading up more wooden boxes, presumably for distribution to other places where the money could be dished out to whoever. There were five of us in my detail and so when we got underway towards our destination I told the driver to pull over. I thought it's now or never, so I told them all what I'd been told and asked them if they wanted to retire rich?

It took me a while to convince them I wasn't kidding around. They really couldn't believe me, and I couldn't blame them. In fact, I still wasn't sure myself. So I suggested we have a look see. We opened one of the crates, and there they were stacks of dollars shrink wrapped just like the guy said. We did a quick count and multiplied the number of crates we had on the truck and came up with a figure of forty million dollars and change. We went back, sat in the cab and let it sink in. As much as it was, I found out later it was chicken feed, compared to the total amount of the money shipped over, somewhere north of eleven billion dollars.'

'Jesus Christ,' said Frankie

'That's not the big story,' said Joe, 'the real story is that most of it disappeared and was never accounted for.'

'Never' said Billy Ray, 'I mean eleven billion dollars just goes missing like that, fuck, never?'

'It's the truth,' said Joe 'look it up. Might have been even more? Anyway, long story short. We all decided we deserved a share of the money, but there were a few knotty logistical issues you might say. Like where to store it and how to get it back to the good old US of A. Also we weren't sure if this was a one off opportunity or if we'd be asked to transport any more of the cash.

And the big question, how good was the accounting for the money? Would they know if we helped ourselves to some? We figured out that if this was bent money, and it had to be the way it was being shipped in cash. I mean what government would use cash instead of bank transfers or some other legitimate means of transferring such huge sums of money.' Joe got up and poured the rest of the coffee into his cup, then continued.

'So, we all decided we'd help ourselves. Like I said, war does things to your perspective. I don't think any of the guys involved would have been thieves had we all stayed at home, but we hadn't, maybe we should've? So, we stopped just outside a small village a few miles from Sabaa Al Bour and offloaded some of the crates next to a derelict bombed out building. We estimated that to represent about thirty million. We left two of the guys with the crates and carried on to the delivery place. We were met by some guy who knew we were due to deliver the stuff, but it soon became clear he hadn't really got an idea of how many crates we were supposed to deliver. He kept asking for a delivery manifest or at least that's what I thought he wanted, but we played it dumb. He gave up eventually, muttering in Arabic or whatever, and we hightailed it back, collected the loot and the two guys, and made our way back to Bagdad.

We never got to take another load, so that was all we ever had the chance to steal. Still, it was enough. We had to use quite a lot to bribe people, but then we thought, that's what the money was for anyway. Naturally, we didn't tell anyone it was cash in the boxes. We wrapped all the dollars in blankets and found some bits of this and that to form a top layer, just in case anyone got nosey and had a peek. If anyone asked, we said it was stuff we'd stolen from the Iraqis. No one was bothered about that overmuch, lots of guys took what you might call 'souvenirs', happens in all wars.

Still, it cost us a small fortune to have it stored in Iraq, and a bigger small fortune to have it flown back to the base in the US. Freddy, one of my fellow thieves, had a cousin working on the US airbase back home, so there goes another million. One of the five guys didn't make it, so the main money, or what was eventually left of it, was split among the four of us. That amounted to a net seven million each, in the end, give or take.' Joe stopped talking for a while to let the information sink in.

'Jesus Joe.' Was all Frankie could think of to say.

'I'm going to make me some more coffee, talking's thirsty work,' said Joe and got up to go to the kitchen. 'Anyone else?'

'Bathroom break for me,' said Billy Ray.

'Me too,' said Frankie, 'after you.'

Joe poured new coffees, and they all sat back down. Frankie had recovered from the shock of finding out about what he'd unwittingly become a part of.

'Okay Joe, how does all this relate to Billy Ray going missing and you calling me?'

'I'm coming to that. See it's all very well getting yourself a load of cash. And you can have some fun spending it, giving some away and all that sort of stuff, but you've got to be careful. You can only spend so much in cash before it looks suspicious. Get caught with that amount of contraband cabbage, and you're in big trouble, not just with the IRS but the cops too. And I'm coming to the time of life when I have to think about leaving what I have to my daughter and my two grandkids. Can't leave illegitimate money. So I kept thinking about how to get it laundered.

'Then shipwreck diving nut and nephew Billy Ray here, asks me to lend him a boat and fund him to look for buried treasure. At first I'm skeptical, but then Billy Ray shows me evidence, stuff on the web, confirming that all these people had made fortunes, not everyone of course, but enough to get me interested. He then shows me some websites set up which invite investors to have a punt and back these sorts of guys.

Course they have to provide proof it isn't a scam, and I guess some of them are, but you know these days, everything's done online, most of it I just don't understand. I mean look at that crazy Bitcoin thing, people piling money in like there's no tomorrow and I say to myself, investing in what? All looks like fresh air to me. Anyways back to the plot. Where was I? Oh yeah, so I start to form an idea in my mind.

Let's roll back the clock....

CHAPTER 35

FIVE YEARS EARLIER

Joe noticed that Belinda had seemed a bit preoccupied the last couple of days. He searched his mind for any recent event that might have caused this but couldn't pin anything down. He mentally shrugged and decided to wait. He knew Belinda well and whatever it was would either go away by itself or surface and be dealt with. She didn't seem unhappy, so that was okay; he loved his wife. He opened the door to leave.

'Just going to the boatyard honey, be back around one, love ya, bye.' He shouted.

'Bye Joe, oh Joe wait, I need to ask you something?' *And so it surfaces* thought Joe. He stepped back inside the hall, closed the door and waited for Belinda to walk the rest of the way down the stairs

'Yes honey, what is it?'

'Business is okay isn't it?'

'Great yeah, never better, why?'

'Well, I wanted to ask you something. Something and nothing really. But I think we should start going on some nice vacations.'

'Okay, but what's brought this on? We already live in one of the nicest places in the world as it is, beaches, beautiful ocean an' all.'

'I know, but we're not getting any younger, and I'd like to go on some vacations, see different places. I thought we might try cruising around the Caribbean islands, that sort of thing to begin with. I've got brochures. Then maybe sometime in the future, we can go to Europe, visit places our ancestors came from. Be good fun. What do you say Joe?'

'Yeah, why not Belinda? Great idea; let's talk more tonight.' Belinda ran to him and planted a big fat kiss on his lips.' Joe smiled and gave her a hug. 'See ya later hon,' he said as he walked out of the house, *the Caribbean?* an idea forming in his mind.

They left Fort Lauderdale on one fine February day, for a seven day cruise of the western Caribbean on the Holland America Line cruise ship MS Eurodam. Joe had insisted on doing his own packing which Belinda thought unusual, but then Joe agreeing to go on a cruise had also surprised her. She wasn't complaining. This new fun version of Joe suited her just fine.

Their first port of call was Half Moon Cay in the Bahamas, a little island only accessible by boats.

Joe played along and even agreed to go on an excursion to Stingray Cove see the tame stingrays. They even made friends with a Dutch couple, Andro and Mila. Andro was also a fisherman, so he and Joe swapped stories of the ones caught and the ones that got away. After a day at sea, their next port of call was Georgetown in the Cayman Islands.

Georgetown, the capital of the Cayman Islands, located in the west of the largest island, Grand Cayman, is mainly known as a port of call for cruise ships, but also as an international financial hub. After breakfast, Belinda asked Joe if he'd like to go for a walk around the town with Mila and Andros, look around the tax free shops, maybe get some lunch in one of the local restaurants?

'You go honey, I've got a meeting, business thing.'

'A meeting, but we're on vacation, what kind of meeting, I don't understand Joe.'

'It won't take long Belinda, but when you chose this cruise, and I saw it included Grand Cayman I thought I'd take the opportunity to set up a bank account here. Just put some funds out here, you know, not good to have all your eggs in one basket. I'll only be an hour or so, so you go with Mila and Andros, and I'll see you back on board later.'

'Okay hon,' she said beginning to wonder if

it had really been her who chose this particular cruise.

Joe caught a taxi and told the driver where to go. He'd made the appointment some time ago and had already had a few telephone conversations with Harry Barns to make sure he was on the right track. Harry enthusiastically welcomed Joe into his smart offices, located in a white clapperboard two story building in the financial district. They sat down in Harry's private office and after the initial formalities, discussed the amount of cash involved, and Joe's aspirations, Harry Suggested he set up a number of brass plate companies and bank accounts for Harry to deposit money into.

'So this money will be safe?' asked Joe.

'Couldn't be safer Joe. Away from prying eyes and remember there's zero tax in this financial paradise. Be assured Joe, this is the safest place to store your hard earned cash, and more to the point, any unearned cash.' He laughed at his own joke. *If only you knew* thought Joe, but laughed along nevertheless. 'So how much do you want to deposit?' Joe leaned down and opened the bag on the floor. He took out bundles of cash and put them all on the desk.

'I brought just $700,000 this time, but I'd like to bring more out another time. Don't want to be too obvious, so it might take a while. Another cruise next year, or maybe a vacation to a nearby island before then, and hop over here and deposit some more?'

'Okay, sounds like a plan. I'll get you a receipt for the cash, then set things up and distribute the cash amongst all the companies and accounts. I'll call you to let you know details, and I'll use the normal mail to confirm everything. I don't use email if I can help it, you'll understand why,' then he picked up the phone and spoke to his assistant. 'Jodie, please make out a cash receipt for $700k to a Mr. Joe Nelson Naples Florida. He'll collect it on his way out.' Joe stood, and they shook hands.

'Been a pleasure to meet you Joe, give my best to Mr.s Nelson won't you?'

'I will and likewise it's been a real pleasure.' Joe left and made his way back to the cruise ship. Next stop Cozumel, Mexico.

CHAPTER 36

PRESENT – FLORIDA

7 APRIL

Joe continued…
'Over the years we've made a few trips involving the Cayman Islands, then other cruises to that same area, plus some vacations to nearby islands where I could get to Grand Cayman on a local flight, or a charter a little private plane. Anyway, over the years I managed to take out various amounts of the cash and deposit it in my company bank accounts, all in all just over three million dollars.' Frankie looked at Billy Ray.

'News to me too Frankie, this bit anyway.'

'So back to the present, or to be more accurate, the very recent past,' said Joe. Like I say I get this idea in my mind and I say to Billy Ray here that he has to get a website up inviting investors, similar to the other guys, but all the investors will be me. Some of the dummy companies I set up in GC would each invest in the venture to a total of one million dollars.' Billy Ray spoke.

'I had no idea Uncle Joe had that kind of money,' said Billy Ray, 'He told me it was undeclared profit from the boat sales business and I had no reason to doubt it, and to be honest I didn't really care. I was just so happy that I was now going to be in a position to really have a go at finding some serious treasure.' Joe nodded and continued.

'I told Billy Ray we'd tell anyone else who wanted to invest, that the deal was no longer available. The website was just to prove to anyone who looked at the operation, namely the IRS, that it was all a legit setup. The original idea was pretty straightforward. I would back Billy Ray and Jerry in the hope that by being fully funded, they would find treasure and then they'd sell it, pay whatever taxes applicable, maybe no taxes if the shipwreck was found in the right place, but whatever was left would be legitimate money.

'So, we set up the website and put the plan into action. After a couple of weeks, Billy Ray calls me and says they'd found a wreck that looked promising. Big plus was, it was in international waters, just. So, this wreck was potentially free of any kind of jurisdiction, taxes and so on. Plus, it was an old Spanish galleon, so age and location meant it would be deemed treasure and not salvage. Perfect according to Billy Ray here. That was the good news. The bad news was that when they went back a second time to search more thoroughly, there was no treasure. Been picked clean.'

'Plenty of skeletons though,' said Billy Ray, 'a real bummer.' Joe slurped some more coffee then set it down on the desk.

'Yeah, real bummer,' said Joe smiling broadly. Frankie wondered why the smile.

'Obviously, there's more,' said Frankie.

'Yup, that's when I had my second brainwave,' said Joe, standing up and rubbing his hands together. 'A bigger brainwave. Supposing I thought,' he said walking behind his chair and putting both hands on the back of it. 'Just supposing I could buy treasure and seed the galleon with it, then Billy Ray could discover it?' said Joe, raising his arms and using the first two fingers of each hand as quote marks, 'then that find would be legitimate, tax free, any treasure sellable, and the funds generated would, therefore, be legit as well. And,' he said, 'maybe I could use the cash I still had left over here and wash that too. Is that genius or what?' said Joe looking at Frankie.

'In theory, I guess it is, but the obvious question is, where and how do you get this treasure to seed the galleon with?'

'Exactly,' said Joe, pointing at Frankie and warming to the tale with relish. 'Like I said, when Billy Ray first got into this treasure hunting business, I thought he was crazy until he told me just how much stuff was found. Then I asked him about who got to keep the stuff these diving nuts found. He explained it depended, if it was considered treasure or salvage and where it was found could matter. Inshore or international waters and so on. So, ownership and taxes payable depended on all these factors.

Then he said, course lots of divers didn't bother reporting stuff they found unless it was a really big find and worth reporting the wreck so it could be officially designated as theirs. That right Billy Ray?'

'That's right. I told Joe, that even the unofficial finds amounted to millions and millions of dollars, collectively.'

'And that last bit of information formed the most important part of my second brainwave plan,' said Joe. 'When Billy Ray told me he'd found the wreck, in international waters, with no treasure on it, I saw the opportunity to launder all my Iraq money clean. Wash it in the sea I suppose you could say.' Joe laughed at his own joke, then continued. 'I asked Billy Ray how much black-market treasure, he thought he could buy. How much you want me to buy? Was his answer. How's about seven million dollarsworth, I said. At that time Billy Ray had no idea I'd got all this money out of Iraq, so the look on his face was something else,' said Joe. pointing a finger at Billy Ray and grinning.

'I still can't believe the government would send billions of dollars to Iraq in cash then lose it, I mean...just crazy,' said Billy Ray shaking his head.

'You'd better believe it son,' Joe replied. 'So, to continue, where was I? Oh yes, so first Billy Ray asks me if I'm serious and I convince him I am. He asks me how come I can get my hands on all that money, and I tell him to mind his own business. At the time I didn't want to tell him where the money came from. Not that I didn't trust you Billy Ray, but I thought, well, the fewer people who knew, the better. I'm only telling the truth now because after all you've both been through, I think you deserve to know.'

Billy Ray held up his good hand in acknowledgement. Joe continued. 'So Billy Ray here says, no problem. A lot of these guys are desperate to convert their ill-gotten gains into cash but are naturally cautious about exposing the fact that they may have illicit treasure for sale.'

'See,' said Billy Ray, 'I know them, and they know me, so there's trust.' Joe picked up his story again

'So now I have a workable, feasible plan, a suitable wreck available, a guy I can trust to buy the stuff, the treasure, a place to store it. I have a huge secret basement downstairs ideal for the purpose. So, we're all set to go when this guy here lets his wiener get priority over his brain and falls for a mobster's wife. Of all the women to choose from in this world, and on the eve of being able to make a fortune for himself and launder my dirty money to boot, he decides to get involved with this woman. And surprise surprise, her husband isn't too happy about it, and comes after them, guns blazing.' Billy Ray nodded then looked at the floor. 'Sorry Billy Ray, but Frankie wanted the truth, and you wanted me to tell it, so... but listen, we all make mistakes when we get infatuated or whatever.'

'Woah,' said Frankie, 'so you knew all this when you sent me chasing off to see Max in Fort Lauderdale. You pretended to have no idea what had happened to Billy Ray and Jerry? Why didn't you tell me about the wreck and Billy Ray getting involved with this mobster's wife?'

'Yeah, I'm really sorry about that. See if I'd told you any of it, I'd have had to tell you the lot, the whole story. Me stealing millions of dollars, my plan for laundering the money, all that stuff. I couldn't take the risk. You might have walked, or worse, told the authorities and then walked. I thought if I pointed you in the general direction, you could maybe pick up the trail... And well look, I was right wasn't I. You did pick up the trail, you found Billy Ray and you rescued him, got him free.'

'Yes, and I could have been killed by a murderous Miami gangster. What is it with you Joe? You send people into danger without any hint of what they might be walking into, what I was walking into? You think that's okay do you, as long as it serves your purpose?' That's some fucking twisted logic if you don't mind me saying so Joe, the end justifying the means.'

'Well when you put it like that Frankie, I guess it was irresponsible. I guess I wasn't thinking straight. I'm really sorry Frankie, I really am.'

'Yes, you should be Joe. I really don't know what to say,' said Frankie shaking his head. 'Anyway, you're telling me the whole story now aren't you,' continued Frankie, 'so what's changed? I could still choose to tell the authorities.'

'Yes, you could, but I don't think I have any choice now with all that's happened. And yes, you still might report me to the authorities.' Joe looked at Frankie obviously hoping for some indication of his intentions.'

'If you're looking for an answer Joe, let's just say that decision's on hold. Carry on with the story and let's see where it goes, okay?' Joe looked uncomfortable but took a deep breath and carried on.

'Okay, fair enough. So when Billy Ray disappeared, I'm worried crazy on two levels. One, I love Billy Ray here like a son and although I could've killed him for being so... well, let's just say getting carried away. And of course, he's just fucked up my plan big time. So, I hire this PI Chuck Mainous, who a friend of mine says is the best. Mainous is an ex Miami cop, so he knows his way around and finds out quite a lot about this guy Meszaros through his connections. He tells me what this guy is capable of, so I'm naturally concerned and at the same time impressed, I think I have the right guy. Then he goes looking for Billy Ray, then nothing, no contact at all, didn't answer his phone, no returning text messages, nothing.

So, I contacted the agency I hired him from, and they said they hadn't heard from him either and they were worried. I asked them if I could hire another PI, but they said no one else would want to work the case, at least while Chuck's fate was unknown. I tried another couple of detective agencies, but they didn't have anyone. I got the impression word had got around, and no one else was willing to take the risk of going up against this Meszaros. Like I say, Mainous was considered one of the best, so if he'd come to a sticky end, then no one else was going to take a chance.

So, I report Billy Ray as missing to the cops, but not much hope there. And that's where you come in. And yes Frankie, I did lie to you and not just the once I admit. I'd kind of kept tabs on you via Google the last few years, just out of curiosity, you know the way you do? You think one day *hey, I wonder how that guy's going on, the limey whose ass I saved in Iraq.*

So, I looked you up and found you'd started security outfit. So, I'm in bed one night, can't sleep thinking *who the hell am I going to get to help me find Billy Ray,* and your name popped into my head. And then I thought, how could I possibly get you to come all this way to help? And then I thought, moral blackmail. The guy said he owed me and would do anything to help me if I asked. So, I asked, and you came. Must admit I was a bit stunned that you agreed so easily, got the impression something else was going on. Am I wrong?'

'I suppose if we're all telling the truth here, the answer's yes; there was something else going on as you put it. My wife had just left me.'

'Oh', said Joe, 'hey, I'm sorry to hear that Frankie, didn't mean to pry.

'It's okay, I'm over it now, thanks largely to you and this crazy situation. Took my mind off it, helped me to re-focus. Anyway, forget my personal problems, we're still missing a significant part of the story. Come on Billy Ray. You have some questions to answer as well. Like how did your friend Jerry get killed and dumped in the sea? And do you know what happened to the PI Chuck Mainous?'

'Okay, but I need another black coffee,' he said. The coffee was poured and served. Billy Ray took a deep breath then started.

'Okay, well, when Valentina escaped and came

running to me, I decided that it would be too easy for her husband to find us in Fort Pierce. We'd been there long enough for lots of people to know I moored the boat there, so we left and went north to a place called Melbourne Harbor. Jerry had to come with us as I assumed this Meszaros guy would know he was my best buddy and if he couldn't find me, he'd find Jerry and do whatever to get a lead on me. So, there we were, all on the boat in Melbourne Harbor, that's Me, Jerry and Valentina.

I thought we'd be safe there, give us time to think about a more permanent place to hide, but I fucked up. Used my credit card to buy fuel when we arrived and that was enough for the PI you sent after me to find us.'

'And?' said Joe.

'Well, the problem was that one of Meszaros's henchmen, a guy called Lenny, had access to the same credit card information and he tracked us down as well. This hoodlum found us just as we were questioning this Mainous guy. Jerry had hit the PI thinking he was one of Meszaros's hoods and we had him tied to a chair. Long story short, Jerry attacked this Lenny character, and he shot Jerry in the head, then he shot the PI. I'll tell you in more detail later. I really don't want to talk about it. I just...' Billy Ray hung his head to hide his tears. It was plain to see he was too distressed to go on. Joe went over to him and patted him gently on the back.

'Sorry Joe but I have to ask Billy Ray a couple of more questions.'

'It's okay,' said Billy Ray, 'ask away.'

'So how did you get away from this Lenny character and why has he disappeared?'

Billy Ray told them about the trip out to sea to dispose of the bodies of the PI and Jerry and how he and Valentina had eventually overpowered Lenny and had thrown him in the ocean wrapped in chains.

'He'd killed two people, one of them the best friend I ever had, so I had no problem in doing what I did. He'd have killed us as well if we'd caused him any problems. Maybe it would be considered wrong in the eyes of the law, but I'm glad I did it.'

'So unlikely anyone will ever find his body?'

'That would be my guess yes. We did the same with the PI. I couldn't risk his body washing up and being linked to me. I feel bad about that. Joe, is there any way we could find some way of letting his family know?'

'Not sure Billy Ray, not without it being linked to you. I guess if we wait a while then send an anonymous note to say he was killed? Might be better than leaving them wondering. I'll think on it,' said Joe, 'you satisfied now Frankie, any more questions?'

'No, no questions, but there are a few potential problems for Billy Ray here. Once the police know you're back in the land of the living, they're going to come and question you about where you've been, who took you and Valentina from the survivalist place, all that stuff, and about Jerry, so what are you going to tell them?'

'Yeah, been thinking about that. I can't tell them the truth about Jerry. That would involve telling them all the rest of the stuff, including killing the gunman. Justified or not I'd be in big trouble, so I thought I'd tell them that Jerry was into gambling and I think he owed a lot of money to someone, but I don't know who to. And the truth is, Jerry did go gambling, he loved it. It's where most of his money went. So, if they dig, they'll find out its true.'

'I think I can help here as well,' said Frankie. 'Detective Sharkey told me he had information that I wasn't the only person looking for you and Jerry and when I asked him who it might be, he said not the kind of person you wanted on your tail, something like that anyway. And when I asked why such people might be looking for you, he said gambling debts would be the usual reason, so your story could fit in nicely with that.'

'Even better Frankie,' said Billy Ray, 'that takes care of that. I'll say we were all hiding out on the boat, from Lola's husband and Jerry went to get some supplies one day, and just never came back.'

'Okay, said Frankie, that takes care of the Jerry situation, but you should know that Jerry's trailer got burnt down and his dog Banjo died in the fire.'

'Oh, shit no! Why?'

'I don't know the answer, said Frankie, 'but my guess is, one of Meszaros's goons did it, but it could help support your story about Jerry being hounded by people he owed money to, so there is that.'

'I can see that helps, yeah,' said Billy Ray, 'poor old Banjo.'

'Okay, so what about the rest, what are you going to tell them about Valentina and being kidnapped, have you worked anything out on that score?' asked Frankie

'I have, and it sure gets a bit more complicated don't it? But I've been thinking that through, and the cops don't know who the woman was I ran away with, or who her husband is. Luckily, we used a false name for Valentina at the camp, called her Lola.'

'Lola, jeez,' said Joe.

'Yeah, she wasn't too thrilled with the name herself, said it made her sound like a stripper. Anyhow, lucky break really. I'll tell the cops that's what she told me her name was, but now I'm not sure she was being honest about that, or about her abusive husband. I thought I'd say I had a big fall out with Lola at the camp, and I think she must have called her husband, asked him to take her back, to come and get her. And that it was obviously her husband who sent in the heavies.

I'll say I was blindfolded and bundled into the trunk of their car and when they stopped, they beat me up, told me to stay clear of Lola and dumped me somewhere in Miami. Then I managed to borrow a phone from someone and called Joe. And you came to get me Uncle Joe. We need to agree on those details in case they question you as well. I'll say Lola hasn't been in touch and I have no idea where she is or what's happened to her.

'And the hand?'

'Hopefully, the big bandages will be off in the next day or so. As soon as it's not so obvious, I'll call the cops and tell them I'm here if they want to come talk to me. And if they ask about my hand, I'll make up something, say I cut myself on a knife by accident, something....'

'You really think they'll accept all that?'

'What choice do they have? I mean who's going to contradict me? Valentina sure isn't going to go running to the cops and apart from her, only you two know what really happened, apart from that Zaros guy and he sure as hell isn't going to get involved.'

'Sounds like you've thought it all through Billy Ray.'

'Maybe, I sure hope so.'

'You've been through a lot Billy Ray,' said Frankie. Billy Ray said nothing more and looked down at the floor.

CHAPTER 37

PRESENT – FLORIDA

7 APRIL

'Okay, your turn now Frankie,' said Joe, 'you still haven't explained how you got this Zaros guy to let Billy Ray here go, and without it costing a cent. I really can't wait to hear this story.' Billy Ray had recovered his composure and was smiling.

'Neither can I,' said Billy Ray, 'neither can I.'

'And I don't normally drink till sundown,' Joe said getting up from behind his desk, 'but I really need a beer now. Anyone else join me?' They both said yes. Beers were served, and the story was told, both Joe and Billy Ray frequently interrupting him with questions, asking him to stop occasionally to replenish their beers or to use the bathroom. Eventually, Frankie finished the story up to the point where they dropped Billy Ray off that morning.

'You are one of the most devious motherfuckers I have ever had the pleasure to have known, Frankie boy. And as for your feigned heart attack in the casino,' Joe using his fingers to make quotes as he said it, 'boy what I'd give to have been there, 'said Joe, and began laughing. It was infectious, and they all joined in until they couldn't laugh any more.

'Okay,' said Frankie when they'd all calmed down, 'So where do we go from here?

'Well, said Joe, 'that depends a lot on you. Thing is, now you know everything, you must realize you're in possession of knowledge of a felony. I purposely didn't say I was telling you all this in confidence, for one, it wouldn't mean much really, not if you intend to report me to the authorities. And two, I don't want you to feel obligated in any way. The only thing I would say in my defense is that this money was going to be stolen anyway. Almost certainly by some bent Iraqi officials.

It was never going to be used for legit purposes, so we stole it instead, convinced ourselves we deserved it for fighting in that shitty war. Anyway, whether or not that's a good excuse, doesn't matter. We are where we are, and one thing I'm not going to do, is give it back. No one really owns it. But doesn't matter what I think, only what you think Frankie. Your call.'

'And if I say I don't have any view on this, nothing to do with me, what happens then?'

'Okay, well then that depends on this man here. If he wants to carry on where we left off?' Joe looked at Billy Ray. 'Do you?' Billy Ray grinned.

'You really need an answer Uncle Joe? Hell yes.' The office door opened, and a woman stood there, Charlie in tow.

'Sorry Joe honey, didn't realize you had...' then she saw Billy Ray. 'Billy Ray, you're back. Where have you been? You've had us worried to....' then she saw his bandaged hand. 'What's happened; you're hurt.' Billy Ray stood and hugged her in a one armed embrace.

'I'm okay really, nothing, honest, looks worse than it is.' Charlie was up on his hind legs pawing at Billy Ray's legs. 'Hey little fella, how ya doin'?' He said and bent down to pat Charlie's head. Charlie's tail was wagging furiously; then Charlie spotted Frankie who was still sitting in his chair. The dog bounded over to him jumped onto his lap and stayed there looking up adoringly at Frankie. Billy Ray looked over his aunt's shoulder. Joe laughed

'Looks like you lost out again Billy Ray. Frankie here looked after Charlie most of the time you were gone, and they got real attached to each other.' Billy Ray looked disappointed.

◆ ◆ ◆

Melinda left them to finish their meeting and took Charlie with her.

'So, Frankie,' said Joe, where do you go from here?'

'Not sure Joe, but to put your mind at ease, the money you, what shall we say, you purloined? Nothing to do with me, that's between you and your conscience. If you can justify taking it and keeping it, well like I say, not my business.'

'Okay,' said Joe, 'I've said my piece on why I think I'm justified, so I won't labor the point, but let me just say thanks for your understanding, and leave it at that.' Frankie nodded and stood.

'So, any plans Frankie, you gonna stay a while, relax, do some fishing? Happy to pay for you to stay as long as you want.'

'That's kind of you, but I don't know what I'm going to do Joe. Probably go and have a few beers and a think.'

'Now look I know, well the money thing, you might not like where it came from, but you've got to let me show my appreciation for all your help and you know I can well afford to pay, so are you going to let me show my appreciation?'

'No Joe I don't personally want any money from you, but there are a couple of things you can do for me....' After they'd talked some more,

Frankie gave the car keys back to Billy Ray and ordered a cab back to the Cove Inn. As he sat in the taxi, he tapped out a text. *Text back to me with details of your bank or your parent's bank. Account name, number, routing number etc. Don't ask any questions. Good luck to Nikita and have a good life x Frankie*

CHAPTER 38

PRESENT – FLORIDA

7 APRIL

Frankie, having said his goodbyes to Joe and Billy Ray, just wanted to rest. Have a few days relaxing on the beach before deciding what to do, short term and long term. Back at the Cove he changed and walked to the beach. Lying in the sun, he went over the recent past in his mind, sometimes laughing out loud at some of the memories. It had been a strange couple of weeks. He fell asleep.

He woke when something screeched in his ear. He sat bolt upright and found two seagulls fighting over a piece of dead fish right next to where he lay. He closed his eyes again and suddenly felt homesick. He got up and made his way back to the Cove and called Derek.

'Hi Barnsie, sorry to call so late. I suppose the nerd's filled you in on what happened,'

'He has, and I'm still trying to take it all in. You sure this guy isn't going to put a contract out on you?'

'He has, sort of but it's a conditional one. If I don't reveal his data to the authorities, he doesn't have me killed, and vice versa. He kills me, and the authorities will get all the data.'

'Right, is that what they call a Mexican stand-off?'

'I guess it is Barnsie, or maybe a Florida stand-off? Frankie laughed. 'Listen I've decided I'm coming home, for a while anyway, try and work out what I'm going to do with the rest of my life. I can't do that here. I need to get back home.'

'Okay, understand. Just let me know your flight details and when it arrives, and I'll be at the airport to collect you. Be great to see you Frankie. You can fill me in on all the details, over many pints of beer.'

'Will do Derek.' And he cut the line. His next call was to Joe to tell him he was leaving. Joe insisted he would pay Frankie's flight back home and to book himself first class.

'It isn't up for discussion partner,' said Joe, 'put it on my credit card.' And he gave Frankie his credit card details. Frankie went online to book his flights then walked round to the Dock Pub for a couple of beers. They did a passable takeaway fish and chips, which he took back his room and washed down with another couple of beers while watching an old John Wayne movie on TCM. The next morning, he walked down to Naples Pier for a last look, then back to the Cove Inn Coffee Shop for a full bacon, sausage, pancakes, fried tomato and eggs breakfast.

Later on, Joe came to pick him up to take him to Fort Myers Airport for his flight to Atlanta. As Joe navigated his way through Golden Gate and on to the Interstate 75 towards Fort Myers airport, he said.

'I guess you're looking forward to getting back Frankie?'

'Mixed feeling Joe. I'll miss Naples, the weather, the beaches, the people.'

'Yeah, it's a tough place to leave.'

'There's something I wanted to ask you Joe' Joe turned to Frankie.

'Shoot,' he said, 'ask anything you like. You already know all my dirty secrets.'

'Well, when I got back to the Cove, after listening to your story. And not that I doubted you, but you saying the US government sent all that money in cash to Iraq, well I mean it was so hard to take in. So, I did some research on the net, and of course, you were right. And even though I read about it and saw the official confirmation. I still find it hard to believe that the US government sent so much cash over there, and then had no real idea where it all went, I mean billions and billions of dollars in cash.'

'Yup, like I said twelve billion dollars Frankie. Do I sense a but coming?'

'No, no buts Joe, well other than I also read about some other US soldiers who allegedly stole some of the money, twenty five million I think it said, but they died in an explosion on their way to be interrogated about it. At least three of them did.'

'Wouldn't know Frankie. Lots of soldiers were blown up. Those fucking roadside IED's were everywhere, I should know. And like I said, there were lots of other little piggies with their noses in the trough Frankie, the guy who put me on to it in the first place for instance?'

'Yes, I remember that Joe.' Frankie continued, 'The suggestion was that the fourth man, the guy behind that particular robbery, got away and took the money with him. No trace of either.'

'That so Frankie? Well, can't say I recall that sort of detail. Lots of things happen in the fog of war as you know only too well Frankie.' They drove along in silence for a while then Joe spoke.

'It wasn't me Frankie.'

'No Joe I didn't really mean to imply....'

'It's okay Frankie,' Joe interrupted, 'at the end of the day what I did was wrong, strictly speaking, so I can understand how you might assume I might go further, but killing my fellow soldiers, my buddies? No Frankie, not me.'

'No, like I said Joe, I didn't mean to suggest you

did. On another subject, how's Billy Ray doing, how's his hand?'

'Gone for a check-up at the Naples NCH hospital today to for a check up on his hand. Says he can still feel sensations in his little finger, even though it's not there anymore, weird or what? Anyhows, he tried to change his appointment so he could come say goodbye to you. You'll never know just how grateful that boy is Frankie. And so am I.'

'Well let's hope he keeps away from mobster's wives in future.'

'Amen to that. But you know, he's still as nervous as a cat Frankie. I try to tell him it's okay, that you've got the guy buttoned down, but I wonder if Billy Ray will ever stop looking over his shoulder?'

'Yes, I know the feeling,' replied Frankie.

'You still worried Meszaros will try something? I mean, would the guy be willing to take the risk of all that incriminating stuff being released to the authorities?'

'You'd hope not Joe. And I think I've made as good a provision as I can to ensure that should anything untoward happen to any of us, Billy Ray, you, me or mine, then Meszaros knows what will happen. You've got all the details of who to contact in the event?'

'I have Frankie thanks. Gave a copy to my sis, Billy Ray's mom, so that covers both me and Billy

Ray, you know, should, by any chance both of us have an accident... Told her to keep it safe, not to open it unless, you know. She's solid my sis, so no problem there.'

'Good thinking. Well let's just hope it never comes to that, and that the guy has enough self-interest, or survival instinct, whatever, to stick to the deal.'

'Sure hope so Frankie, I sure do, but...' Frankie looked across at Joe who now seemed lost in thought.

'What are you thinking Joe?'

'Nuthin, just thinking is all.'

They exited the Interstate and were soon driving up the ramp to departures Joe insisted on dropping Frankie at the outside check-in booth and despite Frankie's protests, said he would park the car in the short stay area and bring Frankie's luggage to the check in himself. Once Frankie and his bag were checked in, they shook hands, then Joe gave Frankie a big hug.

'Travel safe buddy. Keep in touch and don't be a stranger,' said Joe as he stood back and saluted Frankie. Then he turned and walked away. Frankie walked towards through the airport entrance and towards the security queue where he handed his passport and boarding card to the security man.

CHAPTER 39

PRESENT – MANCHESTER UK

12 APRIL

Frankie had been home just under a week and finally shaken off the jet lag. Waking up at three in the morning, with little prospect of getting back to sleep made him too tired to think or function properly for a few days, but now he was back on track. A couple of sessions in the gym and some brisk walks and he was feeling as fit as ever. It took a while to catch up with his correspondence, pay some overdue bills and generally get up to date with domestic issues.

He was still wondering how to deal with the package he'd found when he unpacked his suitcase. He now understood why Joe had insisted on bringing his bags to the airport check-in desk. Stuffed inside his clothes was a plastic bag full of one hundred-dollar notes. He counted fifty thousand dollars in all. *He'd obviously put the money in the case when he parked at the airport!* Frankie found an old shoe box and hid the money in the bottom of his wardrobe.

When he'd gone to Florida, he'd left in such a hurry, he'd forgotten to empty the fridge so after dumping the rotting contents he had to give it a thorough clean. He went to the supermarket to re-stock. Now he was on his own he had to adjust his shopping to suit, and it reminded him how his life was going to be in the future.

The day after he'd arrived back Frankie went into the office for a day to get up to speed on any outstanding business issues, but he needn't have worried, Derek had managed the business well in his absence. Frankie thanked Gareth for all his help and handed over Joe's cheque for $25,000. And for the first time in Frankie's experience, the normally garrulous Gareth was struck dumb. After he'd recovered, Gareth insisted on taking both him and his uncle Derek to the pub at lunchtime where they insisted Frankie re-tell them the story of his encounter with Zsolt Meszaros blow by blow.

Frankie told Derek he'd be back full time in the office in the near future and had some ideas for a new division. Derek pressed him for details, but Frankie said it would have to wait.

'I need to get my mind clear first, and I can't do that until I've got all my personal affairs sorted out.'

'Understood Frankie,' said Derek, 'take your time, no rush.' They shook hands

Frankie said goodbye to Gareth.

'And don't forget to declare Joe's cheque to the taxman Gareth,' he said as he was leaving.

'I guess so Frankie, course there's always the offshore option? Might use it to start up my tax free stash.'

'Yeah right,' said Frankie laughing, and wondered once again *what the fuck am I going to do with all that cash Joe put in my suitcase?*.

He spent the next couple of days getting up to speed with everything else, paying overdue bills and then decided he couldn't put off dealing with the thing he'd been dreading. He could easily afford to re-mortgage, pay Penny off and stay in the house, but it had too many memories. A fresh start required a new place to live. *Hell, I don't even know if I'll stay around here, or even stay in the country.* Memories of sunny Naples and walks with Charlie kept coming back to him whenever he looked out at the summer weather, or what passed for weather in the north west of England.

There were some nice days, but nothing like the weather he'd left behind. He wondered if he could maybe go and live in Naples permanently, but parked the thought. *I'll wait until everything's sorted and think about it more seriously then.*

Although he'd got back into some sort of routine, being on his own meant Frankie had nothing or no one to remind him about mealtimes, other than suddenly feeling hungry, which he did now. He looked at his watch, six thirty. He had food in the fridge but just couldn't be bothered cooking. *A pizza with a beer and a couple of glasses of red wine is the obvious answer*

He started looking for the address book where Penny kept all the phone numbers, including the local takeout pizza place. He found it and was about to call when his phone rang. The name Penny appeared on the screen. *Shit!* He hadn't wanted to speak to her until he'd got things going with the lawyers and the estate agent, didn't want her to think he was delaying things. He picked up.

'Hi, Penny, how are you?'

'Fine thanks Frankie, heard you were home.'

'Yeah, about a week now, and sorry I haven't been in touch about the house, but it was next on my list. I'm not just saying that, but I've had a few...' Penny interrupted,

'It wasn't about the house. I just called to see how you were.'

'Oh, right, I'm fine thanks, you?'

'Great thanks, you on your own?'

'Yes, I'm on my own; why?'

'Sorry, I mean on your own as in you didn't bring anyone back with you. None of my business I realize, but...'

'No, on my own as in, on my own. No one came

back with me. What's this all about Penny?'

'I wanted to come round to see you, have a chat, that was all.'

'Well okay, but I thought we'd done all, the chatting necessary. I'm not going to be difficult about anything. Sell the house, go fifty-fifty on the proceeds. You can have the furniture or whatever, so no problems there. Not sure how we start the divorce thing, but either you can ask a lawyer, or I can. Just let me know, okay?'

'I'd still like to pop round if that's all right with you, won't take up much of your time?'

'Okay. Listen I was just about to order a pizza, from that place we used to use Pepe's. Does a fantastic Pepperoni special remember? If you're hungry, I'll order a large.' Frankie heard a sob. 'Penny, you okay?'

'Frankie, I've made the worst mistake of my whole life.'

'What have you done?'

'You idiot, you, I left you,' then she stopped talking, he could swear she was crying. He listened not knowing what to say or do.

'Sorry, Frankie, I just meant come round and talk to you. I wasn't going to say anything, just try to get an idea if there was still anything there. Now I've made a complete fool of myself, sorry. Listen I'll call tomorrow.

'The offer of that pizza's still good. You can drive round, or jump in a taxi if you're going to have a drink. Or I can come and get you?'

'This is exactly what I didn't want to do. The last thing I want is pity.'

'I'm offering a slice of pizza, not pity. We can just have a chat, okay?' There was a long silence, 'Penny, you still there?'

'I'll jump in a cab.' She replied

'I'll order the large pepperoni. Anchovies?'

'Yes please.'

◆ ◆ ◆

The doorbell chimed. Frankie felt a little awkward answering the door to his wife. He was sure she still had a key, but probably thought it wouldn't be appropriate to use it in the circumstances. He also didn't know how to greet his estranged spouse, and it seemed neither did she. They settled for an awkward kiss on the cheek. They went to the kitchen where Frankie had set the table.

'Beer or wine?' he asked opening the fridge

'Beer please.' He got two beers and poured. The doorbell rang again.

'Pizza, won't be a mo.' He came back and left the cardboard box on top of the cooker and sat back down.

'You look well, nicely tanned, suits you.'

'Yeah, I really enjoyed the sun.'

'I heard you had a bit of an adventure, but I

think some of what I heard must be a bit of exaggeration.'

'I'd guess it was' He took a swig of beer. 'Look Penny, you know I've never been good at the small talk, so why don't I put the pizza on the table, and we can talk while we're eating okay?' she nodded. He opened the box, and they each took a slice.

'Okay, so what's happened, you had a fight with Jill?'

'Boy, you don't change, do you, straight in the deep end?'

'Sorry, but you were the one who said...'

'I know, sorry but I'm feeling pretty stupid. No, no argument with Jill. It just happened a few days ago.'

'What happened a few days ago?'

'I was on a half day off, doing a bit of housework and that Joni Mitchell song came on the radio, you know, the big yellow taxi, the one we used to sing to, a bit?'

'Yes, I remember, and?'

'Well there I was, cleaning away humming to the tune, and it, well it invoked memories, then she sang a particular line and the next thing I know I'm in floods of tears. I sat down and something, I don't know what, but it was like the dam burst. I couldn't stop blubbing. And you know me, I'm not a blubber. That doesn't sound right does it, a blubber? Anyway, you know what I mean? So, after I'd stopped crying, everything became clearer.'

'Clearer?'

'Yes, look I'm not making much sense, but ever since I left, I've had this feeling, as though it wasn't me making those decisions, doing those things. Know what I mean?'

'If I'm honest, no I haven't got the foggiest, but carry on.'

'Well let's ditch the confused me. I'm really too old for making excuses based on; I don't know what. I know you probably can't forgive me, and I don't expect you to just say, oh it's okay Penny, no problem, move back in why don't you? But I wondered if you might think about it? There, I've said what I've been wanting to say and dreading to say it.' She took a swig of her beer and nibbled at her slice of pizza. Frankie put his glass down.

'I don't know what to say. I've built a bit of armor around me since you left. I had to. Either that or go to pieces. The trip to Florida saved me, and you were right, I was thinking of doing something stupid, but I was saved by the bell you might say, a telephone bell actually.' He laughed at his own weak joke. Penny pulled a face.

'Still the same crap sense of humor then?' she said. He laughed. 'Bottom line Frankie, I can't tell you how sorry I am that I put you through all that stuff, but could you consider it at least?'

'Depends. If there's the remotest chance you might do this again, then the answer's no. I know no one knows what the future holds, but...' Penny stopped eating and put her head down, then looked up.

'I can guarantee nothing would ever make me leave again, one thousand percent, gold plated guarantee. But that's it Frankie. I'm not going to beg. I've said my piece.' They were both silent for a beat.

'Okay,' said Frankie, 'well let me get used to the idea. I have to try to come to terms with what I've been through. Maybe what we've both been through. You understand?'

'I do Frankie. I wasn't expecting a miracle. I'm going to go now. I've said what I came to say. I still love you and never stopped loving you. I miss you and miss our life, including the sex, just in case you had any doubts on that score.'

'You sure, you don't want to stay, finish your beer and pizza?'

'No, I need to go now while I still have a shred of self respect left. I'll see myself out, and I'm going to walk. It's a nice evening.' Frankie knew better than to argue. They went to the front door, and Penny opened it. 'Do you think you'll have decided by tomorrow Frankie? I'd rather know sooner than later, and I promise I won't be difficult if it's a no'.

'Promise I'll call you tomorrow, whatever,

okay?'

'Sure, that's fine. I wasn't sure how tonight would go, but now that I know you're willing to think about it, can I just ask you a couple of questions before I go?'

'Go ahead,' Frankie said, holding the door open.

'If I was a betting woman, should I put my money on a good outcome?'

'Well to be fair, I'm still... in shock I suppose. And I vowed I would never put myself in a vulnerable situation ever again. So my immediate response is that my head says no, but my heart, it might say different. I honestly don't know. Second question.'

'What about this Charlie? You said it was love at first sight, or something like that anyway. What's happened to that relationship?'

'I think it's fair to say we're still extremely fond of each other. In fact, he's coming to live here in about six months' time.' Her face fell.

'Here as in Manchester?' she asked.

'Yes, here as in here with me, but it takes six months to comply with the regulations on travelling abroad after having a rabies jab.'

'A what?'

'A rabies jab, Charlie's a dog, you'll love him.' She turned and walked down the path, then turned round and pointed at him, tears streaming down her face.

'Frankie Armstrong, I'll swing for you. Don't you ever, ever, do anything like that to me again.' He walked down the path and facing her said.

'It's a deal, you neither, okay?' then he put his arms around her shoulders, and they walked back together into the house.

CHAPTER 40

PRESENT – MANCHESTER
SUMMER/AUTUMN 2017

He and Penny soon fell back into the old routine, but maybe with a little less taking each other for granted. Flowers featured more often. Jill resigned her job and moved out of the area. Penny never heard from her since moving back in with Frankie. Two weeks after they'd got back together Penny suggested they resumed going out on Friday nights to a nice restaurant. Penny referred to it as their weekly date. On the first such date since Frankie's return, they took a taxi to Manchester to dine at Da Vittorio, one of their Favorites.

'So,' said Penny after they'd got their drinks and ordered their meal, 'you've never really told me what happened over there in Florida. You told me about finding Joe's nephew, but not much about how you did it, so come on.' Frankie had given Penny the potted version but knew she would want more detail eventually.

'Okay,' he said, swilling the gin and ice round in his glass, 'well some of it might sound a bit farfetched, but I guess you deserve to know. So where do I start?' It took Frankie until the pudding menu was presented to tell Penny the whole story. She had lots of questions and variously gasped and laughed as he told her the details but frowned as he told her about the threats from Zaros. Her face paled and became taut as she asked.

'So, you mean you're under some sort of threat, you have a contract out on you? Frankie, you have to tell someone, the police, the authorities or someone.'

'It doesn't work like that Penny. Look it's okay, the guy knows if anything happens to me, any kind of attack, or God forbid, something worse. Then all his incriminating data will be released to the appropriate authorities. I've taken steps to make sure that happens regardless of my ability to do it.'

'You mean if you're killed, murdered? Frankie, I can't believe I'm hearing this.' Penny's voice had risen and was attracting the attention of other diners. Frankie leaned in to speak.

'Look Penny, that's the way it is. I can't turn back the clock. I quite understand if you want to leave, if you feel threatened as well, I mean by association. I don't want you to leave, but neither do I want you to be frightened. It was my choice to do what I did, so why should you live with the consequences?' Penny leaned back, then took a gulp of her wine. She closed her eyes briefly, then looked at Frankie.

'You don't get rid of me that easily Frankie Armstrong. We're in this life together, forever, whatever,' then she laughed. 'Jesus Christ, it's like living with James Bond,' then she grabbed the menu, 'now let's see, what's for pudding?' Frankie thought he'd never loved her more than at that moment.

'I believe they have one called a chocolate bomb,' he said, and they both burst out laughing.

◆ ◆ ◆

'What's new in paradise?' asked Penny one day when Frankie was online reading the Naples Daily News. She called it that in response to Frankie's description, which she said always sounded like paradise the way he described it.

'It's the nearest I've come to paradise that's for sure,' said Frankie in response. 'The only thing missing was Eve, but you can pick them up easy, ten a penny.' She'd cuffed him and replied.

'Don't forget; you promised to take me there soon.'

'I will I promise, but in the meantime, I have some spare cash that needs spending, so I think we need to think about a few holidays anyway. Not Florida though, not for now. I thought we'd save that until Charlie's due to come here then we can go a couple of weeks beforehand and all fly back together, albeit with Charlie in the hold, but still?'

'Sounds good to me, but can you afford to take all that time away from the business?'

'As much time as I like. Since I came back from Florida, I feel like a spare part at the office.'

'Are you serious Frankie?'

'Yep, just think about where you want to go.'

'I'm on it,' said Penny and went to search for ideas on Google.

'Penny.' She stopped and turned back. 'Don't choose any package deals, we'll need to pay for the flights here, but I want to pay for the hotels in wherever we go in cash, you understand? And book the most expensive five star hotels you can find.'

'Are you kidding me Frankie Armstrong?'

'Nope deadly serious. Let me know where we're going and when.'

'I'll wake up in a minute,' she said, and went to do her research.

◆ ◆ ◆

Frankie once again wondered about the cash and Joe's story. He went on to Google and researched the subject of cash being sent to Iraq by the USA. He'd looked once before and found out that Joe's claims were true, America had sent enormous amounts of cash to Iraq, and most of it was unaccounted for.

Once again, he read about Henry Waxman, a fierce critic of the war, who said the way the cash had been handled was mind-boggling. "The numbers are so large that it doesn't seem possible that they're true. Who in their right mind would send three hundred and sixty three tonnes of cash into a war zone?"

Frankie looked further and found various reports to support these amazing claims. One report which caught his eye was about some American servicemen who, it was alleged, had hijacked a huge amount of cash while it was being transferred to a new location, said to be in the region of twenty five million dollars. A similar story to Joe's.

Three of them had been arrested, but they'd been killed along with their escorts when an IED had blown up their armored vehicle while on its way to headquarters for further interrogation. He closed the browser and leaned back in his chair. *Surely not?* He dismissed the idea almost as soon as it had crossed his mind.

Frankie got the odd email from Joe, keeping him up to speed on progress with his *project* as he referred to it, but by necessity, the details were couched in obscure language. *Doing well on the buying front. Initial part of project nearly complete. Billy Ray has a new partner, business partner, thankfully not the other kind. Now playing the field, much safer, ha! Start planting soon and looking forward to exporting the crop. Yours Joe. Keep well and don't be a stranger.* Joe always signed off the same way. Frankie replied and told him the good news about getting back together with Penny and asked how Billy Ray's hand was and how he was looking forward to Charlie coming to live with them in the UK.

Frankie continued to keep abreast of events in Naples via The Naples News, with the, all the latest developments, the weather and all manner of happenings, including photographs and reports of the big fish catches. He also regularly went on to the Naples Pier online webcam and could almost feel the warmth of all that beautiful sunshine. There were still some months to go before Charlie arrived and he began to wonder how the little dog would take to the British climate.

Frankie and Penny went on their vacations, weekends in Paris and Brussels. In early August, just as they'd arrived back from their latest trip, two weeks in Mallorca where they'd spent their honeymoon, Frankie got another update email.

Billy Ray completed seeding the farm. Leaving things to mature and settle for a few weeks, before registering the crop as ready to reap. Expecting a

bumper harvest.
Get yourself out here soon and bring that wife of yours – beers are on me. Best Joe
PS Charlie all okay.

Out of guilt, Frankie went into the office for a couple of weeks, but found he was unable to make any useful contributions. He'd developed an idea whilst he'd been away on their various holidays and discussed with Penny who gave her tacit approval. He pulled Derek aside.

'I'm not having much input these days Barnsie, so I have a proposal, you know the idea I mentioned a while ago?'

'Okay, and that is?

'We go international. I realize this is going to sound a bit corny, but based on my experience in Florida, I've been researching the missing people business, and you'd be surprised just how much potential business there is out there.'

'Really? I thought government agencies would do most of that sort of thing, Interpol that sort of thing?'

'That's more about criminals, but there are all sorts of other business opportunities Beneficiaries of wills who went to live abroad, kidnap victims, family members who disappear after a fallout, all sorts of stuff. I also think Gareth could be a significant help in this. So much detection work is technology based these days. What do you say?'

'Okay, I'm open to the idea. Let me have some facts and figures, and we can take it forward. In the meantime, piss off and relax. You've earned your corn Frankie, so stop feeling guilty about not coming in. You're a partner in a highly successful security company. Enjoy the benefits of your hard graft.' Frankie left looking forward to doing the research and business plan. He began to feel useful again.

❖ ❖ ❖

Anything interesting happening in Paradise this week?' said Penny looking over his shoulder as he read the Naples News online.

'Not sure about interesting, replied Frankie but it looks as if there's a hurricane building up in the Caribbean that could impact on Florida. They're saying it could be heading for Miami then up the east coast.'

'But Naples is on the west coast, right?'

'Yes, thankfully.' Over the next few days, Frankie kept an eye on Hurricane Irma. It seemed to be gathering strength and had now been described as a monster storm. On the 31st August, Irma intensified into a hurricane, with winds gusting up to ninety eight miles an hour, as it swept across the Caribbean, wreaking havoc as it progressed inexorably towards Florida. Although initial indications were that Irma would hit Miami full on, it veered towards south west Florida, with Naples now directly in its path.

On the evening of September 11th, Frankie turned on CNN to watch Irma's destructive progress. Live reports were coming from both Miami and Naples. The potential damage for both places was huge. By the time he went to bed, Hurricane Irma was well into her stride, with forecasts of fifteen foot storm surges in Naples. Frankie wondered what would happen to the Cove Inn and Joe's boatyard.

The next morning, Frankie turned on the TV to find that the worst forecasts for Naples had been overdone, but nevertheless, the damage to the infrastructure was huge. Less so in Miami, but seriously bad nevertheless. In his concern about Naples, he'd forgotten about Joe's plan and the Spanish Galleon. He didn't see any point in calling Joe so soon after the hurricane had hit, so he waited. A week later he called

Joe answered the phone immediately.

'It's me Joe.'

'Frankie, how's it going buddy?'

'Okay, you Joe?'

'Well partner, you know what they say? The Lord giveth and the Lord taketh away. And boy has the Lord taketh away this time.'

'The wreck's gone?'

'Done gone, well let's say redistributed. Billy Ray reckons he can still get to it. It slipped off the shelf into deeper water. Going to be a fuckin nightmare to retrieve the treasure now, but we'll do it. In some ways, makes it look more authentic. Luckily Billy Ray registered the find just a few days before that bitch Irma came to visit. Got to say, Frankie, I sometimes do wonder if it's all worthwhile, then I think, fuck, yes it is.' And he started laughing. Frankie waited for him to stop.

'Glad you're taking it so well Joe.'

'At the end of the day Frankie, it's only money.'

'You're right Joe, it's only money, talking of which, I haven't really had the chance to thank you for the little bundle you put in my suitcase when I left. I didn't want to say anything on email for obvious reasons.'

'Think nothing of it Frankie, you earned it. Keep well and give my love to your wife Penny. I'm looking forward to meeting her one of these days. Can't wait till you come back to visit.'

'Me neither Joe.'

◆ ◆ ◆

Ten days later, Frankie was sitting at the kitchen table with his laptop.

'Coffee Frankie?' asked Penny.

'Please,' replied Frankie opening up the browser to read the Naples News online. Penny came back with his coffee and set it down on the table. She was walking away when Frankie gasped.

'Oh, sweet Jesus,' said Frankie.

'What is it Frankie?' said Penny coming back to look over his shoulder.

'Read that,' said Frankie pointing. She looked at the headline.

◆ ◆ ◆

Miami Millionaire and wife die in mid-air explosion

Florida police and air traffic authorities are investigating an unexplained explosion that blew a Beechcraft airplane out of the sky over the Everglades. Wreckage was strewn over a large area. The owner of the aircraft, a Mr. Zsolt Meszaros was believed to be on board, along with his wife and their pilot. Police say there were no survivors. Mr. Meszaros and his wife were well loved, and respected members of Miami society.
"The Meszaros were generous charity donors and supported many worthy causes". A spokesman said. "They will be sorely missed. Many people will be grieving at the loss of these two wonderful and caring human beings....

◆ ◆ ◆

'Meszaros? That's the man who kidnapped Joe's nephew, the man who threatened to kill you if you ever told?'

'That's the man,' said Frankie closing the lid of his laptop.

'Jesus Christ Joe...!'

AFTERWORD

FACT

In 2004 Uncle Sam in his wisdom, decided to ship over to Iraq, approximately $12 billion in cash - shrink wrapped bundles of untraceable US dollars. Over three hundred and fifty tonnes of the stuff. It was ostensibly intended for distribution to overseas contractors and Iraq ministries. Henry Waxman, a long-time critic of US involvement in Iraq, was claimed to have said; "The way the cash had been handled was mind-boggling. The numbers are so large that it doesn't seem possible that they're true. Who in their right mind would send 363 tonnes of cash into a war zone?" (8th Feb. 2007)

ABOUT THE AUTHOR

Kerry Costello

Kerry Costello was born near Manchester UK. He has worked as a printer, a salesman, a building site labourer, a waiter - and for a while as one half of a singing-guitar duo appearing in nightclubs up and down the UK. Costello then went into the travel business and eventually started his own successful tour operation. He sold the company and retired to take up his ambition to become an author.

The setting for his later novels is Naples Florida, a place Costello knows well. "There are just so many larger than life characters in Florida," says Costello, "a rich seam for any author to mine."

BOOKS BY THIS AUTHOR

No Way Back

Jack's in the wrong place at the wrong time. It could happen to anyone – it could happen to you!

One beautiful sunny morning in May, Jack Brandon takes his dog Bess for their usual early morning walk in the Cheshire countryside, and suddenly Jack's pleasant and peaceful world turns into a violent nightmare. A chance meeting changes his life forever. Jack now has a secret or two, and is pursued by some powerful people who want answers - they'll stop at nothing to get what they're after.

The Long Game

A dramatic story fuelled by years of unresolved bitter hatred, and revenge - with a shocking twist that that will elude you until the very last page.

Police Sergeant Gibson investigates what appears to be an elderly man's death by natural causes.

Using instinct, good old fashioned detective work and a dogged determination to get at the truth - Sergeant Gibson pieces together an intricate puzzle of long awaited retribution.

Florida Shakedown

Jack paid the ransom, but they executed Rick anyway!
"An exciting read, with a terrific ending that won't disappoint"

Retired ex British detective Gibson travels to Florida to recover from a tragic family bereavement. All he wants is peace and quiet, but Jack, a resident of the holiday condo he's staying at, has other ideas. He persuades Gibson to look at the death of his business partner in bizarre and brutal circumstances. Gibson is hooked, and against his better judgement, agrees to help. He's soon drawn into a violent corrupt and terrifying world where his very own survival is at risk.

Florida Clowns

Lorna's life depends on Gibson believing her incredible story. He knows anyone in her situation would lie. in just a few short weeks, Lorna faces execution by lethal injection.

Ex British detective Gibson returned to Florida to find work as a Private Eye, but didn't expect his first assignment to be so tough. He's tasked to rescue a fellow Brit from death row. Lorna claims she's been set up. Does Gibson believe her, or is Lorna sending him on a wild goose chase? Will Gibson find the truth out in time – and what evil might lurk behind a clown's painted smile?

To find out - buy this spine-chilling thriller now!

Condo

After attempting to rescue a woman attacked by a gator in an otherwise peaceful Florida condo community, ex British soldier Frankie Armstrong becomes suspicious. Was it a freak accident, or was it something more sinister?
The more he looks into the lives of his fellow condo residents, the more troubled Frankie becomes. Nothing and no one are as they seem. Using all the resources at his disposal to expose the truth, he attempts to hunt down the killer and bring him to justice... But will he succeed, or will the killer find him first?

CONDO is an edge-of-your-seat crime thriller. If you like fast-paced storytelling with twists that keep you guessing until the end, then you'll enjoy this gripping tale.

A BIG THANK YOU

Thank you for reading You Owe Me. I trust you enjoyed it. When you have a few minutes to spare, I'd be very grateful if you'd leave a review on Amazon.

◆ ◆ ◆

And if you'd like to be kept up to date with any new books, or special offer etc., please go to kerrycostellobooks.com and sign up for the newsletters.

Excerpt from my latest novel

CONDO

By

Kerry Costello

Copyright © 2020 Kerry Costello

All rights reserved - ISBN 9 781916 425958

All rights reserved. No part of this book may be reproduced or transmitted, in any form, or by any means, mechanical or electronic or, by photocopying, recording, or by any storage and retrieval system, without the express permission, in writing, from Kerry J Costello, the owner of all copyright to this work. This book is a work of fiction. Names, characters, places and incidents, are either the product of the writer's imagination or are being used fictitiously. Any resemblance to any actual persons, living or dead, and events or locations, is entirely coincidental.

CHAPTER 1

2019 Day 1

Tuesday evening

Frankie

Frankie was sitting in his favorite chair on the lanai, talking to his business partner over Skype. The ceiling fans rotated with a gentle thropping noise, his little dog Charlie lay at his feet and yelped occasionally as he dreamed. Every now and then Frankie leaned down to stroke Charlie's head.

"So how hot is it there now Frankie, at what, seven in the evening?"

Frankie looked at the thermometer.

"Seventy-five," said Frankie

"So that's about twenty-four?"

"I guess so," said Frankie.

"Well lucky you. It's colder than a witch's tit here. We'll be lucky if the temperature gets above freezing this week."

"Hang on a minute Barnsie, got to open one of the sliders, let some cool air in."

"Yeah, rub it in why don't you? Anyway, don't you have air con?"

"I do," said Frankie getting up from his chair, "but I don't turn it on 'til I go to bed."

Frankie slid one of the floor to ceiling windows along, letting the evening breeze waft into the lanai. His condo was on the second floor, offering an uninterrupted view over Venetian Bay. He stopped briefly to watch the sunset, the sky now a mixture of blues, burnished copper and red swirls The sun was a red molten ball descending behind the high-rise buildings opposite, heralding another spectacular Naples sunset. He sighed, then lowered his gaze to look out over the condo gardens. About 150 yards away, he could just about make out a couple on the other side of the swimming pool, silhouetted in the fading light.

His view was partially obscured by the branches of the poolside bottle brush tree. The couple were standing on one of the boat docks having an animated discussion. Odd for anyone to be out there this time of night? He shrugged, went to sit down and resumed his conversation with Derek, Barnsie his business partner and friend. He took another sip of his cold Michelob.

"Okay Derek, I'm concentrating now."

"Okay, so, as I was saying... Do you think it's too soon to make Gareth a director? He's worked hard and really improved the IT department.

We're getting loads of recommends from existing clients. Pen testing and cyber security in general is more in demand than ever. We're in a great position to make a killing. My suggestion is we make Gareth a director, move Jimmy up to office manager and employ a couple more techies. What do you think?"

"Yeah, sounds like a good move." Charlie suddenly woke up, went to the open window and started barking, "Just hold on Barnsie, give me a minute."

"What's up Frankie?"

"Not sure, something's going on outside," said Frankie putting his beer down. He stood and pushed the mosquito screen aside to get a clearer view, and straining to try to hear what was going on. The discussion between the two people had become more animated, but he was too far away to see properly and couldn't hear anything distinctly. They'd moved further along the boat dock. The woman appeared to be gesticulating, then seemed to stumble backwards. Frankie heard her scream, then a splash as she fell off the dock into the water. Frankie watched transfixed. A split second later another louder and more horrific scream rent the air. Did the man push her, why isn't he helping her? Frankie turned back to the laptop, then looked back briefly to where the couple had been. The man had gone. He turned back to the laptop.

"Sorry Derek, got to go, someone's just fallen in the bay," and with that Frankie rushed for the door, stopping only briefly to grab his cell.

He opened the condo door, ran along the walkway to the stair's door, opened it then dashed down the stairs two at a time and out through the ground floor door. He suddenly realized he didn't have any shoes on but didn't stop. Turning left and left again, he passed under the breezeway and along the path through the gardens, and on round the swimming pool towards the boat dock where he'd seen the woman go into the water.

He got to the dock and ran to the end. The docks were wooden pier-like structures, about thirty feet long. A boat was moored on the right-hand side of the dock, but no boat on the left-hand side where the woman had gone in. He couldn't see any sign of the woman. The sun had now disappeared beyond the horizon and illumination was limited to a small dim light on the dock, the security lights around the pool and some reflected light from the houses and condos alongside the bay.

Frankie ran back down the dock to the rear of the pool where there was an extending pole kept in a plastic tube holder. It had a large hook on the end. He took it out and quickly returned to the dock, nearly bumping into a man holding a flashlight. He recognized him as Hector Carmouche, one of the other residents.

"Frankie is that you?" the man asked, shining the torch in Frankie's face.

"Yes, it is," said Frankie holding up his hand to shield his eyes from the blinding glare.

"Oh, sorry," said Hector, "what's going on? I heard a scream," he said as he followed Frankie to the far end of the dock.

"Not sure Hector, but I saw a woman fall off the dock and into the water, or maybe she was pushed?"

"Pushed! Sweet Jesus, by who?"

"No idea." Frankie replied

Hector shone his light across the water

"Keep shining that light Hector."

Frankie got down on all fours, then flattened himself out on the wooden deck and leaned over trying to look underneath the dock. They were joined on the dock by another two of the residents who'd come to see what was going on.

"Anything?" asked Hector, waving his flashlight and trying to provide some light underneath the structure.

"Nothing," Frankie replied. "You know, when I got into the garden, Hector, I'd swear I could hear a sort of thrashing, not like somebody struggling in the water, something more, I don't know, a sort of heavy slapping sound, something violent."

"Oh, shit," said one of the others who had joined them.

"What?" asked Frankie.

"You heard about the gator?"

"What gator? no I didn't hear about any gator. I haven't been around the pool the last few days, been sorting out some business stuff. You're not saying...?"

"A few folks have seen an alligator near the docks in the last couple of days. Not every day but... Tom and Marge saw it and they reckoned it was a bull gator, well over twelve feet long, but then you know how people exaggerate?"

"Oh Christ," said Frankie, scanning the water as he took out his cell. "Did anyone call 911?" he asked the little group, now joined by one of the women residents.

They all looked at each other.

"No," said one of the men who Frankie recognized as Bill Ferenczi "I thought someone else would have."

"Jesus," said Frankie in frustration. He took out his cell and punched in the numbers 911.

"Yes, an emergency, someone fell, or was pushed into the bay, Venetian Bay that is. Anyway, we can't see her. Yes, Venetian Bay," he said again, then proceeded to give the operator the address and zip. "They'll be here shortly," he said to others. He looked around and saw some more people had come down to see what the fuss was. One shouted.

"Can we help?"

"I don't think so," Frankie shouted back. There were already enough people doing nothing useful he thought. "Someone fell in the water," he shouted back to them, "the emergency services are on the way." There was a collective gasp. Frankie turned his attention back to scanning the bay.

"Look, over there Hector, out there," Frankie said pointing "shine your flashlight. See that red thing?"

"Yeah, I see, can't see what it is though, clothing maybe?" said Hector,

"Might be the woman," one of the others said. Frankie went to the end of the dock and dove in.

◆ ◆ ◆

Buy CONDO on Amazon now!
www.Amazon.com

Printed in Great Britain
by Amazon